MARCHING SANDS

MARCHING SANDS BY
HAROLD LAMB

With a new introduction by
L. SPRAGUE de CAMP

HYPERION PRESS, INC.
WESTPORT, CONNECTICUT

Library of Congress Cataloging in Publication Data

Lamb, Harold, 1892-1962.
    Marching sands.

    Reprint of the 1930 ed. published by Jacobsen
Pub. Co., New York.
    I. Title.
PZ3.L165Ma6 [PS3523.Z4235] 813'.5'2   73-13258
ISBN 0-88355-113-6
ISBN 0-88355-142-X (pbk.)

Reproduced from an edition published in 1930
by Jacobsen Publishing Company, Inc., New York
Copyright 1920 by D. Appleton and Company; copyright 1919
by Frank A. Munsey Company

Hyperion reprint edition 1974

Library of Congress Catalogue Number 73-13258

ISBN 0-88355-113-6 (cloth ed.)
ISBN 0-88355-142-X (paper ed.)

Printed in the United States of America

HAROLD LAMB

By L. Sprague de Camp

The time between the two world wars was the golden
age of the pulp magazines. There were dozens: war
stories, sea stories, flying stories, westerns, and so on.

Among these pulps a few, such as *Blue Book* and
Adventure Magazine, were recognized as aristocrats.
While the stories in all pulps varied widely in quality,
these leading magazines maintained a consistently high
standard. If short on characterization, social con-
sciousness, and sex, the stories were long on action,
humor, suspense, and plain entertainment. The disappearance of the pulps, during and after the Second
World War, and their replacement by the paperbacked
novel brought about a drastic shrinkage in the market for
the American short story.

In the 1920s, Harold Lamb was one of the most
talented, prolific, and consistent contributors to *Adventure Magazine*. Born in Alpine, New Jersey, in 1892,
Harold Albert Lamb graduated from Columbia University
in 1916. In the First World or Kaiserian War he served in
the American Army as an infantryman.

After the war, recently married, Lamb soon settled
down to a full-time writing career. In the 1920s, he con-
tributed a huge volume of tales of historical adventure to
Adventure and other magazines. All concerned the
milieu that Lamb made particularly his own: the conflict
between East and West, between Europe and Asia. He
told of the bloody incursions of Turks and Mongols into
Europe and of Crusaders and Cossacks into Asia.

About forty loosely linked novelettes in *Adventure*
narrated the adventures of several Cossack heroes in the
early seventeenth century, in the times of Boris Godunov
in Russia and Akbar in India. A few of these stories have
been reprinted by Doubleday in recent years. They are
tales of wild adventure, full of swordplay, plots, treachery,
startling surprises, mayhem, and massacre, laid in the
most exotic setting that one can imagine and still stay in a
known historical period on this planet. Lamb influenced

other writers of adventure fiction, notably Robert E. Howard, creator of the mighty prehistoric barbarian hero, Conan.

Making his home in California, Lamb also traveled in the Orient, although details of his journeys are scarce. A shy man who disliked crowds and social events, he avoided publicity and self-promotion. He became prodigiously learned in Asian history and languages. I met him once, when he came to New York about 1958 to consult with his editors at Doubleday. In his sixties, he was a big, well-built, handsome man with close-cut gray hair and a hearing aid. Having just studied ancient Persian for a historical novel, I greeted him in that language, to which he replied without hesitation in the same.

In 1927, Lamb published his first best-selling book, a biography of Genghis Khan. Thenceforth he gave less and less time to fiction and more to popular history and biography, always on his favorite theme of East-versus-West. He wrote histories of the Crusades and of the conquests of the Turks, the Mongols, and the Cossacks. He wrote biographies of leaders on both sides of this millennial struggle, such as Cyrus, Alexander, Hannibal, Justinian, Charlemagne, Timur, and Süleyman the Magnificent. His last book was a life of Babur, the first Mogul emporer of India. In the Second World or Hitlerian War, he traveled in the Arab lands on behalf of the Office of Strategic Services. He died after a brief illness in1962, aged seventy-nine.

Marching Sands (originally published in 1920) is very early Lamb—in fact, probably his first published book. The setting is China and Mongolia, but in modern times. The story contains several elements that were then common in science fiction and fantasy writing but have since dropped out of general use. This, however, should not interfere with our enjoyment of the story.

For instance, there is the lost-race plot, a staple of adventure fiction of half a century ago. It has since been made obsolete by the perfection of the airplane, as a result of which scarcely a square mile of the earth's surface has not been viewed from the air. No room is left for lost cities and lost races to hide in.

There are touches of the now discredited idea of "the

white man's burden" and references to the "Aryan race." This latter concept was subsequently made infamous by Hitler and exploded by advances in anthropology and genetics.

Finally, there is the exemplary sexual purity of the leading characters, which in our promiscuous age seems quaint. Such a convention, however, had its uses. The sexual revolution has more or less ruined the old-fashioned love story. A storyteller used to be able to make a whole novel out of the efforts of a young couple to overcome legal, financial, moral and other obstacles to achieve union. Now it is all to simple and predictable. Boy no sooner meets girl than they are racing off to the bedroom. End of story. The old way was really more fun for the reader.

CONTENTS

MARCHING SANDS

CHAPTER I

THE LOST PEOPLE

"You want me to fail."

It was neither question nor statement. It came in a level voice, the words dropping slowly from the lips of the man in the chair as if he weighed each one.

He might have been speaking aloud to himself, as he sat staring directly in front of him, powerful hands crossed placidly over his knees. He was a man that other men would look at twice, and a woman might glance at once—and remember. Yet there was nothing remarkable about him, except perhaps a singular depth of chest that made his quiet words resonant.

That and the round column of a throat bore out the evidence of strength shown in the hands. A broad, brown head showed a hard mouth, and wide-set, green eyes. These eyes were level and slow moving, like the lips—the eyes of a man who

Marching Sands

could play a poker hand and watch other men without looking at them directly.

There was a certain melancholy mirrored in the expressionless face. The melancholy that is the toll of hardships and physical suffering. This, coupled with great, though concealed, physical strength, was the curious trait of the man in the chair, Captain Robert Gray, once adventurer and explorer, now listed in the United States Army Reserve.

He had the voyager's trick of wearing excellent clothes carelessly, and the army man's trait of restrained movement and speech. He was on the verge of a vital decision; but he spoke placidly, even coldly. So much so that the man at the desk leaned forward earnestly.

"No, we don't want you to fail, Captain Gray. We want you to find out the truth and to tell us what you have found out."

"Suppose there is nothing to discover?"

"We will know we are mistaken."

"Will that satisfy you?"

"Yes."

Captain "Bob" Gray scrutinized a scar on the back of his right hand. It had been made by a Mindanao *kris,* and, as the edge of the *kris* had been poisoned, the skin was still a dull purple. Then he smiled.

"I thought," he said slowly, "that the lost people

2

The Lost People

myths were out of date. I thought the last missing tribe had been located and card-indexed by the geographical and anthropological societies."

Dr. Cornelius Van Schaick did not smile. He was a slight, gray man, with alert eyes. And he was the head of the American Exploration Society, a director of the Museum of Natural History—in the office of which he was now seated with Gray—and a member of sundry scientific and historical academies.

"This is not a *lost* people, Captain Gray." He paused, pondering his words. "It is a branch of our own race, the Indo-Aryan, or white race. It is the Wusun—the 'Tall Ones.' We—the American Exploration Society—believe it is to be found, in the heart of Asia." He leaned back, alertly.

Gray's brows went up.

"And so you are going to send an expedition to look for it?"

"To look for it." Van Schaick nodded, with the enthusiasm of a scientist on the track of a discovery. "We are going to send you, to prove that it exists. If this is proved," he continued decisively, "we will know that a white race was dominant in Asia before the time of the great empires; that the present Central Asian may be descended from Aryan stock. We will have new light on the development of races—even on the Bible——"

"Steady, Doctor!" Gray raised his hand. "You're

getting out of my depth. What I want to know is this: Why do you think that I can find this white tribe in Asia—the Wusuns? I'm an army officer, out of a job and looking for one. That's why I answered your letter. I'm broke, and I need work, but——"

Van Schaick peered at a paper that he drew from a pile on his desk.

"We had good reasons for selecting you, Captain Gray," he said dryly. "You have done exploration work north of the Hudson Bay; you once stamped out dysentery in a Mindanao district; you have done unusual work for the Bureau of Navigation; on active service in France you led your company——"

Gray looked up quickly. "So did a thousand other American officers," he broke in.

"Ah, but very few have had a father like yours," he smiled, tapping the paper gently. "Your father, Captain Gray, was once a missionary of the Methodists, in Western Shensi. You were with him, there, until you were four years of age. I understand that he mastered the dialect of the border, thoroughly, and you also picked it up, as a child. This is correct?"

"Yes."

"And your father, before he died in this country, persisted in refreshing, from time to time, your knowledge of the dialect."

The Lost People

"Yes."

Van Schaick laid down the paper.

"In short, Captain Gray," he concluded, "you have a record at Washington of always getting what you go after, whether it is information or men. That can be said about many explorers, perhaps; but in your case the results are on paper. You have never failed. That is why we want you. Because, if you don't find the Wusun, we will then know they are not to be found."

"I don't think they can be found."

The scientist peered at his visitor curiously.

"Wait until you have heard our information about the white race in the heart of China, before you make up your mind," he said in his cold, concise voice, gathering the papers into their leather portmanteau. "Do you know why the Wusun have not been heard from?"

"I might guess. They seem to be in a region where no European explorers have gone——"

"Have been permitted to go. Asia, Captain Gray, for all our American investigations, is a mystery to us. We think we have removed the veil from its history, and we have only detached a thread. The religion of Asia is built on its past. And religion is the pulse of Asia. The Asiatics have taught their children that, from the dawn of history, they have been lords of the civilized world. What would be the result if it were proved that a

5

white race dominated Central Asia before the Christian era? The traditions of six hundred million people who worship their past would be shattered."

Gray was silent while the scientist placed his finger on a wall map of Asia. Van Schaick drew his finger, inland from the coast of China, past the rivers and cities, past the northern border of Tibet to a blank space under the mountains of Turkestan where there was no writing.

"This is the blind spot of Asia," he said. "It has grown smaller, as Europeans journeyed through its borders. Tibet, we know. The interior of China we know, except for this blind spot. It is——"

"In the Desert of Gobi."

"The one place white explorers have been prevented from visiting. And it is here we have heard the Wusun are."

"A coincidence."

Van Schaick glanced at his watch.

"If you will come with me, Captain Gray, to the meeting of the Exploration Society now in session, I will convince you it is no coincidence. Before we go, I would like to be assured of one thing. The expedition to the far end of the Gobi Desert will not be safe. It may be very dangerous. Would you be willing to undertake it?"

Gray glanced at the map and rose.

"If you can show me, Doctor," he responded,

The Lost People

"that there is something to be found—I'd tackle it."

"Come with me," nodded Van Schaick briskly.

The halls of the museum were dark, as it was past the night hour for visitors. A small light at the stairs showed the black bulk of inanimate forms in glass compartments, and the looming outline of mounted beasts, with the white bones of prehistoric mammals.

At the entrance, Van Schaick nodded to an attendant, who summoned the scientist's car.

Their footsteps had ceased to echo along the tiled corridor. The motionless beast groups stared unwinkingly at the single light from glass eyes. Then a form moved in one of the groups.

The figure slipped from the stuffed animals, down the hall. The entrance light showed for a second a slender man in an overcoat who glanced quickly from side to side at the door to see if he was observed. Then he went out of the door, into the night.

CHAPTER II

LEGENDS

THAT evening a few men were gathered in Van Schaick's private office at the building of the American Exploration Society. One was a celebrated anthropologist, another a historian who had come that day from Washington. A financier whose name figured in the newspapers was a third. And a European orientologist.

To these men, Van Schaick introduced Gray, explaining briefly what had passed in their interview.

"Captain Gray," he concluded, "wishes proof of what we know. If he can be convinced that the Wusun are to be found in the Gobi Desert, he is ready to undertake the trip."

For an hour the three scientists talked. Gray listened silently. They were followers of a calling strange to him, seekers after the threads of knowledge gleaned from the corners of the earth, zealots, men who would spend a year or a lifetime in running down a clew to a new species of human beings or animals. They were men who were gatherers of the treasures of the sciences, indifferent to the ordinary aspects of life, unsparing in their

8

efforts. And he saw that they knew what they were talking about.

In the end of the Bronze Age, at the dawn of history, they explained, the Indo-Aryan race, their own race, swept eastward from Scandinavia and the north of Europe, over the mountain barrier of Asia and conquered the Central Asian peoples—the Mongolians—with their long swords.

This was barely known, and only guessed at by certain remnants of the Aryan language found in Northern India, and inscriptions dug up from the mountains of Turkestan.

They believed, these scientists, that before the great Han dynasty of China, an Indo-Aryan race known as the Sacæ had ruled Central Asia. The forefathers of the Europeans had ruled the Mongolians. The ancestors of thousands of Central Asians of to-day had been white men—tall men, with long skulls, and yellow hair, and great fighters.

The earliest annals of China mentioned the Huing-nu—light-eyed devils—who came down into the desert. The manuscripts of antiquity bore the name of the Wusun—the "Tall Ones." And the children of the Aryan conquerors had survived, fighting against the Mongolians for several hundred years.

"They survive to-day," said the historian earnestly. "Marco Polo, the first European to enter

China, passed along the northern frontier of the
Wusun land. He called their king Prester John
and a Christian. You have heard of the myth of
Prester John, sometimes called the monarch of
Asia. And of the fabulous wealth of his kingdom,
the massive cities. The myth states that Prester
John was a captive in his own palace."

"You see," assented Van Schaick, "already the
captivity of the Wusun had begun. The Mongolians have never tolerated other races within their
borders. During the time of Genghis Khan and
the Tartar conquerors, the survivors of the Aryans
were thinned by the sword."

"Marco Polo," continued the historian, "came as
near to the land of the Wusun as any other European. Three centuries later a Portuguese missionary, Benedict Goës, passed through the desert near
the city of the Wusun, and reported seeing some
people who were fair of face, tall and light-eyed."

Van Schaick turned to his papers.

"In the last century," he said, "a curious thing
happened to an English explorer, Ney Elias. I
quote from his book. *An old man called on me
at Kwei-hwa-ching, at the eastern end of the Thian
Shan Mountains, who said he was neither Chinaman, Mongol, nor Mohammedan, and lived on
ground especially allotted by the emperor, and where
there now exist several families of the same origin.
He said that he had been a prince. At Kwei-hwa-*

*ching I was very closely spied on and warned
against asking too many questions.*"

Van Schaick peered over his spectacles at Gray.

"The Thian Shan Mountains are just north of
this blind spot in the Gobi Desert where we think
the Wusun are."

The historian broke in eagerly.

"Another clew—a generation ago the Russian explorer, Colonel Przewalski, tried to enter this blind
spot from the south, and was fought off with much
bloodshed by one of the guardian tribes."

Gray laughed frankly.

"I admit I'm surprised, gentlemen. Until now
I thought you were playing some kind of a joke
on me."

Van Schaick's thin face flushed, but he spoke
calmly.

"It is only fair, sir, that you should have proof
you are not being sent after a will-o'-the-wisp. A
few days ago I talked with a missionary who had
been invalided home from China. His name is
Jacob Brent. He has been for twenty years head
of the college of Chengtu, in Western China. He
heard rumors of a captive tribe in the heart of the
Gobi. And he saw one of the Wusun."

He paused to consult one of his papers methodically.

"Brent was told, by some Chinese coolies, of a
tall race dwelling in a city in the Gobi, a race that

11

was, they said, 'just like him.' And in one of his trips near the desert edge he saw a tall figure running toward him over the sand, staggering from weariness. Then several Chinese riders appeared from the sand dunes and headed off the fugitive. But not before Brent had seen that the man's face was partially white."

"Partially?" asked Gray quizzically.

"I am quoting literally. Yes, that was what Brent said. He was prevented by his native bearers from going into the Gobi to investigate. They believed the usual superstitions about the desert—evil spirits and so forth—and they warned Brent against a thing they called the pale sickness."

Gray looked up quietly. "You know what that is?"

"We do not know, and surmises are valueless." He shrugged. "You have an idea?"

"Hardly, yet—you say that Brent is ill. Could he be seen?"

"I fancy not. He is in a California sanitarium, broken down from overwork, the doctors informed me."

"I see." Gray scrutinized his companions. The same eagerness showed in each face, the craving for discovery which is greater than the lust of the gold prospector. They were hanging on his next words. "Gentlemen, do you realize that three great difficulties are to be met? Money—China—and a knowledge of science. By that I mean my own qualifications. I am an explorer, not a scientist——"

At this point Balch, the financier who had not spoken before, leaned forward.

"Three excellent points," he nodded. "I can answer them. We can supply you with funds, Captain Gray," he said decisively.

"And permission from the Chinese authorities?"

"We have passports signed, in blank, for an American hunter and naturalist to journey into the interior of China, to the Gobi Desert."

"You will not go alone," explained Van Schaick. "We realize that a scientist must accompany you."

"We have the man," continued Balch, "an orientologist—speaks Persian and Turki—knows Central Asia like a book. Professor Arminius Delabar. He'll join you at Frisco." He stood up and held out his hand. "Gray, you're the man we want! I like your talk." He laughed boyishly, being young in heart, in spite of his years. "You're equal to the job—and you can shoot a mountain sheep or a bandit in the head at five hundred yards. Don't deny it—you've done it!"

"Maps?" asked Gray dryly.

"The best we could get. Chinese and Russian surveys of the Western Gobi," Balch explained briskly. "We want you to start right off. We know that our dearest foes, the British Asiatic So-

ciety, have wind of the Wusun. They are fitting
out an expedition. It will have the edge on yours
because—discounting the fact that the British know
the field better—it'll start from India, which is
nearer the Gobi."

"Then it's got to be a race?" Gray frowned.

"A race it is," nodded Balch, "and my money
backs you and Delabar. So the sooner you can
start the better. Van Schaick will go with you to
Frisco and give you details, with maps and passports on the way. We'll pay you the salary of
your rank in the army, with a fifty per cent bonus
if you get to the Wusun. Now, what's your answer—yes or no?" He glanced at the officer sharply, realizing that if Gray doubted, he would not be
the man for the expedition.

Gray smiled quizzically.

"I came to you to get a job," he said, "and here
it is. I need the money. My answer is—yes. I'll
do my best to deliver the goods."

"Gentlemen," Balch turned to his associates, "I
congratulate you. Captain Gray may or may not
get to the Wusun. But—unless I'm a worse judge
of character than I think—he'll get to the place
where the Wusun ought to be. He won't turn
back."

Their visitor flushed at that. He was still young,
being not yet thirty. He shook hands all around
and left for his hotel, with Balch and Van Schaick

Legends

to arrange railroad schedules, and the buying of an outfit.

This is a brief account òf how Robert Gray came to depart on his mission to the Desert of Gobi, as reported in the files of the American Exploration Society for the summer of 1919.

It was not given to the press at the time, owing to the need of secrecy. Nor did the Exploration Society obtain authority from the United States Government for the expedition. Time was pressing, as they learned the British expedition was getting together at Burma. Later, Van Schaick agreed with Balch that this had been a mistake.

But by that time Gray was far beyond reach, in the foothills of the Celestial Mountains, in the *Liu Sha,* and had learned the meaning of the pale sickness.

CHAPTER III

DELABAR DISCOURSES

GRAY had meant what he said about his new job. Van Schaick pleaded for haste, but the army officer knew from experience the danger of omitting some important item from his outfit, and went ahead with characteristic thoroughness.

He assembled his personal kit in New York, with the rifles, medicines and ammunition that he needed. Also a good pair of field glasses and the maps that Van Schaick furnished. Balch made him a present of twenty pounds of fine smoking tobacco which was gratefully received.

"I'll need another man with me," Gray told Van Schaick, who was on edge to be off. "Delabar'll be all right in his way, but we'll want a white man who can shoot and work. I know the man for the job—McCann, once my orderly, now in the reserve."

"Get him, by all means," agreed the scientist.

"He's in Texas, out of a job. A wire'll bring him to Frisco in time to meet us. Well, I'm about ready to check out."

16

Delabar Discourses

They left that night on the western express.

Gray was not sorry to leave the city. Like all voyagers, he felt the oppression of the narrow streets, the monotony of always going home to the same place to sleep. Wanderlust had gripped him again at thought of the venture into another continent.

He took his mission seriously. On the maps that Van Schaick and Balch had given him they had pointed out a spot beyond the known travel routes, a good deal more than a thousand miles into the interior of China. To this spot Gray was going. He had his orders and he would carry them out.

Van Schaick talked much on the train. He explained how much the mission meant to the Exploration Society. It would give them world-wide fame. And it would add enormously to the knowledge of humankind. Gray, he said, would travel near the path of Marco Polo; he would tear the veil of secrecy from the hidden corner of the Gobi Desert. It would be a victory of science over the ancient soul of Mongolia.

It would shake the foundation of the great jade image of Buddha, of the many-armed Kali, of Bon the devil-god, and the ancient Vishnu. It would strengthen the hold of the Bible on the Mongolian world.

If only, said Van Schaick wistfully, Gray could find the Wusun ahead of the expedition of the

Marching Sands

British Asiatic Society, the triumph would be complete.

Gray listened silently. It was fortunate, in the light of what followed, that his imagination was not easily stirred.

He looked curiously at the man who was to be his partner in the expedition. Van Schaick introduced them at the platform of the San Francisco terminal.

Professor Arminius Delabar was a short, slender man, of wiry build and a nervous manner that reminded Gray of a bird. He had near-sighted, bloodshot eyes encased behind tinted glasses, and a dark face with well-kept beard. He was half Syrian by birth, American by choice, and a denizen of the academies and byways of the world. Also, he spoke at least four languages fluently.

The army man's respect for his future companion went up several notches when he found that Delabar had already arranged competently for the purchase and shipment of their stores.

"You see," he explained in his room at the hotel to Gray, "the fewer things we must buy in Shanghai the better. Our plan is to attract as little attention as possible. Our passport describes us as hunter and naturalist. Foreigners are a common sight in China as far into the interior as Liangchowfu. Once we are past there and on the interior plains, it will be hard to follow us—if we have attracted no attention. Do you speak any Chinese dialects?"

It was an abrupt question, in Delabar's high voice. The Syrian spoke English with only the trace of an accent.

"A little," admitted Gray. "I was born in Shensi, but I don't remember anything except a baby white camel—a playmate. Mandarin Chinese is Greek to me."

Some time afterward he learned that Delabar had taken this as a casual boast—not knowing Gray's habit of understating his qualifications. Fortune plays queer tricks sometimes and Gray's answer was to loom large in the coming events.

Fortune, or as Gray put it, the luck of the road, threw two obstacles in their way at Frisco. Van Schaick had telegraphed ahead to the sanitarium where the missionary Brent was being treated. He hoped to arrange an interview between Brent and Gray.

Brent was dying. No one could visit him. Also, McCann, the soldier who was to accompany them, did not show up at the hotel,—although he had wired his officer at Chicago that he would be in Frisco before the appointed time.

Gray would have liked to wait for the man. He knew McCann would be useful—a crack shot, a good servant, and an expert at handling men—but Delabar had already booked their passage on the next Pacific Mail steamer.

"Van Schaick can wait here," Delabar assured Gray, "meet McCann, and send him on by the boat following. He will join you at Shanghai."

"Very well," assented Gray, who was checking up the list of stores Delabar had bought. "That will do nicely. I see that you've thought of all the necessary things, Professor. We can pick up a reserve supply of canned foodstuffs at Shanghai, or Hankow." He glanced at Van Schaick. "There's one thing more to be settled. It's important. Who is in command of this party? The Professor or I? If he's to be the boss, all right—I'll carry on with that understanding."

Van Schaick hesitated. But Delabar spoke up quickly.

"The expedition is in your hands, Captain Gray. I freely yield you the responsibility."

Gray was still watching Van Schaick. "Is that understood? It's a good thing to clear up before we start."

"Certainly," assented the scientist. "Now we'll discuss the best route——"

Van Schaick stood at the pier-head the next day when the steamer cast off her moorings, and waved good-by to the two. Gray left him behind with some regret. A good man, Van Schaick, an American from first to last, and a slave to science.

During the monotonous run across the Pacific when the sea and the sky seemed unchanged from day to day, Delabar talked incessantly about their trip. Gray, who preferred to spend the time doing and saying nothing, listened quietly.

The officer was well content to lie back in his deck chair, hands clasped behind his curly head, and stare out into space. This was his habit, when off duty. It satisfied him to the soul to do nothing but watch the thin line where the gray-blue of the Pacific melted into the pale blue of the sky, and feel the sun's heat on his face. It made him appear lazy. Which he was not.

The energetic professor fancied that Gray paid little attention to his stream of information about the great Gobi Desert. In that, he did the other an injustice. Gray heeded and weighed Delabar's words. Ingrained in him from army life and a solitary existence marked by few friendships was the need of reticence, and watchfulness. Nor was his inclination to idle on the voyage mere habit. Unconsciously, he was storing up vital strength in his strongly knit frame—strength which he had called on in the past, and which he would need again.

"You don't seem to appreciate, my young friend," remarked the professor once, irritably, "that it is inner Asia we are invading. Also, we are going a thousand miles beyond your American gunboats."

"The days of the *Ih-hwo-Ch'uan* are past."

Delabar shrugged his shoulders, surprised at his

companion's pertinent remark. "True. China is a republic and progressive, perhaps. But the Mongolian soul does not change overnight. Moreover, there are the priests—Buddhists and Taoists. Fear and superstition rule the mass of the Dragon Kingdom, my friend, and it is these priests who will be our enemies."

Gray had spoken truly when he said he remembered nothing of China, except a white camel, but, subconsciously, many things were familiar to the soldier.

"At the border of the Gobi Desert, where we believe the Wusun to be," continued the scientist warmly, as Gray was silent, "a center of Buddhism existed in the Middle Ages. The three sects of Buddhist priests—Black, Yellow and Red—are united in the effort to preserve their power. They preach the advent of the Gautama in the next few years. Also, that the ancient Gautama ruled the spiritual world before the coming of Christianity.

"So you can see," he pointed out, "that the discovery of a white race—a race that did not acknowledge Buddha—in the heart of China would be a blow to their doctrine. It would contradict their book of prophecy."

Gray nodded, puffing at his pipe. Presently, he stirred himself to speak.

"Rather suspect you're right, Professor. You know the religious dope. And the religions of

Delabar Discourses

Asia are not good things to monkey with. But, look here." He drew a map from his pocket and spread it out on his knee. "Here's the spot where Van Schaick located the Wusun—our long-lost but not forgotten cousins. Well and good. Only that spot, which you and your friends call the 'blind spot' of Asia, happens to be in the middle of the far Gobi Desert. How do you figure people existed there for several centuries?"

Delabar hesitated, glancing up at the moving tracery of smoke that rose from the funnel, against the clouds. They were on the boat deck.

"The Ming annals mention a city in that place, some two thousand years ago. A thousand years later we know there were many palaces at this end of the Thian Shan—the Celestial Mountains. Remember that the caravan routes from China to Samarcand, India and Persia are very old, and that they- or one of the most important of them—ran past this blind spot."

"Marco Polo trailed along there, didn't he?"

"Yes. We know the great city of the Gobi was called Sungan. The Ming annals describe it as having 'massive gates, walls and bastions, besides underground passages, vaulted and arched.' "

"European travelers don't report this city."

"Because they never saw it, my friend. Brent, who was at the edge of the Gobi near there, states that he saw towers in the sand. And the Mohammedan annals of Central Asia have a curious tale."

"Let's have it," said Gray, settling himself comfortably in his chair.

"It was in the sixteenth century," explained Delabar, who seemed to have the myths of Asia at his tongue's end. "A religious legend. A certain holy man, follower of the prophet, was robbed and beaten in a city near where we believe Sungan to be. After his injury by the people of the city—he was a *mullah*—he climbed into a minaret to call the hour of evening prayer."

Delabar's voice softened as he spoke, sliding into more musical articulation.

"As he cried the hour, this holy man felt something falling like snow on his face. Only it was not snow. The sky and the city darkened. He could not see the roofs of the buildings. He went down and tried the door. It was blocked. Then this man saw that it was sand falling over the city. The sand covered the whole town, leaving only the minaret, which was high. The people who had done him the injury were buried—became white bones under the sand."

"That story figures in the Bible," assented Gray, "only not the same. You don't consider the myth important, do you?"

"The priests of Asia do," said the professor seriously. "And I have seen the memoirs of Central Asian kingdoms which mention that treasure was dug for and found in ruins in the sands." He glanced at his companion curiously. "You do not seem to be worried, Captain Gray, at entering the forbidden shrine of the Mongols."

Having been born thereabouts, the idea amused Gray.

"Are you?" Gray laughed. "The Yellow Peril is dead."

"So is Dr. Brent."

"You don't connect the two?"

"I don't attempt to analyze the connection, Captain Gray. Remember in China we are dealing with men who think backward, around-about, and every way except our own. Then there are the priests. All I know is that Dr. Brent entered on forbidden ground, fell sick, and had to leave China. Do you know what he died of?"

"Do you?"

Delabar was silent a moment; then he smiled. "I have imagination—too much, perhaps. But then I have lived behind the threshold of Asia for half my life."

"I suspect it's a good thing for me you have," Gray admitted frankly.

Before they left their chairs that afternoon a steward brought the officer a message from the wireless cabin.

Van Schaick had sent it, before the steamer passed

the radio limit.   Gray read it, frowned, and turned to Delabar.

"This is rather bad luck, Professor," he said. "McCann, the fellow I counted on, is not coming. He was taken sick with grippe in Los Angeles on his way to Frisco.   It looks as if you and I would have to go it alone."

CHAPTER IV

THE news of McCann's loss, so important to the officer, Delabar passed over with a shrug. Gray wondered briefly why a man obviously inclined to nervousness should ignore the fact that they were without the services of a trustworthy attendant. Later, he came to realize that the scientist considered that McCann's presence would have been no aid to him, that rifles and men who knew how to use them would play no part in meeting the hostile forces surrounding the territory of the Wusun.

From that moment he began to watch Delabar. It was clear to him that the professor was uneasy, decidedly so. And that the man was in the grip of a rising excitement.

It manifested itself when the steamer stopped at a Japanese port. Gray would have liked to visit Kyoto, to see again the little brown people of the island kingdom, to get a glimpse of the gray castle of Oksaka, and perhaps of peerless, snow-crowned Fujiyama.

But Delabar insisted on remaining aboard the steamer until they left for China. The nearing

gateway of Asia had a powerful effect on him.
Gray noticed—as it was unusual in a man of mildly
studious habits—that the scientist smoked quantities
of strong Russian cigarettes. Indeed, the air of
their cabin was heavy with the fumes.

"We must not make ourselves conspicuous,"
Delabar urged repeatedly.

At Shanghai they passed quickly through the
hands of the customs officials. Their preparations
progressed smoothly; the baggage was put on board
a waiting Hankow steamer, and Delabar added to
their stores a sufficient quantity of provisions to
round out their outfit. In spite of this, Delabar
fidgeted until they were safely in their stateroom
on the river steamer, and passing up the broad,
brown current of the Yang-tze-kiang—which, by
the way, is not called the Yang-tze-kiang by the
Chinese.

Gray made no comment on his companion's misgivings. He saw no cause for alarm. There were
a dozen other travelers on the river boat, sales
agents of three nations, a railroad engineer or two,
a family of missionaries, several tourists who stared
blandly at the great tidal stretch of the river, and
commented loudly on the comforts of the palatial
vessel. Evidently they had expected to go up to
Hankow in a junk. They pointed out the choco-
late colored sails of the passing junks with their
half-naked coolies and dirty decks.

Warning

For days the single screw of the Hankow boat churned the muddy waste, and the smoke spread, fanwise, over its wake.

The Yang-tze was not new to Gray. He was glad he was going into the interior. The fecund cities of the coast, with their monotonous, crowded streets, narrow and overhung with painted signs held no attraction for him. The panorama of Mongolian faces, pallid and seamed, furtive and merry was not what he had come to China to see. In the interior, beyond the forest crowned mountains, and the vast plains, was the expanse of the desert. Until they reached this, the trip was no more than a necessary evil.

Not so—as Gray noted—did it affect Delabar. The first meeting with the blue-clad throngs in Shanghai, the first glimpse of the pagoda-temples with their shaven priests had both exhilarated and depressed the scientist.

"Each stage of the journey," he confided to Gray, "drops us back a century in civilization."

"No harm done," grunted the officer, who had determined to put a check on Delabar's active imagination. "As long as we get ahead. That's the deuce of this country. We have to go zig-zag. There's no such thing as a straight line being the shortest distance between two points in the land of the Dragon."

Delabar frowned, surprised by these unexpected

displays of latent knowledge. Then smiled, waving a thin hand at the yellow current of the river.

"There is a reason for that—as always, in China. Evil spirits, they believe, can not move out of a straight line. So we find screens put just inside the gates of temples—to ward off the evil influences."

"Look at that," Gray touched the other's arm. A steward stood near them at the stern. No one else was in that· part of the deck, and after glancing around cautiously the man dropped over the side some white objects—what they were, Gray could not see. "I heard that some fishermen had been drowned near here a few days ago. That Chink—for all his European dress—is dropping overside portions of bread as food and peace offering to the spirits of the drowned."

"Yes," nodded Delabar, "the lower orders of Chinamen believe the drowned have power to pull the living after them to death. Centuries of missionary endeavor have not altered their superstitions. And, look—that does not prevent those starved beggars in the junk there from retrieving the bread in the water. Ugh!"

He thrust his hands into his pockets and tramped off up the deck, while Gray gazed after him curiously, and then turned to watch the junk. The coolies were waving at the steward who was watching them impassively. Seeing Gray, the man hurried about his duties. For a moment the officer hesitated, seeing that the junkmen were staring, not at the bread in their hands, but at the ship. Then he smiled and walked on.

In spite of Delabar's misgivings, the journey went smoothly. The banks of the river closed in on them, scattered mud villages appeared in the shore rushes. Half naked boys waved at the "fire junk" from the backs of water buffaloes, and the smoke of Hankow loomed on the horizon. From Hankow, the Peking-Hankow railway took them comfortably to Honanfu, after a two-day stage by cart.

Here they waited for their luggage to catch up with them, in a fairly clean and modern hotel. They avoided the other Europeans in the city. Gray knew that they were beyond the usual circuit of American tourists, and wished to travel as quietly as possible.

"We're in luck," he observed to Delabar, who had just come in. "In a month, if all goes well, we'll be in Liangchowfu, the 'Western Gate' to the steppe country. What's the matter?"

Delabar held out a long sheet of rice paper with a curious expression.

"An invitation to dine with one of the officials of Honan, Captain Gray—with the vice-governor. He asks us to bring our passports."

"Hm," the officer replaced the maps he had been overhauling in their case, and thrust the missive on top of them. He tossed the case into an open valise. "A sort of polite invitation to show our cards—to explain who we are, eh? Well, let's accept with pleasure. We've got to play the game according to the rules. Nothing queer about this invite. Chinese officials are hospitable enough. All they want is a present or two."

He produced from the valise a clock with chimes and a silver-plated pocket flashlight and scrutinized them mildly.

"This ought to do the trick. We'll put on our best clothes. And remember, I'm a big-game enthusiast."

Delabar was moody that afternoon, and watched Gray's cheerful preparations for the dinner without interest. The army man stowed away their more valuable possessions, carefully hanging the rifle which he had been carrying in its case over his shoulder under the frame of the bed.

"A trick I learned in Mindanao," he explained. "These towns are chuck full of thieves, and this rifle is valuable to me. The oriental second-story man has yet to discover that American army men hang their rifles under the frame of their cots. Now for the vice-governor, what's his name? Wu Fang Chien?"

Wu Fang Chien was most affable. He sent two sedan chairs for the Americans and received them at his door with marked politeness, shaking his

Warning

hands in his wide sleeves agreeably when Delabar introduced Gray. He spoke English better than the professor spoke Chinese, and inquired solicitously after their health and their purpose in visiting his country.

He was a tall mandarin, wearing the usual iron rimmed spectacles, and dressed in his robe of ceremony.

During the long dinner of the usual thirty courses, Delabar talked with the mandarin, while Gray contented himself with a few customary compliments. But Wu Fang Chien watched Gray steadily, from bland, faded eyes.

"I have not known an American hunter to come so far into China," he observed to the officer. "My humble and insufficient home is honored by the presence of an enthusiast. What game you expect to find?"

"Stags, antelope, and some of the splendid mountain sheep of Shensi," replied Gray calmly. Wu Fang Chien's fan paused, at the precision of the answer.

"Then you are going far. Do your passports permit?"

"They give us a free hand. We will follow the game trails."

"As far as Liangchowfu?"

"Perhaps."

"Beyond that is another province." The man-

33

darin tapped his well-kept fingers thoughtfully on the table. "I would not advise you, Captain Gray, to go beyond Liangchowfu. As you know, my unhappy country has transpired a double change of government and the outlaw tribes of the interior have become unruly during the last rebellion." He fumbled only slightly for words.

Gray nodded.

"We are prepared to take some risks."

Wu Fang Chien bowed politely.

"It might be dangerous—to go beyond Liangchowfu. Your country and mine are most friendly, Captain Gray. I esteem your welfare as my own. My sorrow would greaten if injury happen to you."

"Your kindness does honor to your heart."

"I suggest," Wu Fang Chien looked mildly at the uneasy Delabar, "that you have me *visé* your passports so that you may travel safely this side of Liangchowfu. Then I will give you a military escort who will be protection against any outlaws you meet on the road. In this way I will feel that I am doing my full duty to my honored guests."

"The offer is worthy," said Gray, who realized that the sense of duty of a town official was a serious thing, but did not wish an escort, "of one whose hospitality is a pleasure to his guests."

Wu Fang Chien shook hands with himself. "But we have little money to pay an escort——"

"I will attend to that."

Warning

"Unfortunately, an escort of soldiers would spoil my chances at big game. We shall pick up some native hunters."

Wu Fang Chien bowed, with a faint flicker of green eyes.

"It shall be as you wish, Captain Gray. But I am distressed at the thought you may suffer harm. The last American who went beyond the Western Gate, died."

Gray frowned. He had not known that one of his countrymen had penetrated so far into the interior.

"Without doubt," pursued the mandarin, stroking his fan gently across his face, "you have a good supply of rifles. I have heard much of these excellent weapons of your country. Would you oblige me showing them to me before you leave Honan?"

"I should be glad to do so," said Gray, "if they were not packed in our luggage which will not be here before we set out. But I have two small presents——"

The gift of the clock and electric light turned the thread of conversation and seemed to satisfy Wu Fang Chien, who bowed them out with the utmost courtesy to the waiting sedan chairs. Then, as the bearers picked up the poles, he drew a small and exquisite vase from under his robe and pressed it upon Gray as a token, he said, to keep fresh the memory of their visit.

At their room in the hotel Gray showed the vase to Delabar. It was a valuable object, of enamel wrought on gold leaves, and inscribed with some Chinese characters.

"What do you make of our worthy Wu Fang—

hullo!" he broke off. Delabar had seized the vase and taken off the top.

"It is what the Chinese call a message jar," explained the scientist, feeling within the vase. He removed a slim roll of silk, wound about an ebony stick. On the silk four Chinese characters were delicately painted.

"What do they mean?" asked Gray, looking over his shoulder.

36

Warning

The Syrian glanced at him appraisingly, under knitted brows. His companion's face was expressionless, save for a slight tinge of curiosity. Delabar judged that the soldier knew nothing of written Chinese, which was the truth.

"Anything or nothing, my friend. It reads like a proverb. The oriental soul takes pleasure in maxims. Yet everything they do or say has a meaning—very often a double meaning."

"Such as Wu Fang's table talk," smiled Gray.

"Granted. Is this any particular dialect?"

"Written Chinese is much the same everywhere. Just as the Arabic numerals throughout Europe." He scanned the silk attentively, and his lips parted. "The first ideograph combines the attribute or adjective 'clever' or 'shrewd' with the indicator 'man.' A shrewd man—*hua jen.*"

"Perhaps Wu Fang: perhaps you. Go on."

"The second character is very ancient, almost a picture-drawing of warning streamers. It is an emphatic 'do not!' "

"Then it's you—and me."

"The third character is prefixed by *mu,* a tree, and signifies a wooden board, or a wall. The fourth means 'the West.' "

"A riddle, but not so hard to guess," grinned Gray, taking up his maps from the table and filling his pipe preparatory to work. *"A wise guy doesn't climb the western wall."*

"You forget," pointed out Delabar sharply, "the negative. It is the strongest kind of a warning. *Do not, if you are wise, approach the western wall.* My friend, this is a plain warning—even a threat. To-day Wu Fang Chien hinted we should not go to Liangchowfu. Now he threatens——"

"I gathered as much." Gray took the slip of fine silk and scanned it quizzically. "Delabar, do you know the ideograph for 'to make' or 'build?'"

The scientist nodded.

"Then write it, where it seems to fit in here."

Delabar did so, with a glance at his companion. Whereupon the soldier folded the missive and replaced it in the jar. He clapped his hands loudly. Almost at once a boy appeared in the door.

To him Gray handed the vase with instructions to carry it to His Excellency, the official Wu Fang Chien. He reënforced his order with a piece of silver cash. To the curious scientist he explained briefly.

"Wu Fang is a scholar. He will read our reply as: *A wise man will not build a wall in the west.* It will give him food for thought, and it *may* keep His Excellency's men from overhauling our belongings a second time during our absence."

Delabar started. "May?"

"Yes. Remember I left that message of Wu's on top of these maps. I find it underneath them. The maps are all here. We locked our door, carefully. Some one has evidently given our papers the once over and forgotten to replace them in the order he found them. I say it *may* have been at Wu's orders. I think it probably was."

"Why?" Delabar licked his thin lips nervously.

"Because nothing has been taken. A Chinese official has the right to be curious about strangers in his district. Likewise, his men wouldn't have much trouble in entering the room—with the landlord's assistance. The ordinary run of thieves would have taken something valuable—my field glasses, for instance."

Delabar strode nervously the length of the room and peered from the shutters.

"Captain Gray!" he swung around, "do you know there are maps of the Gobi, of Sungan, in your case. The person who broke into our room must have seen them."

"I reckon so."

"Then Wu Fang Chien may know we are going to the Gobi! I have not forgotten what he said about the last American hunter. What hunter has been as far as the Gobi? None. So——"

"You think he meant——"

"Dr. Brent."

Gray shook his head slowly. "Far fetched, Delabar," he meditated. "You're putting two and two together to make ten. All we *know* is that Wu has sent us a polite motto. No use in worrying ourselves."

But it was clear to him that Delabar was worried, and more. Gray had been observing his companion closely. Now for the first time he read covert fear in the professor's thin face.

Fear, Gray reflected to himself, was hard to deal with, in a man of weak vitality and high-strung nerves. He felt that Delabar was alarmed needlessly; that he dreaded what lay before them.

For that reason he regretted the event of that night which gave shape to Delabar's apprehensions.

At the scientist's urging, they did not leave the room before turning in. Gray adjusted Delabar's walking stick against the door, placing a string of Chinese money on the head of the stick, and balancing the combination so a movement of the door would send the coins crashing to the floor.

"Just in case our second-story men pay us another visit," he explained. "Now that we know they can open the door, we'll act accordingly."

CHAPTER V

INTRUDERS

IT was a hot night.

Gray, naked except for shirt and socks, lay under the mosquito netting and wished that he had brought double the amount of insect powder he had. Across the room Delabar had subsided into fitful snores. The night was not quiet.

In the courtyard of the hotel some Chinese servants were at their perpetual gambling, their shrill voices coming up through the shutters. On the further side of the street a guitar twanged monotonously. Somewhere, a dog yelped.

The warm odors of the place assaulted Gray's nostrils unpleasantly. They were strange, potent odors, a mingling of dirt, refuse, horses, the remnants of cooking. Gray sighed, longing for the clean air of the plains toward which they were headed.

They were still far from the Gobi's edge. The distance seemed to stretch out interminably. It is not easy to cross the broad bosom of China.

He wondered what success they would have. What was the city of Sungan? How had it escaped observation? How did a city happen to be in the desert, anyway?

What was the pale sickness Brent had spoken of? Brent had died. From natural causes, of course. Gray gave little heed to Delabar's wild surmises. But the conduct of Wu Fang Chien afforded him food for thought.

Had the vice-governor actually known of their mission? His words might have had a double meaning. And they might not. The silk scroll meant little. Delabar had read warning into it; but was not that a result of his imagination?

Gray turned uncomfortably on his bed and considered the matter. How could Wu Fang Chien have known they were bound for Sungan? Their mission had been carefully kept from publicity. Only Van Schaick and his three associates knew of it. Men like Van Schaick and Balch could keep their mouths shut. And Delabar was certainly cautious enough.

Gray cursed the heat under his breath, with added measure for the dog which seemed bound to make a night of it. The chatter at the hotel door had subsided with midnight. But the guitar still struck its melancholy note, accompanied by the intermittent wail of the sorrowing dog.

No, Gray thought sleepily, Wu Fang Chien could not have known of their mission. He had let Delabar's nerves prey on his own—that was all. Dela-

Intruders

bar was full of this Asia stuff, especially concerning the priests——

Gray's mind drifted away into vague visions of ancient and forgotten temples. The guitar note became the strum of temple drums, echoing over the waste of the desert. The dog's plaint took form in the wailing of shrouded forms that moved about gigantic ruins, ruins that gave forth throngs of spirits. And the spirits took up the wail, approaching him.

A green light flamed from tae temple gate. The gongs sounded a final crash—and Gray awoke at the noise of the stick and coins falling to the floor.

He became fully conscious instantly—from habit. And was aware of two things. He had been asleep for some time. Also, the door had been thrown open and dark forms were running into the room.

Gray caught at his automatic which he always hung at his pillow. He missed it in the dark. One of the figures stumbled against the bed. He felt a hand brush across his face.

Drawing up his legs swiftly he kicked out at the man who was fumbling for him. The fellow subsided backward with a grunt, and the officer gained his feet. His sight was not yet cleared, but he perceived the blur of figures in the light from the open door.

He wasted no time in outcry. Experience had taught him that the best way to deal with native assailants was with his fists. He bent forward from the hips, balanced himself and jabbed at the first man who ran up to him.

His fist landed in the intruder's face. Gray weighed over a hundred and seventy pounds, and he had the knack which comparatively few men possess of putting his weight behind his fists. Moreover, he was not easily flurried, and this coolness gave his blows added sting.

At least four men had broken into the room. The other two hesitated when they saw their companions knocked down. But Gray did not. There was a brief rustle of feet over the floor, the sound of a heavy fist striking against flesh, and the invaders stumbled or crawled from the room.

Gray was surprised they did not use their knives. Once they perceived that he was fully awake they seemed to lose heart. The fight had taken only a minute, and Gray was master of the field.

He had counted four men as they ran out. But he waited alertly by the door while Delabar, who had remained on his bed, got up and lit the lamp. Gray's first glance told him that no Chinamen were to be seen.

He was breathing heavily, but quite unhurt. Having the advantage of both weight and hitting power over his light adversaries, he took no pride in his prompt clearing of the room. Delabar, however, was plainly shaky.

44

Intruders

"What did they want?" the professor muttered, eyeing the door. "How——"

"Look out!" warned Gray crisply.

From the foot of his bed a head appeared. Two slant eyes fixed on him angrily. A Chinaman in the rough clothes of a coolie crawled out and stood erect.

In one hand he held Gray's rifle, removed from the case. With the other he was fumbling at the safety catch with which he seemed unfamiliar.

Gray acted swiftly. Realizing that the gun was loaded and that it would go off if the coolie thought of pulling the trigger, inasmuch as the safety catch was not set, he stepped to one side, to the head of the bed.

Here he fell to his knees. The man with the rifle, if he had fired, would probably have shot over the American, who was feeling under the pillow.

As it happened the coolie did not pull the trigger of the gun. A dart of flame, a *crack* which echoed loudly in the narrow room—and Gray, over the sights of the automatic which he had recovered and fired in one motion, saw the man stagger.

Through the swirling smoke he saw the coolie drop the gun and run to the window.

Gray covered the man again, but refrained from pressing the trigger. There was no need of killing the coolie. The next instant the man had flung open the shutters and dived from the window.

45

Marching Sands

Looking out, Gray saw the form of his adversary vaguely as the coolie picked himself up and vanished in the darkness.

The street was silent. The guitar was no longer to be heard.

Gray crossed the room and flung open the door. The hall was empty. He closed the door, readjusted the stick and string of coins and grinned at Delabar who was watching nervously.

"That was one on me, Professor," he admitted cheerfully. "The coolie who bobbed up under the bed must have been the one I kicked there. Fancy knocking a man to where he can grab your own gun."

Delabar, however, saw no humor in the situation.

"They were coolies," he said. "What do you suppose they came after?"

"Money. I don't know." Gray replaced the shutters and blew out the light. "We'll complain to our landlord in the morning. But I don't guess we'll have much satisfaction out of him. The fact that my shot didn't bring the household running here shows pretty well that it was a put-up job."

His prophecy proved true. The proprietor of the hotel protested that he had known nothing of the matter. Asked why he had not investigated the shot, he declared that he was afraid. Gray gave

46

Intruders

up his questioning and set about preparing to leave Honanfu.

"The sooner we're away from Wu Fang's jurisdiction the better," he observed to Delabar. "No use in making an investigation. It would only delay us. Our baggage came this morning, and you've engaged the muleteers. We'll shake Honanfu."

Delabar seemed as anxious as Gray to leave the town. Crowds of Chinese, attracted perhaps by rumor of what had happened in the night, followed them about the streets as Gray energetically assembled his two wagons with the stores, and the men to drive the mules.

He made one discovery. In checking up the list of baggage they found that one box was missing.

"It's the one that had the rifles and spare ammunition," grunted Gray. "Damn!"

He had put the rifle that had been intended for McCann with his own extra piece and ammunition in a separate box. In spite of persistent questioning, the drivers who had brought the wagons to Honanfu denied that they had seen the box.

A telegram was sent to the railway terminal. The answer was delayed until late afternoon. No news of the box was forthcoming.

"It's no use," declared Delabar moodily. "Remember, you told Wu Fang Chien that our rifles were with the luggage. Probably he has taken the box."

47

Marching Sands

"Looks that way," admitted Gray, who was angered at the loss. "Well, there's no help for it. We'll hike, before Wu Fang thinks up something else to do."

He gave the word to the muleteers, the wagons creaked forward. He jumped on the tail of the last one, beside Delabar, and Honanfu with its watching crowds faded into the dust, after a turn in the road.

From that time forth, Gray kept his rifle in his hand, or slung at his shoulder.

While they sat huddled uncomfortably on some stores against the side of the jogging cart—nothing is quite so responsive to the law of gravity as a springless Chinese cart, or so uncomfortable, unless it be the rutted surface of a Chinese imperial highway—both were thinking.

Delabar, to himself: "Why is it that an imperial road in China is not one kept in order—in the past —for the emperor, but one that can be put in order, if the emperor announced his intention of passing over it? My associate, the American, who thinks only along straight lines, will never understand the round-about working of the oriental mind. And that will work him evil."

Gray, aloud: "Look here, Delabar! We can safely guess now that Wu Fang would like to hinder our journey."

"I have already assumed that."

48

Intruders

"Hm. Think it's because the Wusun actually exist, and he wants to keep us from the Gobi?"

Delabar was aroused from his muse.

"A Chinese official seldom acts on his own initiative," he responded. "Wu Fang Chien has received instructions. Yes, I think he intends to bar our passage beyond Liangchowfu. By advancing as we are from Honanfu, we are running blindly into danger."

Gray squinted back at the dusty road, nursing his rifle across his knees. His brown face was impassive, the skin about the eyes deeply wrinkled from exposure. The eyes themselves were narrow and hard. Delabar found it increasingly difficult to guess what went on in the mind of the taciturn American.

"I've been wondering," said Gray slowly, "wondering for a long time about a certain question. Admitting that the Wusun are there, in the Gobi, why are they kept prisoners—carefully guarded like this? It doesn't seem logical!"

The Syrian smiled blandly, twisting his beard with a thin hand.

"Logic!" he cried. "Oh, the mind of the inner Asiatic is logical; but the reasons governing it, and the grounds for its deductions are quite different from the motives of European psychology."

"Well, I fail to see the reason why the Wusun people should be guarded for a good many hundred years."

49

Marching Sands

"Simply this. Buddhism is the crux of the oriental soul. Confucius and Taoism are secondary to the advent of the Gautama—to the great Nirvana. Buddhism rules inner China, Tibet, part of Turkestan, some of India, and—under guise of *Shamanism,* Southeastern Siberia."

Gray made no response. He was studying the face of Delabar—that intellectual, nervous, unstable face.

"Buddhism has ruled Central Asia since the time of Sakuntala—the great Sakuntala," went on the scientist. "And the laws of Buddha are ancient and very binding. The Wusun are enemies of Buddhism. They are greater enemies than the Manchus, of Northern and Eastern China. That is because the Wusun hold in reverence a symbol that is hateful to the priests of the temples."

"What is that?"

Delabar hesitated.

"The symbol is some barbarian sign. The Wusun cherish it, perhaps because cut off from the world, they have no other faith than the faith of their forefathers." The scientist's high voice rang with strong conviction. "In the annals of the Han dynasty, before the birth of Christ, it is related that an army under the General Ho K'u-p'ing was sent on plea of the Buddhists to destroy the Huing-nu—, the 'green-eyed devils' and the Wusun—the 'Tall Ones,' of the west. The military expedition failed.

But since then the Buddhists have been embittered against the Wusun—have guarded them as prisoners."

"Then religious fanaticism is the answer?"

"A religious feud."

"Because the Wusun will not adopt Buddhism?"

"Because they cling to the absurd sign of their faith!"

Gray passed a gnarled hand across his chin and frowned at his rifle.

"Sounds queer. I'd like to see that sign."

Delabar settled himself uneasily against the jarring of the cart.

"It is not likely, Captain Gray," he said, "that either of us will see it."

Whereupon they fell silent, each busied with his thoughts, in this manner.

Delabar, to himself: My companion is a physical brute; how can he understand the high mysteries of Asian thought?

Gray: Either this Syrian has a grand imagination, or he knows more than he has been telling me—the odds being the latter is correct.

CHAPTER VI

NEAR Kia-yu-kwan, the western gate of the Great Wall, the twin pagodas of Liangchowfu rise from the plain.

In former centuries Liangchowfu was the border town, a citadel of defense against the outer barbarians of the northern steppe and Central Asia. It is a walled city, standing squarely athwart the highway from China proper to the interior. Beyond Liangchowfu are the highlands of Central Asia.

In exactly a month after leaving Honanfu, as Gray had promised, the wagons bearing the two Americans passed through the town gate.

Gray, dusty and travel-stained to his waist, but alert and erect of carriage, walked before the two carts. He showed no ill effects from the hard stage of the journey they had just completed.

Delabar lay behind the leather curtain of one of the wagons. His spirits had suffered from the past month. The monotonous road, with its ceaseless mud villages had depressed him. The groups of natives squatting in the sun before their huts, in the never-ending search for vermin, and the throngs of staring children that sought for horse dung in

52

the roads to use for fuel, had wrought on his sensitive nerves.

They had not seen a white man during the journey. Gray had written to Van Schaick before they left Honanfu, but they expected no mail until they should return to Shanghai.

"If we reach the coast again," Delabar had said moodily.

The better air of the hill country through which they passed had not improved his spirits, as it had Gray's. The sight of the forest clad peaks, with their hidden pagodas, from the eaves of which the wind bells sent their tinkle down the breeze, held no interest for the scientist.

Glimpses of brown, spectacled workmen who peered at them from the rice fields, or the vision of a tattered junk sail, passing down an estuary in the purple quiet of evening, when the dull yellow of the fields and the green of the hills were blended in a soft haze did not cause Delabar to lift his eyes.

China, vast and changeless, had taken the two Americans to itself. And Gray knew that Delabar was afraid. He had suspected as much in Honanfu. Now he was certain. Delabar had taken to smoking incessantly, and made no attempt to exercise as Gray did. He brooded in the wagon.

The calm of the army officer seemed to anger Delabar. Often when two men are alone for a long stretch of time they get on each other's nerves.

But Delabar's trouble went deeper than this. His fears had preyed on him during the month. He had taken to watching the dusty highway behind them. He slept badly.

Yet they had not been molested. They were not watched, as far as Gray could observe. They had heard no more from Wu Fang Chien.

The streets of Liangchowfu were crowded. It was some kind of a feast day. Gray noted that there were numbers of priests who stared at them impassively as he led the mule teams to an inn on the further side of the town, near the western wall, and persuaded the proprietor to clear the pigs and children from one of the guest chambers.

"We were fools to come this far," muttered Delabar, throwing himself down on a bamboo bench. "Did you notice the crowds in the streets we passed?"

"It's a feast, or bazaar day, I expect," observed Gray quietly, removing his mud caked shoes and stretching his big frame on the clay bench that did duty as a bed.

"No." Delabar shook his head. "Gray, I tell you, we are fools. The Chinese of Liangchowfu knew we were coming. Those priests were Buddhist followers. They are here for a purpose."

"They seem harmless enough."

Delabar laughed.

"Did you ever know a Mongol to warn you, before he struck? No, my friend. We are in a nice trap here, within the walls. We are the only Europeans in the place. Every move we make will be watched. Do you think we can get through the walls without the Chinese knowing it?"

"No," admitted Gray. "But we had to come here for food and a new relay of mules."

"We will never leave Liangchowfu—to the west. But we can still go back."

"We can, but we won't."

Gray turned on the bed where he sat and tentatively scratched a clear space on the glazed paper which formed the one—closed—window of the room. Ventilation is unknown in China.

He found that he could look out in the street. The inn was built around three sides of a courtyard, and their room was at the end of one wing. He saw a steady throng of passersby—pockmarked beggars, flaccid faced coolies trundling women along in wheelbarrows, an astrologer who had taken up his stand in the middle of the street with the two tame sparrows which formed his stock-in-trade, and a few swaggering, sheepskin clad Kirghiz from the steppe.

As each individual passed the inn, Gray noticed that he shot a quick glance at it from slant eyes. An impressive palanquin came down the street. A fat porter in a silk tunic with a staff walked before the bearers. Coming abreast the astrologer, the man with the staff struck him contemptuously aside.

As this happened, Gray saw the curtain of the palanquin lifted, and the outline of a face peering at the inn.

"We seem to be the sight of the city," he told Delabar, drawing on his shoes. "The rubberneck bus has just passed. Look here, Professor! No good in moping around here. You go out and rustle the food we need. I'll inspect our baggage in the stable."

When Delabar had departed on his mission, Gray left the inn leisurely. He wandered after the scientist, glancing curiously at a crowd which had gathered in what was evidently the center square of the town, being surrounded by an array of booths.

The crowd was too great for him to see what the attraction was, but he elbowed his way through without ceremony. Sure that something unusual must be in progress, he was surprised to see only a nondescript Chinese soldier in a jacket that had once been blue with a rusty sword belted to him. Beside the soldier was an old man with a wrinkled, brown face from which glinted a pair of keen eyes.

By his sheepskin coat, bandaged legs and soiled yak-skin boots Gray identified the elder of the two as a Kirghiz mountaineer. Both men were squatting on their haunches, the Kirghiz smoking a pipe.

"What is happening?" Gray asked a bystander, pointing to the two in the cleared space.

56

Mirai Khan

Readily, the accents of the border dialect came to his tongue. The other understood.

"It will happen soon," he explained. "That is Mirai Khan, the hunter, who is smoking the pipe. When he is finished the Manchu soldier will cut off his head."

Gray whistled softly. The crowd was staring at him now, intent on a new sight. Even Mirai Khan was watching him idly, apparently unconcerned about his coming demise.

"Why is he smoking the pipe?" Gray asked.

"Because he wants to. The soldier is letting him do it because Mirai Khan has promised to tell him where his long musket is, before he dies."

"Why must he die?"

The man beside him coughed and spat apathetically. "I do not know. It was ordered. Perhaps he stole the value of ten *taels*."

Gray knew enough of the peculiar law of China to understand that a theft of something valued at more than a certain sum was punishable by death. The sight of the tranquil Kirghiz stirred his interest.

"Ask the soldier what is the offense," he persisted, exhibiting a coin at which the Chinaman stared eagerly.

Mirai Khan, Gray was informed, had been convicted of stealing a horse worth thirteen *taels*. The Kirghiz had claimed that the horse was his own,

57

taken from him by the Liangchowfu officials who happened to be in need of beasts of burden. The case had been referred to the authorities at Honanfu, and no less a personage than Wu Fang Chien had ruled that since the hunter had denied the charge he had given the lie to the court. Wherefore, he must certainly be beheaded.

Gray sympathized with Mirai Khan. He had seen enough of Wu Fang Chien to guess that the Kirghiz' case had not received much consideration. Something in the mountaineer's shrewd face attracted Gray. He pushed into the cleared space.

"Tell the Manchu," he said sharply to the Chinaman whom he had drawn with him, "that I know Wu Fang Chien. Tell him that I will pay the amount of the theft, if he will release the prisoner."

"It may not be," objected the other indifferently.

"Do as I say," commanded Gray sharply.

The soldier, apparently tired of waiting, had risen and drawn his weapon. He bent over the Kirghiz who remained kneeling. The sight quickened Gray's pulse—in spite of the danger he knew he ran from interfering with the Chinese authorities.

"Quick," he added. His companion whispered to the soldier who glanced at the American in surprise and hesitated.

Gray counted out thirteen *taels*—about ten dollars—and added five more. "I have talked with Wu Fang Chien," he explained, "and I will buy this

58

man's life. If the value of the horse is paid, the crime will be no more."

The blue-coated Manchu said something, evidently an objection.

"He says," interpreted the Chinaman, who was eyeing the money greedily, "that thirteen *taels* will not wipe out the insult to the judge."

"Five more will," Gray responded. "He can keep them if he likes. And here's a *tael* for you."

The volunteer interpreter clasped the coin in a claw-like hand. Gray thrust the rest of the money upon the hesitating executioner, and seized Mirai Khan by the arm.

Nodding to the Kirghiz, he led him through the crowd, which was muttering uneasily. He turned down an alley.

"Can you get out of Liangchowfu without being seen?" the American asked his new purchase. He was more confident now of the tribal speech.

Mirai Khan understood. Later, Gray came to know that the man was very keen witted. Also, he had a polyglot tongue.

"Aye, Excellency." Mirai Khan fell on his knees and pressed his forehead to his rescuer's shoes. "There is a hole in the western wall behind the temple where the caravan men water their oxen and camels."

"Go, then, and quickly."

"I will get me a horse," promised Mirai Khan, "and the Chinese pigs will not see me go."

Gray thought to himself that Mirai Khan might be more of a horse thief than he professed to be.

"The Excellency saved my life," muttered the Kirghiz, glancing around craftily. "It was written that I should die this day, and he kept me from the sight of the angel of death. But thirteen *taels* is a great deal of wealth. It would be well if I found my gun, and slew the soldier. Then the Excellency would have his thirteen *taels* again. Where is he to be found?"

"At the inn by the western wall. But never mind the Manchu. Save your own skin."

Gray strode off down the alley, for men were coming after them. In the rear of an unsavory hut, the Kirghiz plucked his sleeve.

"Aye, it shall so be, Excellency," he whispered. "Has the honorable master any tobacco?"

Impatiently Gray sifted some tobacco from his pouch into the hunter's scarred hand. Mirai Khan then asked for matches.

"I will not forget," he said importantly. "You will see Mirai Khan again. I swear it. And I will tell you something. Wu Fang Chien is in Liang-chowfu."

With that the man shambled off down an alley, looking for all the world like a shaggy dog with

60

unusually long legs. Gray stared after him with a smile. Then he turned back toward the inn.

That night there was a feast in Liangchowfu. The sound of the temple drums reached to the inn. Lanterns appeared on the house fronts across the street. Throngs of priests passed by in ceremonial procession, bearing lights. In the inn courtyard a group of musicians took their stand, producing a hideous mockery of a tune on cymbals and one-stringed fiddles. But the main room of the inn, where the eating tables were set with bowls and chop-sticks, was deserted except for a wandering rooster.

"I'm going out to see the show," asserted Gray, who was weary of inaction.

"What!" The Syrian stared at him, fingering his beard restlessly. "With Wu Fang Chien in the town!"

"Certainly. There's nothing to be done here. I may be able to pick up information which will be useful—if we are in danger."

Delabar tossed his cigarette away and shrugged his shoulders.

"We are marked men, my young friend. I saw this afternoon that a guard has been posted at the town gates. Those musicians yonder are spies. The master of the inn is in the stable, with our men."

"Then we'll shake our escort for a while."

Gray's smile faded. "Look here, Professor. I'm alive to the pickle we're in. We've got to get out of this place. And I want to have a look at that hole in the wall Mirai Khan told me about. For one thing—to see if horses can get through it."

Delabar accompanied him out of the courtyard, into the street. Gray noted grimly that the musicians ceased playing with their departure. He beckoned Delabar to follow and turned down the alley he had visited that afternoon. Looking over his shoulder he saw a dark form slip into the entrance of the alley.

"Double time, Professor," whispered Gray. Grasping the other by the arm he trotted through the piles of refuse that littered the rear of the houses, turning sharply several times until he was satisfied they were no longer followed. As a landmark, he had the dark bulk of the pagoda which formed the roof of the temple.

Toward this he made his way, dodging back into the shadows when he sighted a group of Chinese. He was now following the course of the wall, which took him into a garden, evidently a part of the temple grounds.

He saw nothing of the opening Mirai Khan had mentioned. But a murmur of voices from the shuttered windows of the edifice stirred his interest.

"It is a meeting of the Buddhists," whispered

Mirai Khan

Delabar. "I heard the temple messengers crying the summons in the street this afternoon."

Gray made his way close to the building. It was a lofty structure of carved wood. The windows were small and high overhead. Gray scanned them speculatively.

"We weren't invited to the reunion, Professor," he meditated, "but I'd give something for a look inside. Judging by what you've told me, these Buddhist fellows are our particular enemies. And it's rather a coincidence they held a lodge meeting to-night."

He felt along the wall for a space. They were sheltered from view from the street by the garden trees.

"Hullo," he whispered, "here's luck. A door. Looks like a stage entrance, with some kind of carving over it."

Delabar pushed forward and peered at the inscription. The reflected light of the illumination in the street enabled him to see fairly well.

"This is the gate of ceremony of the temple," he observed. "It is one of the doors built for a special occasion—only to be used by a scholar of the town who has won the highest honors of the Hanlin academy, or by the emperor himself—when there was one."

Gray pushed at the door. It was not fastened,

but being in disuse, gave in slowly, with a creak of iron hinges. Delabar checked him.

"You know nothing of Chinese customs," he hissed warningly. "It is forbidden for any one to enter. The penalty——"

"Beheading, I suppose," broke in Gray impatiently. "Come along, Delabar. This is a special occasion, and, by Jove—you're a distinguished scholar."

He drew the other inside with him. They stood in a black passage filled with an odor of combined must and incense. Gray took his pocket flashlight from his coat and flickered its beam in front of them. He could feel Delabar shivering. Wondering at the state of the scientist's nerves, he made out an opening before them in which steps appeared.

They seemed to be in a deserted part of the temple. Gray wanted very much to see what was going on—and what was at the head of the stairs. He ascended as quietly as possible, followed by the Syrian who was muttering to himself.

CHAPTER VII

A SUBDUED glow appeared above Gray's head, as the narrow stairs twisted. The glow grew stronger, and he caught the buzz of voices. Cautiously he climbed to the head of the steps and peered into the chamber from which came the light.

He saw a peculiar room. It was empty of all furniture except a teakwood chair. The light came through a large aperture in the floor. An ebony railing, gilded and inlaid, ran around this square of light. The voices grew louder.

It was clear to Gray that they were in some kind of gallery above the room where the assembly was —for the voices seemed to be rising through the floor.

He walked to the chair—and stopped abruptly.

The opening in the floor was directly above the temple proper. Gray and Delabar could see the shrine, with the usual bronze figure of the almond-eyed god, the burning tapers and the incense bowls.

On the floor by the shrine the gathering of priests squatted. They were facing, not the image of Buddha, but a chair which stood on a daïs at one side. On this chair an imposing mandarin was seated with the red button and silk robe of officialdom.

"Wu Fang Chien!" whispered Delabar.

Gray nodded. It was their friend of Honanfu, with his thin beard, placid face and spectacles.

"What are they doing?" asked Gray softly.

The murmur of voices persisted. For some time Delabar listened. Then he pointed out a man in beggar's dress kneeling beside the mandarin's chair.

"It is some kind of trial," he said doubtfully. "The priest by Wu Fang Chien is an ascetic—what they call a *fakir* in India. But he is not the criminal."

They moved nearer the opening, being secure from observation from below. Gray wrinkled his nose at the mingled scent of incense and Mongolian sweat that floated up through the opening.

"Wu Fang Chien is saying that he has come to Liangchowfu to sit in judgment on the evildoers who are enemies of the god," interpreted Delabar. "He has called the priests to witness the proceedings."

Gray looked at Delabar curiously. He had caught a word or two of the talk.

"Does he name the offenders?" he asked.

"No. He says the priesthood has been informed that two men plan·to desecrate a holy place. He has come to catch them red-handed."

The Door is Guarded

Wu Fang Chien, Gray reflected, could not know they were in the gallery of the temple, by the seat reserved for a distinguished student, or the emperor. The mandarin must have discovered their mission, as Delabar feared. He peered over the rail.

Directly underneath three priests were stripped to the waist. They held a bronze bowl of considerable size.

As Gray watched, a silence fell on the room below.

"They are going to try divination," whispered Delabar, and Gray saw that his face was strained. "The divination of the ivory sticks and the bowl. That is a custom of the sorcerers of the interior. The priests believe in it implicitly. I have seen some wonderful things——"

He broke off as the ascetic prostrated himself before Wu Fang Chien, holding out a sandalwood box. Gray saw the mandarin lean forward and draw what looked like a short white stick from the box.

"That is to determine the distance the criminals are from the temple," explained Delabar. "It is a very short stick—representing perhaps a *li* or one-third of a mile."

"That would include the inn," was Gray's comment. "Hello, the bowl boys are coming into action."

Marching Sands

The three priests were turning slowly on their feet, supporting the bronze bowl above their heads. They moved in a kind of dance, and as they revolved, came nearer to the shrine—then retreated. Delabar watched intently.

"They will keep up the dance for twenty-four hours," he said, "without stopping. Meanwhile the other priests will watch, without taking food or drink. It induces a kind of hypnotism. They believe that at the end of the twenty-four hours, the god will enter the bowl."

Gray nodded. Wu Fang Chien had sat back and was eyeing the dance complacently.

"When this happens," Delabar went on, "the priests will leave the temple, holding the bowl in front of them. They will be followed by the townspeople who do not doubt that the god will conduct them to the criminals."

"I guess we're nominated for the guilty parties."

Gray surveyed the scene curiously, the revolving trio of brown bodies, the silent mandarin and the watching priests. He followed idly the smoke fumes that eddied up from the shrine of the bronze god. Wu Fang Chien, he mused, had decided that it was time to strike. And the mandarin was going about it with the patience of the Mongol, sure of his victim, and his own power.

Wu Fang Chien had warned them. They had not heeded the warning. The attack in Honanfu

68

had been a prelude—possibly to get Gray's weapons away from him. It had failed, but Wu Fang Chien had formed another plan. Why else had he come to Liangchowfu?

Watching the whirling priests, Gray guessed at the plan. In twenty-four hours the sorcery of the bowl would come to a head. The three priests would bear it to the inn—in a state of semi-hypnotism themselves, and followed by a fanatical crowd. They would confront Gray and Delabar. They would search the belongings of the white men, and find the maps of Sungan—the maps that had been seen by the intruder at the Honanfu inn. After that——

Delabar gripped his companion's arm. "Some one is coming," he whispered.

Gray listened, and heard a faint sound of footsteps. It came from the stairs—the soft *pad-pad* of slippered feet ascending the steps. Gray shot a quick glance into the temple below. The scene had not changed, except that the priest in the tattered robe was no longer at Wu Fang Chien's side.

"We are caught," muttered the scientist. "There is no other door."

Gray was aware of this. The only openings in the chamber where they stood were the door and the aperture in the floor. The *pad-pad* came nearer, but more slowly. He was reasonably sure that they had not been seen. It was abominably bad luck that some one should visit the gallery just then.

"We left the temple door open," Delabar whispered, staring at the dark stairs behind them. "One of the priests observed it and came——"

"Steady," Gray cautioned him. He drew the trembling Syrian back into the shadows at one side of the door. Here they were in semi-obscurity. Stepping quietly to arm's reach of the head of the stairs, Gray waited.

He heard the steps approach, then become silent as if the intruder was looking into the room.

A moment passed while Gray silently cursed the heavy breathing of Delabar who seemed possessed by uncontrollable excitement. Then a shaven head appeared in the doorway, followed by a naked shoulder. A pair of slant, evil eyes flickered around the gallery, failing to notice the two white men in the shadow.

Gray's hand went out and closed on the throat of the priest. His grip tightened, choking off a smothered gasp. The man fell heavily to his knees.

The floor echoed dully at the impact. Gray realized that it must have been heard by those in the temple below. Snatching up the frail priest by throat and leg, he lifted him easily and started down the stairs headlong.

"This way, Professor," he called. "Better hurry."

The Door is Guarded

Concealment being useless now, they plunged down the steps. By the time the lower floor was reached, Gray's grip had stilled the struggles of the man—whom he recognized as the ascetic.

The sound of running feet came to him as he waited for Delabar to come up., The professor shot through the temple door like a frightened rabbit.

Gray tossed the unconscious priest on the doorsill, and pushed the heavy portal nearly shut, wedging the man's body in the opening. Then he trotted after Delabar through the garden.

"Let's hope you're right about the penalty for opening the door there," he laughed. "That priest will have his hands full explaining how he happens to be lying on the emperor's threshold—when he comes to. Probably he'll say that devils picked him up."

Looking back at the edge of the temple garden, Gray saw a crowd with lanterns standing inside the door, over the form of the priest. They were some distance away by now. Following the circuit of the city wall, Gray succeeded in gaining the alleys back of the inn without being observed.

Once safely in their room, Delabar threw himself on the bed, panting. Gray took up his rifle and laid it across his knees, placing his chair so that he could command both door and window.

He did not want to sleep. And he feared to trust

71

Delabar to watch. Throughout the remaining hours until daylight whitened the paper of the window, he sat in his chair. But nothing further happened. The festivities in the streets had ended and the inn itself was quiet, unusually so.

Daylight showed Delabar lying on the bed, smoking innumerable cigarettes. The scientist had maintained a moody silence since their arrival at the inn. The sound of excited voices floated in from the courtyard. Vehicles could be heard passing along the street. But the ordinary pandemonium of a Chinese hostelry at breakfast time was subdued.

Gray tossed his rifle on the bed, yawned and stretched his powerful frame. He was hungry, and said so. He brushed the dirt from his shoes, changed to a clean shirt, looked in the pail for water. Finding none, he picked up the pail, strode to the door and flung it open.

On the threshold, his back against the doorpost, was sitting a Buddhist priest. It was an aged man, his face wrinkled and eyes inflamed. His right shoulder and his breast were bared. In one hand he clasped a long knife. His eyes peered up at the white man vindictively.

Gray recognized the ascetic of the temple. He

could see the dark marks where his hands had squeezed the scrawny throat.

He reached for his automatic with his free hand. The priest did not stir. The man was squatting on his heels, fairly over the threshold; the knife rested on one knee. How long he had been there, Gray did not know.

Priest and white man stared at each other intently. Gray frowned. Plainly the man at the door did not mean well; but why did the fellow remain seated, holding the knife passively? He noted fleetingly that the main room of the inn was vacant.

"Don't move!" Delabar's voice came to him, shrill with anxiety. "Don't take a step. Shut the door and come back here."

"Why?" Gray asked curiously. "I want to go out for water, and I'm blessed if this chap is going to keep me in——"

"It's death to move!"

"For me?"

"No, the priest will die." Delabar clutched his companion's arm. "You don't understand. The priest is here on a mission. If you step through the door, he will stab himself with the knife. And if he commits suicide at our door, we'll have the whole of Liangchowfu down on us."

Gray pocketed the automatic with a laugh. "I don't see why we are to blame if this yellow monkey sticks himself with his own knife."

73

Delabar crossed to the door and closed it on the watching Buddhist.

"You know very little of China, my friend," he said gloomily. "One of the favorite methods of revenge is to hire a priest to sit at a man's door, like this. Then, if any one leaves the house, the priest commits suicide. That fixes—or the Chinese believe it fixes—a crime on the man in the house. It's a habit of the Chinese to kill themselves in order to obtain vengeance on an enemy."

Gray whistled. "I've heard something of the kind. But, look here, I could grab that fellow before he can hurt himself."

"It would be useless. As soon as he was free, he'd commit suicide, and the blame would fall on us. By now, all the Chinese in the town know that this priest is here. If he should die, it would be a signal for a general attack on us."

Meditatively, Gray seated himself on the bucket and considered the situation.

"You know the working of the yellow mind, Professor," he observed. "Do you suppose this fellow has marked us out as the guilty parties who manhandled him in the temple and left him in the sacred door?"

"It's more likely that Wu Fang Chien guessed we were the intruders. We were probably watched more closely than you knew. Then, according to the temple law, this priest is guilty of sacrilege in

74

The Door is Guarded

crossing the emperor's door. So Wu Fang Chien has ordered him to guard our door, to wipe out his own sin, and incriminate us at the same time."

Gray grinned cheerfully.

"The working of the Mongol mind is a revelation, Delabar. I guess you're right. This is Wu Fang Chien's way of keeping us quiet in here while the boys with the bowl get their magic primed. Also, it will help to make the townspeople hostile to us."

Slowly, Wu Fang Chien's plan was maturing. Gray saw the snare of the Mongol mandarin closing around them. It was a queer, fantastic snare. In the United States the situation would have been laughable. Here, it was deadly.

Wu Fang Chien had made his preparations carefully. The temple festival had stirred up the Buddhists; the arrival of the bronze bowl, borne by the priests, would implicate the two white men; the discovery of the maps of the forbidden district of the Gobi would do the rest.

Gray could destroy the maps. But then he would have no guide to the course to be followed, if they should escape from Liangchowfu. He was not yet willing to destroy all prospect of success.

He sought out the maps, in one of their packs, and pocketed them.

"Does this hocus-pocus of the bowl in the temple

75

always take twenty-four hours?" he asked Delabar.

"Always."

"Well, Wu Fang won't want to break the rules of the game—not when he has the cards so well in hand. Professor, we have fourteen hours to think up a line of action. We have food enough here to make a square meal or two. Also wine—as a present to the city mandarins—that will keep us from becoming too thirsty."

Delabar shrugged his bent shoulders. He looked ill. His hand was trembling, and it was clear to Gray that the man was on the verge of a breakdown.

"What can we do?" the Syrian asked plaintively. "Except to destroy the maps, which would incriminate us."

"We won't do that."

There comes a time when fatigue undermines weak vitality. Delabar complained, begged, cursed. But Gray refused to burn the papers which meant the success or failure of their expedition.

"You're sick, Delabar," he said firmly. "You seem to forget we're here on a mission. Now, pay attention a minute. I've been getting ready, after a fashion, for a move on Wu Fang's part. I've paid our coolies four times what was owing them, and promised 'em double that if they stick by us. I think they may do it. If so, we stand a good chance of getting clear with our necessary stores—emergency rations, medicines, a few cooking utensils and blankets. But we can't start anything until it's dark. Sleep if you can. If you can't—don't worry."

He cast a curious glance at the scientist—a glance of mixed good-natured contempt and anxiety.

"This guardian of the gate trick works both ways," he concluded. "If we can't get out, no one will want to get in."

He took a few, sparing swallows of the strong wine, a mouthful of bread and rice and tilted his chair back against the wall. The room was hot and close, and he soon dropped off into a nap. Delabar did not sleep.

Gray, from habit, dozed lightly. He was conscious of the sounds that went on in the street. Several times he wakened, only to drop off again, seeing that all was as it should be. Once or twice he heard Delabar go to the door and peer out to see if the priest was still at his post. Evidently he was, for the Syrian maintained his brooding quiet.

As time wore on, Gray thought he heard Delabar laughing. He assured himself that he must have been mistaken. Yet the echo of the laugh persisted, harsh, and bitter. Delabar must have been laughing.

The officer wondered drowsily what had been the cause of the other's mirth—and sat up with a jerk. He caught at the hand that was stealing under his coat, and found himself looking into Delabar's flushed face, not a foot from his own. The scientist drew back, with a chuckle. There was no mistaking the chuckle this time.

Gray felt at his coat pocket and assured himself the maps were still there.

"So you lost your nerve, eh, Professor?" he said, not unkindly—and broke off with a stare. "What the devil——?"

Delabar staggered away from him, and fell on the bed, rocking with mirth. He caught his head in his hands and burst into the laugh that Gray had heard before. Then he lay back full length, waving his hands idiotically.

Gray swore softly. He noticed the wine bottles on the table, and caught them up. He assured himself grimly that one was empty and another nearly so. He himself had taken only a swallow of the liquor.

Delabar had drunk up approximately two quarts of strong wine. And Gray knew that the man was not accustomed to it.

The scientist was drunk, blindly, hopelessly drunk.

The room was dark. A candle, probably lighted by Delabar on some whim, guttered on the floor. Outside the room, the inn was very still.

Gray regretted that his sleep had enabled Delabar to drink up the liquor. But the harm was done. His companion was helpless as a child. He looked

The Door is Guarded

at his watch. It was after eight. As nearly as he could remember, the proceedings at the temple had started about ten o'clock. Not quite two hours of quiet remained to them.

Delabar sat up and regarded him with owl-like wisdom.

"Drink, my friend," he mumbled, "you are a strong man, and it will be hard for you to die if you are not drunk. You were a fool to come here. You are a child before the ancient wisdom of China. The secrets of the Mongols have been before your God had eyes to see the earth. Why did you pry into them?"

A laugh followed this, and Delabar made a futile grab at one of the bottles.

"You think I am afraid of Wu Fang Chien?" the mumble went on. "No, I am not afraid of him. He is only a servant of the slave of Buddha, who is Fate. We can not go where Fate forbids—forbids us."

Gray surveyed him, frowning.

"Look outside the door," chuckled Delabar. "Look—I stepped outside the door, my friend. And I saw——"

Waiting for no more, Gray crossed to the door and opened it. At his feet lay the priest. The slant eyes stared up at him. The knife was fixed in the man's throat, and a dark circle had gathered on the floor behind his head.

79

CHAPTER VIII

DELABAR LEAVES

GRAY stooped and felt the dead man's face. It was still quite warm. The priest could not have killed himself more than a few minutes ago. Probably Delabar, in his drunken wandering, had put his foot across the threshold.

With a tightening of the lips, Gray straightened and surveyed the inn. It was empty and dark except for a lantern with a crimson shade that hung over the door. Either the people of the place had seen the dead Buddhist and fled to spread the news, or they had given the room a wide berth since that afternoon.

He could not know which was actually the case. Gray, however, could afford to waste no time in speculation. He went back into their chamber, fastened his rifle over his shoulder by its sling, and jerked Delabar to his feet.

"It's time we got out of here, Professor," he said, "if you haven't settled our hash for good."

The man was muttering and stumbling—hardly able to keep his feet. He could give no assistance to Gray.

They crossed the main room of the inn without

hindrance, and left the building by the rear. The stable yard was dark, and apparently empty. Gray's flashlight disclosed only a mild-looking donkey, nibbling at the leaves of a plane tree.

"Guess the place isn't exactly popular just now," thought Gray.

Beside the stable, concealed by the manure piles, he found his wagons and mules, hitched up as he had ordered. A glance and a flicker of his light showed him that the surplus supplies were loaded. He pushed Delabar into the stable and whistled softly.

A coolie crept from a pile of dirty straw under the wall against which several mules were standing patiently.

"Where are the others?" demanded Gray sharply.

The other men, said the coolie, had gone.

"Why are not the fresh mules loaded, as I commanded?"

The man kow-towed. "I was afraid. This is an evil place.. The priests are saying that the black mark of ill-omen has descended from Heaven——"

"Five *taels*," broke in the white man crisply, "if you help me to load the mules. The priests will kill you if they find you here. If you come with me you will live. Choose."

From some quarter of the city came the dull thrum of temple gongs. The coolie whined in fear, and hastened to the mules.

Marching Sands

It is no easy task to strap the packs on four mules in the dark. Gray let Delabar, who had subsided into slumber at contact with the cool outer air, slump on the dirt floor of the stable. He adjusted his flashlight in the straw so its beam would help them to see what they were about.

He found as he expected that the other coolies had made away with many of the stores. They had taken, however, the things most valuable to them, which were least necessary to Gray—such as clothing, cooking utensils, and the heavy boxes of Chinese money.

These last were a grave loss, but Gray had a good deal of gold in his money belt, and he knew that Delabar had the same amount.

The two men loaded the remaining boxes on the animals—the provisions that Delabar had purchased in San Francisco, with medicines and several blankets that had been overlooked by the thieves.

This done, Gray left the stable for a survey of the field. The inn yard was still quiet. Even the street on the further side was tranquil. Turning back, he helped the coolie place Delabar astride a mule, and tied the scientist's feet firmly together under the animal's belly. Throwing a blanket over him, Gray gave the word to start.

The Chinaman went ahead by the first animal, for Gray did not want to trust him out of sight. He

Delabar Leaves

followed beside the mule that carried Delabar, giving directions as to their course.

"The loaded wagon at the inn will be a fair puzzle to the searching party from the temple," he thought. "We could never get free of Liangchowfu with the carts. Here's hoping my friend Mirai Khan was right when he said there was a hole in the city wall behind the temple."

It was a slender chance—to work their way through the alleys in the darkness. But, as Gray reasoned, it was the only thing to do. And two things were in their favor. The inn was undoubtedly watched, front and back. The priests' spies would see the mules leaving, and probably decide the coolies were making off with them—especially as the wagons were still in the stable yard.

Also, the attention of the Liangchowfu population—or the most dangerous part of it—would be centered on the temple and the divination in progress there.

Gray had reasoned correctly. By following the odorous and muddy by-ways that he and Delabar had investigated previously, he was able to gain the wall without attracting attention.

Here the lights were fewer, and the trees sheltered them. The coolie, who was badly frightened, could give Gray no information as to the location of the break in the city wall. It was useless, of course, to try a dash for the city gates which would be guarded.

Gray pushed ahead steadily at a slow trot, scanning the bulk of the wall for signs of an aperture. They were well behind the temple by now, at the further side of the garden they had entered the night before. So far they had been very lucky, but Gray's heart sank as he sighted buildings ahead—a huddle of thatched huts, evidently in the poorer section of the town. Still no break in the stone barrier was visible.

"Keep on," he whispered to the coolie, "and don't forget if we are discovered you'll be caught in the act of aiding me to escape."

The man broke into a faster trot, with a scared glance over his shoulder. The sound of the temple gongs was louder, swelling angrily in the wind. Voices came from the huts ahead, and Gray fancied that he heard shouts in the street they had left.

He swore softly. If only they could find the exit he was seeking! Once out on the plain beyond Liangchowfu, their chances of escape would be good. If only Delabar had kept sober——

He swung around alertly at the sound of horses' hoofs. In the faint light a mounted man appeared beside him.

"That was very well done, Excellency," a voice whispered in hoarse Chinese. "I know, for I watched from the dung heaps by the inn stable. One

Delabar Leaves

of the men who fled I caught and took the money he carried."

"Mirai Khan," whispered Gray.

"Aye," admitted the Kirghiz complacently. "I swore that you would see me again, and it has come to pass. I have heard talk in the town. I knew that the priests—may they swallow their own fire—seek you. So I waited for I had the thought you would not easily be snared. Lo, it has happened so. Verily my thought was a true thought. Follow where I lead."

He urged his pony ahead of the mules, motioning Gray to the side of the small caravan away from the huts. Dim faces peered from window openings at them. But the white man was in the shadow of the wall, and Mirai Khan appeared too familiar a figure in this quarter of Liangchowfu to excite comment. Probably the mules bore out the character of the horse-thief, retiring to the plain with a load of ill-gotten spoil.

They passed through the huts in silence, the coolie too frightened to speak. Delabar was muttering to himself under the blanket, but the swaggering figure of the Kirghiz, with his rifle over his arm, seemed to insure them against investigation. Still, Gray breathed a thankful oath as they dipped into a gully through which flowed a brook.

Mirai Khan rode forward, apparently into the very wall. But here the crumbling stone divided—

85

an opening wide enough to permit of the passage of a pack animal with its burden, walking in the bed of the stream.

Once clear of the wall, the sound of the temple gong dwindled and ceased entirely. They pressed ahead at a quick trot, until, glancing behind, Gray saw that the lights of Liangchowfu had disappeared. As nearly as he could tell by the stars he guessed that Mirai Khan was leading them northwest.

When the sky paled behind them and the dawn wind struck their faces, Gray made out that they were in a nest of hillocks. No house was visible. It was waste land, with only an occasional stunted cedar clinging to the side of a clay bank. They had put more than a dozen miles between them and Liangchowfu.

It was now light enough to discern his companions' faces, and Gray halted the cavalcade.

"We will let the mules breathe a bit," he informed the Kirghiz who glanced at him inquiringly. "I will speak with my friend."

He led the animal the scientist was riding a few paces to one side, and tossed off the blanket that enveloped Delabar. The man had awakened, half blue with cold and with retarded circulation due to his cramped position and the effect of the liquor. He peered at Gray from bleared eyes, sobered by the exposure of the past night.

Delabar Leaves

The officer undid the rope that confined Delabar's legs, then seated himself on a stone and lit his pipe.

"Professor," he said meditatively, "you don't know it, but I've been thinking over things in the last few hours. And I've come to a decision. I'll tell you what I've been thinking, because I want you to understand just why I'm doing this."

Delabar was silent, peering at him inquisitively.

"Back on the steamer," resumed Gray, "you showed me that you had nerves—quite a few. Well, lots of men have 'em. Under the circumstances, I can't say I blame you. But at Honanfu your nerves had a severe jolt. Back there"—he jerked his head at Liangchowfu—"you had a bad case of fright. You're all in now."

"I am hungry," complained the scientist. "Why did you tie me to the mule?"

"That skirmish with Wu Fang Chien," continued the officer, ignoring the question, "wasn't more than a good sample of what we may have to face in the Gobi Desert. It showed me you aren't able to go ahead with the trip. You'd be as sick in body as you are now in mind."

"I am not a horse," snapped Delabar. "The Buddhist priests——"

"Precisely, the Buddhist priests. They've got you scared. Badly. Let me tell you some more I've been thinking. Intentionally or not, you have done all you could at Liangchowfu to hinder me. Only luck and Mirai Khan got us out of the place with a whole skin. In the army where I served for a while they shot men who became drunk when on duty."

"This is China, another world," retorted the man moodily.

"China or not, it's my duty to go to the Gobi Desert and find the Wusun if I can. I promised Van Schaick that, and drew up a contract which I signed. I'm going ahead. You, Professor, are going back to the coast and to the States. You can report our progress to Van Schaick."

Mingled relief and alarm showed in the Syrian's keen face.

"You can complain that I sent you back, if you want to. I'll answer to Van Schaick for this." Gray held up his hand as the other tried to speak. "You'll be all right. I've been quizzing Mirai Khan. The coolie can guide you back, to the north of Liangchowfu, where you'll meet some missionaries. Wu Fang Chien will be looking for us to the west, not in the east. You'll take the money you have on you, and two mules with half the supplies. Promise the coolie enough gold, and he'll stick by you—as he'll be safer going back than forward. Any questions?"

It was a long speech for Gray to make. Delabar studied him and shivered in the cold breeze that

Delabar Leaves

swept the plain. Hardship brings out the strength and weakness of men. In his case it was weakness. Yet he seemed curiously alarmed at leaving Gray. Twelve hours ago he had implored his companion to give up the venture into the Gobi.

"Why are you doing this?" he asked.

"For two reasons. I don't want a sick man on my hands. And—you tried to destroy the maps. There's another reason——" Gray hesitated, and broke off. "I don't claim to be your judge. Every man follows his own course in life. But yours and mine don't fit any longer. It's good-by, Professor."

He rose, knocking the ashes from his pipe. Delabar gave an exclamation of alarm.

"Suppose the men of Wu Fang Chien find me?"

"You'll be safer than here with me"

Delabar stared into the steady eyes of his companion, and his gaze shifted. "I can't go back. I must go with you."

"I've said good-by. Your coolie knows what he's to do. Choose your two mules."

"No. I'll be better now——"

Gray smiled slightly.

"I doubt it. I've been watching you. Closer than you thought. Which mules do you want?"

Delabar flushed, and turned his animal back to the waiting group. He was muttering to himself uncertainly. Gray walked beside him. Once he spoke. "Buddhism, Professor, is a bad thing to think about. As Wu Fang Chien said, it is bad to enter forbidden ground. Well, good luck, Delabar. It's better to part now—than later———"

But Delabar passed out of hearing. He did not look again at Gray, who remained talking to the Kirghiz. Later, Gray regretted that he had not watched Delabar.

The Syrian wasted no time in selecting two animals, and turned back at once. Mirai Khan followed the cavalcade with puckered brows as they passed out of sight among the hillocks. Gray waved his hand once when he thought Delabar looked back. But the man did not turn, humping himself forward over his beast, his head between his shoulders.

"It is a pity," said Mirai Khan, stroking his gray beard reflectively, "to lose the two mules, and so much money. However, what will be, will be. Come, I know a *davan* nearby where we can rest until we are ready to go forward, at night."

He conducted Gray along a sheep track for some miles to a ravine well into the hillocks. Here there was a grove of cedars, and a small spring. While Gray built a fire, Mirai Khan, acting on the white man's instructions, unburdened the two remaining mules.

"We have little food, Excellency," he observed suggestively.

Delabar Leaves

"Open one of the boxes," said Gray.

Presently Mirai Khan appeared beside the fire, carrying a heavy object.

"What manner of food is this?" he asked contemptuously. "I have tasted and the flavor is a mingling of salt and sour wine."

Gray stared at the object in surprise. It was one of the boxes, with the cover removed. It was filled with an array of long bottles. One of these had the cork removed, and effused an acrid odor. Gray picked it up.

It was a bottle of a very good kind of vinegar.

Hastily Gray went to the other boxes and opened them, after noting that the fastenings and the seal were intact. They were all filled with vinegar.

Gray gave a soft whistle of bewilderment. These were the boxes that were supposed to contain their emergency rations, that Delabar had purchased in San Francisco. The Syrian's name was written on them.

He wondered fleetingly if Wu Fang Chien had been tampering with their baggage. But the boxes had clearly not been opened since they were packed. Also, the vinegar was of American make, and bore the name of a San Francisco firm.

Had there been a mistake in shipping the order? It might be. Yet Delabar should have checked up the shipment. No, the Syrian must have known what was in the boxes. He had chosen the other two mules—knowing these few boxes were worthless.

"I should have looked at 'em before I let Delabar go," thought Gray. "He is too far away now to follow. Now why——"

That was the question—why? Delabar, from the first, had placed every obstacle in the way of the expedition. Even to buying bogus supplies.

Delabar had not wanted Gray to succeed. He had used every means to keep the American from the Gobi Desert. He had tried to instill into Gray the poison of his own fear. He had attempted to seize the maps, showing the location of Sungan, which were of vital importance.

Delabar had been Gray's enemy. Why?

Gray had guessed much of this, when he ordered the other back to the coast. But he did not know the answer to this "why?" He puzzled over it much in the following days, and gleaned some light from his reasoning.

It was long before he knew the answer to the "why?" It did not come until he had gained the desert, and seen the *liu sha*. Not until he had met with Mary Hastings and seen the guards of Sungan. Not until he had learned the explanation of much that he as yet dimly imagined.

CHAPTER IX

Mirai Khan agreed with Gray that it would be useless to stay where they were until dark. They had no food. In spite of the risk of discovery, they must go forward.

"If we sleep," the hunter agreed, "we will waken with empty bellies and our strength will be less than now. The time will come when we shall need meat; and there is none here. To the west, we may see a village or shoot a gazelle."

Without further delay they unhitched the mules, packing the small remainder of Gray's outfit—a tent, and his personal kit—on one animal. The American mounted the other, not without protest from the beast, who scented water and forage.

With Mirai Khan leading on his shaggy pony they made their way westward out of the hillocks to the plain. They were now on the Mongolian plain—a barren tableland of brown hills and stony valleys. No huts were to be seen.

They had left teeming China behind, and were entering the outskirts of Central Asia and the Gobi Desert. A steady wind blew at their backs. The blue sky overhead was cloudless.

93

Marching Sands

Gray had left the useless boxes of vinegar behind. And as he went he puzzled over the riddle of Arminius Delabar. It was a riddle. Van Schaick and Balch had said little about the man, for they had been in a hurry to get Gray started on his voyage. He remembered they said Delabar was a Syrian or Persian by birth, an inveterate traveler who had been in most of the corners of the earth, and—the only man in America who could speak Chinese, Turki, Persian and Russian, the four languages a knowledge of which might be necessary on their expedition, and who thoroughly understood anthropology, with the history of Central Asia.

This being the case, Gray had taken a good deal on himself when he sent Delabar back. But he had done right. The vinegar boxes proved it.

Gray had a steady, logical mind which arrived at decisions slowly, but usually accurately. He now reasoned out several things.

Delabar, he guessed, had not come willingly on the expedition. Even on the steamer he had shown fear of the Gobi. Why? He must have known something about the desert that he did not tell Gray. What was that? Gray did not know.

This led to another question. Why, if the man was afraid, had he come at all? He might have refused to start. Instead he had bought, purposely, a shipment of worthless stores; he had worked on Gray's mind to the best of his ability.

94

The Liu Sha

Gray suspected that Delabar had come because he wanted to prevent him—Gray—from reaching the Gobi. But Delabar might have stated his objections before they left San Francisco. Why had he not done so?

Possibly because, so reasoned Gray, Delabar had thought if he prevented Gray from starting on the mission, Van Schaick and Balch would engage another man.

Gray checked up the extent of his reasoning so far. He had decided that Delabar had been bent on preventing not him but any American from undertaking the trip to the Gobi. And to do that the Syrian had come along himself, although he was afraid.

Yes, Delabar had certainly been afraid. Of what? Of Wu Fang Chien for one thing; also the Buddhists. He had been on the verge of a breakdown at the inn at Liangchowfu after their experience in the temple.

Gray recalled a number of things he had passed over at the time: Delabar's pretext of purchasing supplies at Shanghai. The scientist had been absent from him for many hours, but had bought nothing. Then the incident of the Chinese steward on the river steamer of the Yang-tze. Something had been thrown overboard which a passing junk had picked up. Had this something been information about Gray's route? It was more than possible.

Marching Sands

And the attack at Honanfu. How had the Chinese known that Gray kept a rifle under his bed—unless Delabar had so informed them? Delabar had been frightened at the attack. Perhaps, because it failed.

Lastly, at Liangchowfu Delabar had tried to steal the all-important maps. Failing that, the man had, literally, collapsed. And—Gray whistled softly—it might have been Delabar who gave the information that led to the delayal of McCann, whom Gray needed, at Los Angeles. No one else, except Van Schaick and Balch, had known that Gray had sent for McCann.

It was reasonably clear that Delabar had sought to turn back Gray. When the American had ordered him back, instead, the man had protested. Obviously, he dreaded this. Yet he was safer than here with Gray. Delabar had said, in an unguarded moment, that he feared to be caught by Wu Fang Chien. Why?

What was Delabar's relation to Wu Fang Chien? When drunk, he had said that the mandarin was only a slave of an unknown master. Who was the master? Obviously a man possessing great power in Central Asia—if a man at all.

This was what Delabar had feared, the master of Wu Fang Chien. Was Delabar also a slave? Gray laughed. His reasoning was going beyond the borders of logic. But he was convinced that his late companion had been serving not Van Schaick but

The Liu Sha

another; that he feared this other; and that his fear had increased instead of diminished when Gray ordered him back.

Gray looked up as Mirai Khan turned, with a warning hiss. The Kirghiz had reined in his mount and Gray did likewise.

A short rise was in front of them. Over this the hunter had evidently seen something that aroused him.

"Look!" he growled. "Take the windows of long sight and look."

It took a moment's puzzling before the American realized that his companion referred to the field glasses slung over his shoulder. He dismounted and crept with Mirai Khan to the top of the rise. Through the glasses he made out, at the hunter's directions, a pair of gazelles moving slowly across the plain some distance away.

Immediately Mirai Khan became a marvel of activity. He tethered the beasts to a stunted tamarisk, loaded his long musket, cut himself a stick in the form of a crotch, and struck out to one side of the trail, beckoning the American to follow.

The gazelles had been feeding across the trail, and Mirai Khan trotted steadily to the leeward of them, keeping behind sheltering hummocks. It was a long run.

From time to time Mirai Khan halted and peered at the animals. Then he pressed forward. Gray was not easily tired; but he had been long without food and he stumbled as he ran after the hardy Kirghiz who was afire with the spirit of the chase.

"Allah has given us meat for our pot this night," he whispered to Gray, "if we are clever and the animals do not get wind of us."

Gray understood how important their quest was. Their shadows were lengthening swiftly on the sand, and the sun, like a red brazier, was settling over the horizon in front of them. If they did not bag a gazelle, they would have no food that night, and—both men were weakened by hunger.

Mirai Khan stalked his prey with the skill of long experience, pushing ahead patiently until the wind blew from the gazelles to them. But darkness falls fast at the edge of the Gobi. The sky had changed from blue to purple when Mirai Khan threw himself in the sand and began to crawl to the summit of a rise, pushing his crotched stick in front of him.

Following, Gray made out the gazelles feeding some hundred and fifty yards in front of them. The light brown and white bodies were barely discernible against the brown plain, but Mirai Khan arranged his stick, and laid the musket on it carefully.

Gray, stretched out beside him, hazarded a guess as to the distance. The hunter touched him warningly.

"Let me have the shot, Excellency," he whis-

The Liu Sha

pered. "If I cannot slay—even at this distance—no other man can."

He said a brief prayer and sighted, gripping his long weapon in a steady hand. He had removed his sheepskin cap and his white hair and bushy eyebrows gave him the appearance of a keen-eyed bird of prey.

Gray waited, watching the gazelles. As Mirai Khan had claimed the first shot, Gray humored him, but at the same time threw a cartridge into the chamber of his own weapon.

The gazelles had sighted or smelled something alarming, for they quickened their pace away from the hunters. Mirai Khan fired, and swore darkly. Both animals were unhurt, and they had broken into a swift run, gliding away into the twilight.

Gray had laid his own sights on the game, and when the Kirghiz missed the difficult shot, the American pressed the trigger.

A spurt of dust this side of the fleeing animals told him his elevation was wrong. Calmly, he raised his rear sight and fired again, as the gazelles appeared in the eye of the sun on a hillock.

The animal at which he had aimed stumbled and sank to earth. It had been a difficult shot at three hundred yards in a bad light, but Gray was an expert marksman and knew his weapon.

A wild yell broke from Mirai Khan. He flung himself at Gray's feet and kissed his shoes.

"A miracle, Excellency!" he chattered joyously. "That was a shot among a thousand. Aye, I shall tell the hunters of the desert of it, but they will not believe. Truly, I have not seen the like. By the beards cf my fathers, I swear it! I did well when I followed you from Liangchowfu——"

Still babbling his exultation, he hurried to the slain animal and whipped out his knife.

By nightfall, the two had made camp in a gully near the tethered animals. Mirai Khan had dug a well, knowing that water was to be found in this manner, and, over a brisk fire of tamarisk roots, was cooking a gazelle steak.

Gray stretched a blanket on the sand near the fire, watching the flicker of the flames. The gully concealed them from observation. He was reasonably sure by now that they had escaped any pursuing party Wu Fang Chien had sent from Liangchowfu—if one had been sent.

Mirai Khan ate enormously of the steak. When the hunger of the two was satisfied and the white man's pipe was alight, he turned to the Kirghiz thoughtfully.

"Have you ever heard," he asked, "of the city of Sungan?"

Mirai Khan, Gray gathered, was a Mohammedan, a fatalist, a skilled horse-thief, and a dweller at the edge of the Gobi, where life was gleaned from hardship. He was a man of the *yurts,* or tents, a nomad who ranged from the mosques of Bokhara to the outskirts of China. Somewhere, perhaps, Mirai Khan had an *aul,* with a flock of sheep, a dog, and even a wife and children.

The Kirghiz glanced at him keenly and shook his head.

"I have heard the name," he responded. "It was spoken by my father. But Sungan I have never seen."

"It is a city a week's ride beyond Ansichow," persisted Gray, "in the Desert of Gobi."

"That is in the sands," Mirai Khan reflected. "No game is found there, Excellency. Why should a man go to such a place?"

"Have you been there?"

"Does a horse go into a quicksand?"

"Have you known others who went there?"

"Aye, it may be."

"What had they to say of the desert?"

"It is an evil place."

The Kirghiz nodded sleepily. Having eaten heavily, he was ready for his blanket.

"Why did they call it an evil place?"

"How should I know—who have not been there?" Mirai Khan yawned and stretched his stocky arms and legs, as a dog stretches. "It is because of the pale sickness, they say."

Gray looked up quickly from his inspection of the fire. He had heard that phrase before. Delabar had used it.

"What is the pale sickness?" he asked patiently. Mirai Khan ceased yawning.

"Out in the sands, in the *liu sha,* hangs the pale sickness. It is in the air. It is an evil sickness. It leaves its mark on those who go too near. I have heard of men who went too far into the *liu sha* and did not return."

"Why?"

"It is forbidden."

"By the priests of the prophet?"

"Not so. Why should they deal with an evil thing? Is it not the law of the Koran that a man may not touch what is unclean? The rat priests of China, who worship the bronze god, have warned us from the region. I have heard the caravan merchants say that men are brought from China and placed out in the sands, the *liu sha."*

Gray frowned. Mirai Khan spoke frankly, and without intent to deceive him. But he spoke in the manner of his kind—in parables.

"Three times, Mirai Khan," he said, "you have said *liu sha.* What does that mean?"

The Kirghiz lifted some sand in his scarred hand, sifting it through his fingers to the ground.

"This is it," he explained. "We call it in my tongue the *kara kum*—dark sands. Yet the *liu sha*

The Liu Sha

are not the sand you find elsewhere. They are the marching sands."

Gray smiled. He was progressing, in his search for information, from one riddle to another.

"You mean the dust that moves with the wind," he hazarded.

Mirai Khan made a decisive, guttural denial. "Not so. It is the will of Allah that moves the sands. Once there was a city that sinned——"

"And a holy mullah." Gray recalled the legend Delabar had related on the steamer. "He alone escaped the dust that fell from the sky. It was long ago. So that is your *liu sha?*"

The hunter's slant eyes widened in astonishment. "By the beard of my father! Are you a reader of the Koran, to know such things as this? Aye, it is so. The *liu sha* came because of a sin, and without doubt that is why the place is still inhabited of a plague. The Chinese priests bring men there —men who are already in the shadow of death."

"Then, Mirai Khan, there must be a city or an encampment, if many men live there."

"I have not seen it. Nor have those who talked to me."

"But you have not been there?"

"How should I—seeing that the place is inhabited of a sin? No Mohammedan will go there."

"What manner of sickness is this—the pale plague?"

"I know not. But for many miles, aye, the space of a week's ride, no men will bring their *yurts* for fear of it."

Gray gave it up with a shrug. The Kirghiz was speaking riddles, twisted recollections of legends, and tales doubtless exaggerated. While Mirai Khan snored away comfortably, the American went over what he had said in his mind.

The night had grown cold, and he threw the last of the wood on the fire, tucking his blanket about his feet. Their camp was utterly silent, except for the occasional splutter of the flames.

Mirai Khan had said positively that he had seen no city in the Gobi where Gray was bound, nor heard of one. The American knew that if buildings existed on the immense plain of the Gobi they would be visible for miles around. Even if the comrades of Mirai Khan had kept away from the place which they considered unhealthy, they would have sighted the buildings, at one time or another.

Yet Brent had declared that he saw the summits of towers. Imagination, perhaps. Although missionaries were not as a rule inclined to fancies.

Here was one contradiction. Then there were the *liu sha*. Mere legend, doubtless. Central Asia was rife with tales of former greatness.

But one thing was clear. The Chinese priests came to this spot in the desert. And the legend of the plague might be framed to keep the Mohamme-

dans away from the place. Since the late rebellion
Mohammedan and Chinese had frequently taken up
arms against each other—they had never been on
friendly terms. Evidently the Buddhists, for some
reason, took pains to keep this part of the desert to
themselves.

They even guarded it against intrusion—as Brent
had discovered.

And Brent had died of sickness. What was the
pale sickness? Were men inflicted with it brought
to the Gobi—the dreariest stretch of land on the
surface of the earth?

Gray nodded sleepily. The riddles presented no
answer. He determined that he would learn the
truth for himself. Wearied with his exertions, he
was soon asleep. Silence held the camp, the brooding silence of great spaces, the threshold of infinity
which opens before the wanderer in the Gobi. The
wind stirred the sand into tiny spirals that leaped
and danced, like dust wraiths across the gully, pow-
dering the blankets of the sleeping men and the
rough coats of the mules.

Along the summit of the ridge a shadow passed
across the stars. It hesitated to leeward of the
embers of the fire, and the jackal crept on. The
crescent moon moved slowly overhead, throwing a
hazy half-light on the surface of the sand, and
picking out the bleached bones of an antelope.

Night had claimed the Mongolian steppe.

CHAPTER X

THE MEM-SAHIB SPEAKS

It was nearly a week later, on the border of the Gobi, that Gray and Mirai Khan sighted the caravan. The day was rainy. During a space when the rain thinned, the Kirghiz pointed out a group of *yurts* surrounded by camels and ponies a mile away.

Gray scanned the encampment through his glasses, and made out that the caravan numbered a good many men, and that the *yurts* were being put up for the night. The rain began again, and cut off his view.

It was then late afternoon. Both men were tired. They had pushed ahead steadily from Liangchowfu, killing what they needed in the way of game, and occasionally buying goat's milk or dried fruit from a wayside shepherd. The few villages they met they avoided. Gray had not forgotten Wu Fang Chien, or the fears of Delabar.

"They are Kirghiz *yurts*," said Mirai Khan when the American described what he had seen. "And it is a caravan on the march, or we would have seen sheep. Many tribes use our *yurts*. They are taken

down and put up in the time it takes a man to
smoke a pipe. But these people are not Kirghiz.
My kinsmen have not wealth to own so many
camels."

"What do you think they are?"

"Chinese merchants, Excellency, or perhaps
Turkestan traders from Kashgar."

Mirai Khan's respect for his companion had increased with the last few days. Gray's accurate
shooting inspired his admiration, and the fortitude
of the man surprised him.

On his part, Gray trusted the Kirghiz. If Mirai
Khan had meant to rob him, he had enjoyed plenty
of chances to do so. But the Kirghiz's code would
not permit him to steal from one who was sharing
his bread and salt.

"If they are Chinese," meditated the American,
"it will not be wise to ride up to their camp. What
say you, Mirai Khan?"

The Kirghiz puffed tranquilly at his noisome pipe.

"This. It is the hour of sunset prayer. When
that is ended you and I will dismount, Excellency,
and stalk the encampment. By the favor of God
we will then learn if these people are Chinese or
Turkomans. If the last, we shall sleep in a dry
aul, which is well, for my bones like not the damp."

Whereupon Mirai Khan removed his pipe and
kneeled in the sand, facing toward the west, where
was the holy city of his faith. So poverty-stricken

was he that he did not even own a prayer carpet. Gray watched, after tethering the three animals.

"Remember," he said sternly when Mirai Khan had finished the prayer, "there must be no stealing of beasts from the camp, whatever it may be."

The Kirghiz's weakness for horseflesh was well known to him. The hunter agreed readily and they set out under cover of the rain. By the time they were half way to the caravan the sudden twilight of the Gobi concealed them.

Guided by the occasional whinny of a horse, or the harsh bawl of a camel, Mirai Khan crept forward, sniffing the air like a dog. Several lights appeared out of the mist, and Gray took the lead.

He could make out figures that passed through the lighted entrances of the dome-shaped felt shelters. Drawing to one side he gained the camels which rested in a circle, apparently without a watcher.

Mirai Khan had been lost to view in the gloom and Gray walked slowly forward among the camels, trying to gain a clear glimpse of the men of the caravan. The few that he saw were undoubtedly servants, but their dress was unfamiliar.

Gray could almost make out the interior of one of the *yurts*, lighted by candles, with silk hangings and an array of cushions on the floor. He rose to his full height, to obtain a better view, and paused as he saw one of the figures look toward him.

The Mem-Sahib Speaks

The camels were moving uneasily. Gray could have sworn he heard a muffled exclamation near him. He turned his head, and a form uprose from the ground and gripped him.

Gray wrenched himself free from the man and struck out. The newcomer slipped under his arm and caught him about the knees. Other forms sprang from among the camels and lean arms twined around the American.

"Look out, Mirai Khan!" he cried in Chinese. "These are enemies."

A powerful white man who can handle his fists is a match for a round half dozen Mongolians, unarmed—if he has a clear footing and can see where to hit. Gray was held by at least four men; his rifle slung to one shoulder by a sling hampered him. He was cast to earth at once.

His face was ground into the sand, and his arms drawn behind his back. He heard his adversaries chattering in a strange tongue. Cold metal touched his wrists. He felt the *click* of a metal catch and realized that handcuffs had been snapped on him.

He wondered vaguely how handcuffs came to be in a Central Asian caravan, as he was pulled roughly to his feet. In the dark he could not make out the men who held him. But they advanced toward one of the tents—the same he had been trying to see into.

Gray, perforce, made no further resistance. He

was fully occupied in spitting sand from his mouth and trying to shake it from his eyes.

So it happened that when he stood in the lighted *yurt,* he was nearly blind with the dust and the sudden glare. He heard excited native gutturals, and then——

"Why, it's a white man."

It was a woman's voice, and it spoke English. Moreover the voice was clear, even musical. It reflected genuine surprise, a tinge of pity—inspired perhaps by his damaged appearance—and no little bewilderment.

"Yes, *chota missy,*" echoed a man near him, "but this, in the dark, we knew it not. And he cried out in another tongue."

Gray reflected that his warning to Mirai Khan had been ill-timed. His eyes still smarted with the sand. It was not possible for him to use his hands to clear them, because of the handcuffs which bound his wrists behind his back. Not for the world would Gray have asked for assistance in his plight.

He winked rapidly, and presently was able to see the others in the tent clearly. The men who had brought him hither he made out to be slender, dark skinned fellows. By their clean dress, and small, ornamented turbans draped over the right shoulder he guessed them to be Indian natives— most probably Sikhs. This surprised him, for he had been prepared to face Dungans or Turkomans.

The Mem-Sahib Speaks

A portable stove gave out a comfortable warmth, beside a take-down table. The rough felt covering of the *yurt* was concealed behind hangings of striped silk. Gray stared; he little expected to find such an interior in the nomad shelter.

The table was covered with a clean cloth. Behind it hung a canvas curtain, evidently meant to divide one corner from the rest of the tent, perhaps for sleeping purposes. In front of the partition, behind the table, was a comfortable steamer chair. And in the chair, watching him from wide, gray eyes was a young woman.

He had not seen a white woman for months. But his first glance told him that the girl in the chair was more than ordinarily pretty—that she would be considered so even in Washington or Paris. She was neatly dressed in light tan walking skirt and white waist, a shawl over her slender shoulders.

She was considering him silently, chin on hand, a slight frown wrinkling her smooth brow. The bronze hair was dressed low against the neck in a manner that Gray liked to see—at a distance, for he was shy in the presence of women.

The eyes that looked into his were clear, and seemed inclined to be friendly. Just now, they were dubious. The small nose tilted up from a mouth parted over even teeth. She was deeply sunburned, even to throat and arms. Ordinarily, women take great pains to protect their skin from exposure to the sun.

There was the stamp of pride in the brown face, and the head poised erect on strong young shoulders. Gray knew horses. And this woman reminded him of a thoroughbred. Later, he was to find that his estimate of her pride was accurate; for the present, he was hardly in the mood to make other and stronger deductions concerning the girl.

He flushed, hoping that it did not show under the sand.

"Right," he admitted with a rueful smile. "Beneath the mud and dirt, I happen to be an Aryan."

"An Englishman?" she asked quickly, almost skeptically, "Or American?"

"American," he admitted. "My name is Robert Gray."

Her glance flickered curiously at this. He was not too miserable to wonder who she was. What was a white woman doing in this stretch of the Gobi? A white woman who was master, or rather mistress of a large caravan, and seemed quite at home in her surroundings?

He wondered why he had flushed. And why he felt so uncomfortable under her quiet gaze. To his utter surprise the frown cleared from her brow, and her lips parted in a quick smile which crept into her eyes. Then she was serious again. But he

The Mem-Sahib Speaks

found that his pulses were throbbing in wrist and throat.

"Where did you find this *feringhi*, Ram Singh?" she asked curiously.

"Among the camels, *mem-sahib*," promptly answered the man who had spoken before. "His servant was making off the while with our horses."

Gray looked around. At the rear of the group, arms pinioned to his sides and his bearded face bearing marks of a struggle, was Mirai Khan. The Kirghiz wore a sheepish expression and avoided his eye.

"The servant," explained Ram Singh in stern disapproval, "had untethered two of the ponies. One he had mounted when we seized him. Said I not the plain was rife with horse thieves?"

Gray glared at Mirai Khan.

"Did I not warn you," he asked angrily, "that there was to be no stealing of animals?"

The Kirghiz twisted uneasily in his bonds.

"Aye, Excellency. But the ponies seemed unguarded and you had need of one to ride. If these accursed Sikhs had not been watching for horse lifters we would have gone free."

The officer swore under his breath, beginning to realize what an unenviable position Mirai Khan had placed him in. Robbing a caravan was no light offense in this country. And the horses had belonged to the woman!

Gray silently thrust his manacled hands further
out of sight, wishing himself anywhere but here.
Covered with the grime of a week's hike across the
plain, with a stubby beard on his chin, eyes bleared
with sand, and his hat lost, he must look the part of
a horse lifter—and Mirai Khan's appearance did
not conduce to confidence.

"Is this true?" the girl asked. Again the elfin
spirit of amusement seemed to dance in the gray
eyes.

"Every word of it," he said frankly. Searching
for words to explain, his shyness gripped him.
"That is, Mirai Khan was undoubtedly taking your
ponies, but I didn't know what he was up to——"

He broke off, mentally cursing his awkwardness.
It is not easy to converse equably with a self-pos-
sessed young lady, owner of a damaging pair of
cool, gray eyes. Especially when one is battered
and bound by suspicious and efficient servants.

"Why didn't you come direct to the *yurt?*" she
observed tentatively.

"Because I thought you might be—a Chinaman."

"A Chinaman!" The small head perched in-
quisitively aslant. "But I'm not, Captain Gray.
Why should I be? Why should you dislike the
Chinese?"

Two things in her speech interested Gray. She
seemed to be an Englishwoman. And she had given
him his army rank, although he himself had not

mentioned it. Most certainly there could be nothing in his appearance to suggest the service.

"I have reason to dislike one Chinaman," returned Gray. "So I was obliged to take precautions," he blundered, and then strove to remedy
his mistake. "If I had known you were the owner
of the *yurt,* I would have come straight here."

Too late, he realized that he had made his blunder
worse. The girl's brows went up, also her nose—
just a trifle.

"Why should you be so cautious, Mr. Gray?"
The civilian title was accented firmly. Yet a minute ago she had addressed him as "captain."
"Surely"—this was plainly ironical—"the Chinese
are harmless?"

Gray thought grimly of Liangchowfu.

"Sometimes," he said, "they are—inquisitive."
The girl glanced at him. Surely she did not take
this as a personal dig? Gray did not understand
women. "Miss"—he hesitated—*"Memsahib"*—
she stared—"you see, I've gone beyond the limits
mentioned in my passport." He was unwilling,
placed in such circumstances, to tell the whole
truth of his mission and rank. So he compromised.
Which proved to be a mistake. "And the governor
fellow of Liangchowfu is anxious to head me off."

"Really? Perhaps the official," and she glanced
fleetingly at Mirai Khan, "thinks you do not keep

115

good company. Will you show me your passport? You don't have to, you know."

No, he did not have to. But in his present plight he felt that a refusal would be a mistake. He moved to reach the papers in his breast pocket, and was checked by the handcuffs. He glanced at Ram Singh angrily. The native looked at him complacently. It was an awkward moment.

"Ram Singh!" The girl spoke sharply. "Have you bound the white man's hands?"

The Sikh grunted non-committally. She pointed at Gray.

"Undo his hands. Is a white man to be tied like a horse-stealing Kirghiz?"

Reluctantly, Ram Singh obeyed, and stood near vigilantly. Gray felt in his pocket with stiffened fingers and produced his passport. This the girl scanned curiously.

"I want to apologize," ventured Gray, "for Mirai Khan's attempt on your horses. He was acting contrary to orders. But I take the blame for what he did."

He spoke formally, even stiffly. The woman in the chair glanced at him swiftly, studying him from under level brows. He felt a great wish that he should be absolved from the stigma of guilt before her. And, man-like, he pinned his trust in formal explanation.

She seemed not to heed his words. She returned

his papers, biting her lip thoughtfully. He would have given much to know what she was thinking about, but the girl's bright face was unreadable.

"Ram Singh," she ordered absently, "the *Sahib's* rifle must be filled with sand. See that it is cleaned. Take him to the store tent where he can wash the sand from his eyes. Will you come back here, Captain Gray? I would like ever so much to talk to you."

While Gray washed gratefully, and while the natives brushed his coat and shoes, his mind was on the girl of the *yurt*. He told himself savagely that he did not desire to be sympathized with. Like a woman, he thought, she had taken pity on his discomfort. Of course, she had to treat him decently, before the natives.

In this, he was more right than wrong.

CHAPTER XI

SIR LIONEL

WHEN Gray returned to the *yurt,* he found the table set with silver and china containing a substantial amount of curried rice, mutton and tea. This reminded him that he was ravenous, since he had not eaten for twenty-four hours. He did not notice that the girl's hair appeared adjusted more to a nicety, or that she had exchanged the shawl for the jacket of her dress.

"You like your tea strong?" she asked politely.

In spite of his hunger, Gray felt awkward as he ate sparingly of the food under her cool gaze. She was non-committally attentive to his wants. He wished that she would say something more or that Ram Singh would cease glaring at the back of his neck like a hawk ready to pounce on its prey.

The food, however, refreshed him. His curiosity concerning his hostess grew. He had seen no other white man in the camp. It was hardly possible that the Englishwoman had come alone to the Gobi. Whither was she bound? And why did she reside in a Kirghiz *yurt* when the caravan was outfitted with European luxuries?

When the natives had removed the plates, he

took out his pipe from force of habit, and felt for matches. Then he reflected that he should not smoke in the woman's tent.

He would have liked to thank her for her hospitality, to assure her of his regret for the tactics of Mirai Khan, to ask her some of the questions that were in his mind. Especially, if she were really alone in the desert. But while he fumbled for words, she spoke quickly.

"I've never taken a prisoner before, Captain Gray. A white man, that is. I believe the correct thing to do is to question you. That fits in most nicely, because I am unusually curious by nature."

He had pulled out a match which he struck absently, then extinguished it. She noted the action silently.

"You are an army officer?"

"In the reserve. Acting independently, now, of course."

"Acting?" She smiled lightly and held out something to him. "So you are a big game hunter? I did not know this was good country for that sort of thing."

"It isn't," he acknowledged bluntly. "That is— not in the ordinary sense. But I have already some trophies bagged. Mirai Khan is my guide——"

"Please do smoke," she said, and he saw that what she offered him was a box of matches. One of the servants struck a light.

"I am quite used to it. My uncle, Sir Lionel, smokes much worse tobacco than yours."

Gray considered her over his pipe.

"Would you mind telling me," he asked gravely, "Miss Niece of Sir Lionel, what you are going to do with me? I'm fairly your prisoner. Your patrol under Ram Singh captured me within your lines."

The girl nodded thoughtfully. Gray wondered if he had caught a glint of laughter in the demure eyes. He decided he was mistaken.

"You are an officer, Captain Gray. You know all prisoners are questioned closely. I still have two more questions, before I decide your case. Are you really alone? And where are you bound?"

"I am," stated Gray methodically. "Ansichow."

"Really? I am going there. I should introduce you, as my prisoner, to Sir Lionel, but he is tired out and asleep, leaving me with Ram Singh."

"Who is an excellent guardian, Miss Niece——"

"Mary Hastings," said the girl quickly. "I have no reason to conceal my name." Gray thought she emphasized the *I*. "My uncle, Sir Lionel Hastings, is head of the British Asiatic Society in India. He is bound for the Gobi."

Gray stared at her. The British Asiatic Society! Then this must be the expedition in search of the Wusun. Van Schaick had said that it was starting from India.

"I begged Sir Lionel to take me," continued Mary

Hastings calmly, "and he finds me very useful. I record his observations, you know, keep the journal of the expedition, and draw the maps. That gives him time for more important work."

"But the desert——" Gray broke off.

"The desert is no place for a woman. I suppose that is what you meant. But I am not an ordinary woman, I warn you, Captain Gray. Sir Lionel is my only relative, and we have traveled together for years. He did say that he anticipated some opposition from the Chinese authorities. But I refused to be left behind." The rounded chin lifted stubbornly. "This is the most important work my uncle has undertaken, and he is always visited with fever about this time of year."

Gray was secretly envious of Sir Lionel. What an ally this girl would make! Yet, in their present positions, she was apt to be his most ardent foe. He glanced up, measuring her, and met her look. For a long moment the slate-green eyes of the man searched hers. They reminded him of the surface of water, sometimes quiet to an infinite depth and then tumultuous.

For a discerning man, Gray was at a sad loss to fathom Mary Hastings.

"To avoid attention from the Chinese," she continued, looking down, "we came up from Burma, along the Tibetan border. Rather a boring trip. But by going around the main towns at the Yang-

tze headwaters, and by using these serviceable native huts—which can be taken down and put up
quickly—we escape questioning."

So that was the explanation of the clumsy *yurts*.

"You were not quite so fortunate, Captain Gray?
Curious, that, isn't it—when you are only a big
game hunter?"

It was on the tip of his tongue to make a clean
breast of it, and say that he, also, was seeking
Sungan. But it seemed absurd to confess to her
that the sole member of the American expedition
had been found among the camels of the Hastings
caravan. Perhaps he was unconsciously influenced
by his desire to be on friendly terms—even such as
at present with Mary Hastings.

Every moment of their talk was a keen pleasure
to him—more so than he was aware. He reflected
how lucky it was that he had run into the other
expedition. It was not altogether strange, since
they had both started at the same time, and Ansichow was the mutual hopping-off place into the
Gobi.

"Will you tell me," he evaded, "how you came
to call me Captain Gray before you saw my
papers?"

Mary Hastings smiled pleasantly.

"It was an excellent guess, wasn't it? But now
I'm quite through my questions." She paused, her
brow wrinkled in portentous thought. "I think

Sir Lionel

I shall not burden myself with a prisoner. You are quite free, Captain Gray. You and Mirai Khan. Doubtless you wish to return to your caravan."

Gray thought of the two waiting mules and the rain-soaked blanket that constituted his outfit, and laughingly mentioned it to her.

"You are very kind," he said, rising.

"Captain Gray," she said impulsively, "it's raining again. If you would care to spend the night with us, I am sure Ram Singh can spare you a cot and blanket. Mirai Khan can fetch your outfit in the morning, and you can go on with us to Ansichow. It's only a day's *trek*."

Gray hesitated, then accepted her offer thankfully.

"You will find your rifle on your cot. Ram Singh cleaned it himself. It needed it. He said it was a 30-30 model, but then you are probably using it for big game because you are accustomed to it." She held out her hand with a quizzical smile. Gray took it in his firm clasp, awkwardly, and released her fingers quickly, lest he should hold them too long. She nodded.

"Good night, Captain Gray."

Not until he was without the tent did he reflect that he had admitted that he was bound for Ansichow. And Ansichow meant the Gobi.

For a space after his departure Mary Hastings remained in her tent. She had dismissed the native servant. She was thinking, and it seemed to please her. But thought, with the girl, required companionship and conversation.

Abruptly she left her chair and stepped through the door of the tent. It was still drizzling without; still, there was a break in the heavy clouds to the west. Mary noted this, and skipped to the entrance of the *yurt* nearest her.

"It's me, Uncle Singh," she called, not quite grammatically. "Can I come in?"

"Of course," a kindly voice answered at once. "Anything wrong?"

A man sat up on the cot, snapping on an electric torch by the head of the bed and glancing at a small clock. He was a tall, spare individual, with the frame of an athlete, polo shoulders, and the high brow of a scholar.

He was well past middle age, yellow-brown as to face, deep hollows under the cheek bones, his scanty hair matching his face, except where it was streaked with white.

The girl installed herself snugly on the foot of the bed, sitting cross-legged.

"You've been sleeping heavily, *Sher Singh*," she observed reproachfully, giving the man his native surname, "and that means you aren't well. I have news." She paused triumphantly, then bubbled spontaneously into speech.

"Such news. *Aie.* Captain Robert Gray is here,

124

in Ram Singh's tent. He is alone, with a servant. He is a big man, not ill-looking, but awkward—very. He stands so much on his dignity. Really, it was quite ridiculous"—she laughed agreeably—"and I was very nicely entertained. He was brought in by the Sikhs, after trying to steal our ponies——"

"Lifting our horses!" Sir Lionel sat bolt upright and flushed. "Why, the scoundrel——"

"I mean his servant was. Captain Gray was innocent, but I was not inclined to let him off easily——"

Mary's conception of important news did not satisfy the explorer's desire for facts. A peculiarly jealous expression crept into the man's open face.

"Has he a well-equipped caravan?"

"Two mules, a gun and a blanket."

"How extraordinary!" Sir Lionel stared at his niece. "No camels?"

"Not one." Mary yawned, and, with a glance at the clock, began to unbind her heavy hair. It was very late. Her fingers worked dexterously, while Sir Lionel weighed her words. Unlike his niece, he was an individual of slow mental process, perhaps too much schooled by routine.

"Mary! How did you—ah—behave to Captain Gray?"

"I took him prisoner." The girl smiled mischievously. "He was *so* humiliated, Uncle Singh."

"I hope," observed Sir Lionel severely, "you warned him of our identity."

"Rather. But he implied he was after big game."

Sir Lionel reached to the light stand and secured a cigarette, which he lit. His eyes hardened purposefully.

"I'll *trek* for Ansichow, at once. I must buy up all the available camels. If you will retire to your tent, and send my *syce*——"

"Indeed, no." She frowned worriedly. "You haven't had your sleep yet."

Sir Lionel caught her hand in his.

"No, Mary. You must be aware what this expedition means to me. I must be first in Ansichow, and into the Gobi. Failure is not to be thought of. Dear girl, I have thrown my reputation into the dice bowl——"

"I know." She patted his hand lightly, and her eyes were serious. "Only I wish you would let me help a little more." She shook free the coils of her bronze hair and placed a small hand firmly over his lips. "I know what you want to say—that you are being ever so kind and indulging to let me come at all. As if I could be left at Simla when you went on your biggest hunt, Uncle Singh. Well," she sighed, "if you must go buy camels, you will. But"—she brightened—"please leave the wandering American to me. I saw him first."

Sir Lionel removed the hand that restricted his

speech, and frowned portentously. Mary beamed, twining her hair into twin plaits.

"Mary!" he said gravely, "please do not annoy Captain—ah—Gray. We must be perfectly fair with him, you know."

"Of course," she assured him virtuously. "Haven't I been? He may not think so when he learns how you've gone camel buying when I offered him sleeping quarters. He'll forever fear the Greeks bearing gifts——"

"*Oolu ka butcha!*" (Child of an owl!)

"But he shouldn't try to deceive me, should he, Uncle? I fancy he'll have a rather wretched time of it. He seems somewhat out of his environment here."

She nodded decisively.

"It's his own fault altogether for coming where he has no business to be and wanting to deprive my *Sher Singh* of what you worked a lifetime for."

"Merely his duty, Mary."

"But he shall not hinder you in yours."

She fell silent, no longer smiling. There was a great tenderness in the glance she cast at the gaunt Englishman. Sir Lionel was her hero, and, lacking father and mother, all the warmth of the girl's affection had been bestowed on the explorer.

She said good-night softly and slipped from the tent. That night she slept lightly, and was afoot with the first streak of crimson in the east.

CHAPTER XII

In his snug quarters Gray slept well for the first time in many nights, feeling the reaction from the constant watchfulness he and Mirai Khan had been forced to exercise. When he turned out in the morning the sun was well up, and the men were breaking camp under the direction of Ram Singh who greeted him coldly.

When he inquired for Miss Hastings he found that she had gone on to join her uncle, on a camel with a single attendant. He was forced to ride with the caravan, after sending Mirai Khan back for the animals. Ram Singh proved an uncommunicative companion and Gray was glad when the flat roofs of the town showed over the sand ridges in the late afternoon.

The caravan halted at the edge of the town, where the Englishman had prepared his encampment. The place was a lonely settlement, populated by stolid Dungans and a few Chinese who ministered to the wants of merchants passing from Liangchowfu to Kashgar and the cities of Turkestan. Gray failed to see either the girl or her uncle and learned that they had gone to pay a visit of ceremony to the *amban*—the governor—of Ansichow.

He went to seek out Mirai Khan. The meeting with the Hastings had put him in a delicate situation. In spite of his own plight, he determined to confess his mission to the Englishman, having decided that was the only fair thing to do. He could not accept aid from the people who were bound to be his rivals in the quest for the Wusun.

He reflected ruefully that Van Schaick had urged him to reach the spot in the Gobi before the expedition from India. Van Schaick and Balch were counting on him to do that—not knowing that Delabar had been working against him.

As it stood, both parties had gained the town on the Gobi edge at the same time. But the Hastings possessed an ample outfit, well chosen for the purpose and ready to go ahead on the instant. Gray had only Mirai Khan and two mules. He would need to hire camels, and bearers, to stock up with what provisions were available, and to obtain a guide.

This would take time, and much of his small store of money. Moreover, if he made clear his purpose to Sir Lionel, it was probable the Englishman would start at once, thus gaining four or five days on him. Gray knew by experience the uselessness of trying to hurry Chinese through a transaction.

And he was not sure if Mirai Khan would go into the desert.

The Kirghiz had served him faithfully, to the best of his ability so far. But Mirai Khan had said that the tribesmen shunned this part of the desert. Then there was the *amban.* It was more than possible that Wu Fang Chien had sent word to Ansichow to head off Gray.

It was a difficult situation, and Gray was pondering it moodily when he came upon Mirai Khan in the bazaar street of the town. The Kirghiz, who seemed to be excited over something, beckoned him into one of the stalls, after glancing up and down the street cautiously.

"Hearken, Excellency," he whispered. "Here I have found a man who knows what will interest you. He has been much into the desert and has dug up writings and valuable things which he will sell—at a good price. His name is Muhammed Bai."

Gray glanced into the stall, and saw a bent figure kneeling on the rugs. It was an old Turkoman, wearing spectacles and a stained turban. Muhammed Bai *salaamed* and motioned his visitor to be seated. Gray scanned him with some interest. It was quite possible the man had some valuable information. Mirai Khan had a way of finding out things readily.

"Will the Excellency rest at ease," chattered the Turkoman, peering at him benevolently, "while his servant shows him certain priceless treasures which he has dug from the sand among the ruins. Mirai Khan has said the Excellency seeks the ruins."

"You have been there?" Gray asked cautiously. He knew the penchant of the Central Asian for exaggeration.

"Without doubt. Far, far to the west I have been. To the ruins in the sand. Other Excellencies have asked concerning them from time to time but none have been there except myself, Muhammed Bai."

"What are the ruins like?"

The merchant waved a thin hand eloquently. "Towers of stone, great and high, standing forth like guide posts. My father knew of them. One of the sultans of his tribe dug for treasure there. He found gold. Aye, he told me the place. I, also, went and dug. Look——"

With the gesture of a *connoisseur* displaying a masterpiece, the Turkoman drew some objects from under a silk rug. Gray stared at them. They were odd bits of wrought silver and enamel ware, stained with age. These Muhammed Bai spread before him.

"They came from the ruins. The Excellency is undoubtedly a man of wisdom. I need not tell *him* how old these things are. There is no telling their value. But I will sell the lot for a very few *taels*— a ten *taels*."

Marching Sands

The American fingered the fragments curiously. They meant nothing to him. They might be the relics of an ancient civilization. Muhammed Bai watched him keenly, and pushed a piece of parchment under his eyes.

"Here is a greater treasure. The Excellency will see the worth of this at a glance. Other foreign merchants have asked to buy this. But I told them that a high price must be paid. Who would sell a sacred object to a dog? See, the strange writing——"

Gray held up the parchment to the light. It was a small sheet, much soiled. It was covered with a fine writing in characters unknown to him. He wished that Delabar might be here to tell him its meaning. If it had come from that section of the Gobi, it was possible that it shed some light on the Wusun.

"Mirai Khan, who is my friend, said that the Excellency sought tidings of the ancient people. Here is such a scroll as may not be found elsewhere. Perhaps it is priceless. I know not."

"Can you read it?"

"Can a servant such as I read ancient wisdom?" Muhammed Bai elevated his hands eloquently. "But I will sell——"

He looked up as a shadow fell across the stall. Gray saw that Mary Hastings was standing in the entrance. Beside her was a tall man, well dressed. He rose.

"This is my uncle, Major Hastings, Captain Gray," she smiled. "We heard that you were in the bazaar. Are you buying curios to take back with your trophies?"

Sir Lionel returned the American's bow politely, glancing from Muhammed Bai to him curiously. Then his eye fell on the parchment. He leaned forward and uttered a sharp exclamation of interest.

"Whence came this?" he asked Muhammed Bai, in the dialect of Western Shensi.

The Turkoman peered up at him from tufted brows, looking like an aged, gray hen guarding one of its brood. "From the desert yonder. I, Muhammed Bai——"

"What language is the writing?"

"How should I know, Excellency?"

"It would be hard to tell." Sir Lionel frowned thoughtfully. "The characters on the parchment are certainly not the cuneiform of Behistun; equally, they are no dialect of the older Kashgaria, or Chinese. These two languages are the only ones we would expect to find here, except possibly——"

He broke off, glancing curiously at Gray.

"Have you a claim to this manuscript, sir? Are you planning to purchase it?"

Gray hesitated, feeling the cool gaze of the girl

on him. Should he buy the parchment it would be useless to him, as he could not interpret the writing. On the other hand, if he let Sir Lionel have it, the parchment might prove an aid to the English expedition. This, naturally, he was bound to prevent.

"I will buy it," he concluded, and added quickly, "as a curio."

"To add to your big game trophies?" asked Mary Hastings calmly.

While he tried to think of an answer, Sir Lionel handed him the parchment.

"It might serve as a curio, Captain Gray. But, in all fairness, I must warn you. The writing is a counterfeit, cleverly done. You see, it is my life's business to know the ancient languages of Central Asia. This is adapted from some inscription which Muhammed Bai has doubtless seen. The parchment is skillfully colored to appear aged. But the black ink is freshly laid on."

Gray smiled grimly, while the Turkoman stared at the white men, endeavoring to guess what they were saying.

"And these bits of silver?" The American motioned to the relics that lay on the rug.

"Are worthless, except—as curios. Being a hunter, Captain Gray, I presume the authenticity of the objects will not affect your desire to purchase them."

134

A Message from the Centuries

Sir Lionel spoke dryly, and the girl scrutinized him with frank amusement.

"My uncle has heard of Muhammed Bai," she volunteered. "He is an old impostor who makes a living selling false manuscripts to travelers in Khotan and Kashgar. Perhaps he had heard we were coming to Ansichow. I rather think your precious Kirghiz is in league with Muhammed Bai."

Mirai Khan caught the drift of what she said—having a slight knowledge of English, and retired discreetly to the bazaar alley. Gray reflected on the curious ethics of Central Asia which permitted a servant to take money from his master by trickery, while he still served him faithfully. It was one of the riddles of Asian ethics—which he had encountered before. He knew that the girl was probably right.

He tossed down the money for the parchment and pocketed it, as he had said that he would buy it. Sir Lionel checked him, as he rose.

"That manuscript is—interesting," he observed thoughtfully. "Because Muhammed Bai must have had a model to copy this writing from. The characters resemble Sanscrit slightly, but they suggest Tokharian, with which this man can not be acquainted." He turned on the blinking merchant sharply. "Tell me, writer of false missives," he said in Turki, "from what did you copy these letters?"

135

Marching Sands

There was something eager and threatening in the face of the tall Englishman that choked off Muhammed Bai's denial.

"It is as I said, Excellency. The writings were found in the desert."

"Where?"

"A week's ride from here, to the west."

"Near Sungan—eh? How did you find them?"

The Turkoman was sullenly silent. Sir Lionel dropped a coin on the rug. It was gold.

"Ah, the Excellency is generous as a prince of the royal household!" cried Muhammed Bai. "It was on a stone—a boundary stone at the place I said—that I found the writings. See, here is the stone."

He scrambled to his feet, bowing, and hastened to the rear of the stall. He cast off some rugs from the top of a pile, disclosing a piece of brown sandstone some three feet high and a foot in thickness. On the surface of the stone Gray saw characters engraved, characters that were strange to him.

But not to Sir Lionel. The Englishman dropped to his knees with an exclamation, whipping out his eyeglasses. He ran his finger over the writing on the sandstone.

"A form of Sanscrit!" he cried. "By Jove— three centuries old, at least. Four, I should judge. And here is the character corresponding to the Chinese word Wusun, the 'Tall Ones.' Remark-

136

able! This evidently was one of the boundary marks of the Wusun land."

He peered at the inscription intently, forgetting the American in his enthusiasm.

"Hm—it was erected by one of the khans of the Tall People. *By a slave of the Chinese Emperor.* It speaks of the captive race of the Wusun. Plainly they were even then under the *kang* of the Chinese priests. 'In the city of Sungan are the captive people . . . greatly fallen since the age when they were conquerors . . . they cling to their hearths and towers . . . in the sand. There they will always be——' "

He broke off his reading and glanced up at Gray. "Splendid! I must take a rubbing of this."

He ordered Muhammed Bai to bring charcoal and a clean sheet of paper. The charcoal he rubbed over the stone. Then he pressed the paper firmly against it, beating the sheet with his fists until the outline of the inscription was imprinted on the paper. This he surveyed triumphantly.

"Excellent! Captain Gray, I am indebted for your"—he smiled—"involuntary assistance. Will you dine with us? Mary will be glad of company, I am sure. I must place this where it will be safe."

He hurried off, followed by the girl and Gray. Neither spoke during the walk to the outskirts of Ansichow. The American was regretting the bad fortune that had concealed the truth of his mission from the Hastings. He was in the position of a culprit obtaining valuable information from his rivals, without intending to do so. This information he was in duty bound to use to his own advantage.

He had determined to set matters right by revealing to his host his purpose in seeking the Gobi. And the dinner would afford him an opportunity to do so.

The camp of the Hastings was located in a garden which surrounded a spring near the *caravanserai* of Ansichow. Sir Lionel, disliking the filth of the *caravanserai* which bore evidence of much use by not over-fastidious Chinese travelers, had pitched his tents in the garden, making his own *dak* bungalow, as he called it.

It was late evening, and the table had been set under the fly of the main tent, used by the girl. It was the quiet hour of evening prayer. Sheep boys were driving their flocks homeward for the night along the road a short distance away. There was a slight breeze—enough to clear the air of the ever-present dust—which barely shook the sides of the tent. Two Indian servants laid an appetizing meal before their masters.

Sir Lionel, elated by his discovery, talked of the

city of Sungan. Once or twice he checked himself, as if he feared he was saying too much. But his eagerness was not to be restrained.

"The stone proves the existence of Sungan, and gives us a rough idea of its location. Judging from the inscription, the Wusun have clung to their heritage. I think we shall find some survivors in Sungan."

"I thought you said the inscription was a form of Sanscrit," objected Gray. "And the Wusun are Chinese——"

"Ah, that is just the point." Sir Lionel reared his blond head, like a setter at scent of game. "Sanscrit is an Aryan language. The white race buried here in the Gobi called themselves the Tall People. Wusun is the Chinese translation of that term. Their own written tongue is probably the dialect we saw on the boundary stone, which is Aryan. A clear chain of proof, Captain Gray."

"But," the American objected honestly, "my follower, Mirai Khan, has hunted the borderland of the Gobi and he says positively no city is to be seen. The stone is four centuries or more old——"

"Mirai Khan," said the girl quickly, "can not see under the sand, can he? He seems to be bent chiefly on stealing horses."

Sir Lionel, however, was not to be turned from the discussion which filled his mind. "You forget the sand that Mary mentions, Captain Gray," he

retorted warmly. "This is, literally, a sea of sand.
And the waves are rising. We are sure that certain towns in the foothills of the Thian Shan have
been buried by these waves. You see, the prevailing
winds here are from the east. They drive the sand
dunes before them. I have noted that the dunes
march westward——"

"Before you go on, Sir Lionel——" protested the
American, remembering his intention to make a
clean breast of things.

"Not a word, sir. Not another word. Be quiet,
Mary"—as the girl started to speak—"I will not be
contradicted. It is a scientific fact that the sands
march. During the *kara burans* or black windstorms they will progress many feet a day. Sungan was built on the great caravan route from
China to Samarcand and Persia, many centuries
ago. Marco Polo followed this route when he
visited the court of Kubla Khan."

"But," Gray broke in, "I want——"

"I say, it is a fact, sir. Prove the contrary.
You can't!" Sir Lionel glared at him hostilely. "I
am right. Without doubt, I am correct. Sungan
has been buried by the marching sands. Only the
towers remain."

Gray thought of the tale Delabar had mentioned
—of the sand that came down on the city of the
Gobi, as retribution for some sin against the religions of Asia. Also, Mirai Khan had said no city

A Message from the Centuries

was to be seen. And Brent had claimed to see some isolated towers.

"These towers," he started to explain what was in his mind.

"Are the summits of the palaces of Sungan, sir. In them I shall find the white race of Asia, the captive people of the Wusun."

"But, Uncle," protested the girl, "the stone was erected four hundred years ago. If the Chinese had wanted to, they might have killed off the remaining Wusun since that time."

"The ancient Chinese annals," observed Sir Lionel tolerantly, "state that the Wusun, the 'Tall Ones,' were formidable fighters. The Sacæ or Scythians from whom they are descended were one of the conquering races of the world. It is this heritage of strength which has preserved the remnant of the Wusun—for us to find."

Gray faced the Englishman across the table. Sir Lionel had changed to a neat suit of clean duck for the meal. Mary was fastidiously dressed in white, a light shawl over her slender shoulders. He felt keenly his own untidy attire. Moreover, the girl seemed bent on making fun of him.

"Captain Gray is a hunter, you know, Uncle," she remarked, glancing coolly at the uncomfortable American. "Really, your talk about the Wusun must bore him. He has come to shoot antelope. Or is it wild camels, Captain Gray?"

141

Gray met her glance steadily. He saw that she was heart and soul with Sir Lionel in the latter's quest, and guessed that his own confession must terminate any possibility of friendship between them.

"Neither," he said gravely. "I have meant to tell you before this. But at first I was so surprised at finding——"

"That we guarded our ponies, Captain Gray?" The girl's eyes twinkled and she bit her lip.

"A white woman instead of a Chinaman—I didn't confess, as I should have done."

"But Mirai Khan confessed."

Gray flushed. "I was sent to the desert, Sir Lionel, to find the Wusun. I am employed by the American Exploration Society. And I am going to do my best to get to Sungan—ahead of you, if possible."

The effect of his words was curious. The girl studied him silently. Sir Lionel stroked his blond mustache, plainly ill at ease. Neither seemed surprised.

"So you see," Gray made the statement as blunt as possible, "I am your rival. I meant to tell you before. Naturally, it is my duty to use the information you have given me. But I want to make my position clear before we go any further."

Sir Lionel's first words were not what Gray expected.

A Message from the Centuries

"You are not a scientist, sir?"

"I am not. Professor Delabar, who was to have come with me, was forced to turn back at Liang-chowfu."

"Then you are alone? Without a caravan?"

"For the present. I'm going to do my best to outfit at Ansichow and get ahead of you, Sir Lionel." Gray rose. "I suppose I'm not exactly welcome here, after what I've told you——"

The Englishman waved his brown hand tolerantly.

"I like your frankness, Captain Gray. Pray be seated. We are rivals, not enemies, you know. But"—the zeal of the enthusiast shone from his mild eyes—"I shall never permit you to reach Sungan ahead of me. I have studied the Wusun for years. I persuaded the British Asiatic Society to send me here. It is the crowning venture of my life, sir."

The girl looked up proudly.

"Indeed, that is true, Captain Gray. My uncle has spent our money on the trip. His reputation is at stake. Because few of the directors of the Asiatic Society believe the Wusun are to be found——"

"They are mistaken, Mary," Sir Lionel assured her. "I know that I am right. The fact that Captain Gray was sent here is proof of it. I shall reach Sungan—the first white man to penetrate the forbidden region of the Gobi. The boundary stone has

143

indicated our course, and I will not yield the right of way to Captain Gray, or any one. Any one, I repeat, sir!"

He struck the table forcibly and rose, mastering his emotion in a moment.

"I pray, sir," he said with the fine courtesy of the English gentleman, "if we are to be rivals, you will not deny us the pleasure of your company while we are at Ansichow. After that, you know, it is each man for himself. Now, I will go to read over my rubbing——"

He bowed stiffly and walked into the adjoining tent. Gray found that the girl was watching him curiously.

"So Delabar went back," she said·musingly. "I wondered why he was not with you when you came to my *yurt* after Ram Singh——"

She colored slightly. Gray noticed how the fading sunlight glinted on her copper hair, and set off the fine lines of her slender figure. A thoroughbred, he thought—like her uncle.

"Ram Singh did exactly right," he admitted. "But how——"

"Did I expect Delabar?" She hesitated. "Well, I have a confession, too, Captain Gray. I knew all along—or rather suspected—what you were. At Calcutta Sir Lionel received this letter."

She felt in her belt and drew out a square of folded paper. This she handed silently to Gray.

A Message from the Centuries

Captain Gray, an American army officer, and Professor Delabar are on their way to the Gobi. It will be useless for you to attempt the expedition, as they will be there before you. Do not waste your time by going into China.

This was the letter. It was written in a neat hand and unsigned.

"Did the envelope have a postmark?" he asked.

"Yes, San Francisco."

He handed it back to her. The writing he recognized as Delabar's. The Syrian, then, had tried to prevent the Hastings from setting out. As he had done his best to keep Gray from reaching the Gobi. Why?

CHAPTER XIII

THE DESERT

THE next day Gray dispatched Mirai Khan to the *amban's* yamen to try to hire the necessary camels. He thought it better not to go himself. Without the consent of the Chinese official nothing could be done, as the *amban* would expect a liberal commission on every transaction in Ansichow. Also the official had a dozen ill-armed and ill-minded soldiery in the town barracks—enough to enforce his authority on Gray, although the Hastings' party was numerous enough to be independent of the Chinese.

Gray himself wandered moodily through the few streets of the village. Since the conversation of the evening before he had been restless. He had slept badly. Although he would not admit it to himself, the thought of Mary Hastings had preyed on him.

So it happened that his wandering took him to the camp of the Hastings.

He found Mary seated under the fly of the stores tent, inspecting and tallying a stock of provisions that Ram Singh had purchased. She looked up and nodded coolly at his approach.

The Desert

"You are busy, Miss Hastings," he observed. "But I want to ask a favor. A half hour of your time."

The girl poised a pencil over her accounts doubtfully. Ram Singh scowled.

"We can talk here, Captain Gray," she compromised, "while I work. Sir Lionel wants these stores——"

"We can't talk here very well," objected Gray. "What I have to say is important. Last night your uncle gave me some valuable information. I want to give you return value for it."

"Where?"

Mary Hastings had the brisk manner of one accustomed to transacting business. Gray learned later—after the disaster that came upon them in the Gobi—that she handled the routine work of her uncle's expeditions, and very capably, too.

"Outside here, in the garden," he suggested. She hesitated; then rose, reaching for her sun helmet. A dilapidated wall encircled the camp, and a few aloes struggled for existence by the tumble-down stones.

Mary climbed the stones, refusing assistance from the American, until she perched on the summit of the garden wall. Here she could overlook the activity in the camp as she listened.

A haze hung in the air—born of the incessant flurries of fine sand that burden the atmosphere in

147

the Gobi. But from their small elevation, beyond the low buildings of Ansichow, Gray could see the plain of dunes that marked the desert. A dull brown they were, stretching to the long line of the horizon in the west.

Gray was silent, admiring the girl's profile. There was something slender and boyish about her. Her dress was plain, and excessively neat. Under the crown of her helmet a few strands of copper hair curled against her tanned cheek.

Mary glanced at the watch on her wrist significantly.

"I'm afraid you are very lazy, Captain Gray," she said frankly. "I warn you that we are going to lose no time in starting from Ansichow."

"I am lazy," he agreed. "But I don't want you to start at all."

She looked at him calmly. "Why?"

"That's what I wanted to tell your uncle. I'm going to be as frank with you as I intended to be with Sir Lionel. Miss Hastings, the Gobi Desert—"

"Is not safe for a woman, I presume?"

"Exactly. If Sir Lionel knew all that I do, he would not want you to go with him. He'll have to go, of course. So will I. But you can stay here with Ram Singh until we get back. The Sikh is a good watchman. Sir Lionel can join you when he returns."

Mary rested her chin on her hands and scrutinized the aloes with friendly interest. "Why do you think it is dangerous for me to go to—Sungan?"

"I have a good reason for my warning, Miss Hastings. Two reasons. One—Sungan seems to be guarded by the Chinese priests. You have avoided them by coming up through Burma into Mongolia. I've had a taste of their kindly disposition."

He told her briefly of the opposition of Wu Fang Chien, the episode of the inn at Liangchowfu, and the fears of Delabar.

"So. your companion turned back because he was afraid?" She smiled curiously. "What is your other reason, Captain Gray?"

"Sickness. That was what Delabar chiefly dreaded, I think. Brent, a missionary, went past the Gobi border here—and died of sickness. I don't say he was killed. He died."

"We are equipped to deal with that. I have means to purify the water we may have to use in the oases."

"It's not a question of water, in this case. Brent had his own. You may think I'm running to fancy a bit, Miss Hastings. But there's Mirai Khan. I've sounded him thoroughly. He is clearly afraid of the Sungan region, and of the pale sickness. I don't know what it is—don't even *know* that it exists. Still, the fact remains that Mirai Khan, who is a fearless sort of rascal, says his countrymen avoided this part of the Gobi on account of the plague—whatever it may be."

"All Kirghiz are liars by birth and environment. Really, you know, Captain Gray, the Buddhist priests invent such stories to keep visitors from their shrines. The coming of foreigners weakens their power."

"That may be true." Gray felt he was stating his case badly. "But you haven't established contact yet with the amiable Wu Fang Chien. Having a woman along would handicap Sir Lionel."

Her brows arched quizzically.

"Really? The *amban* of Ansichow and his men do not seem to be trying to prevent us from going ahead."

"Because they couldn't very well if they wanted to. But, did it strike you that you have already come so far that the Chinese are not worrying about you? That, if you go into the Gobi, they will count you lost. I've gathered as much, and Mirai Khan has listened in the bazaars. Won't you stay at Ansichow, Miss Hastings?"

His blunt appeal had a note of wistfulness in it. The possible danger to the girl had haunted him all that day. It would be useless he felt, to appeal to Sir Lionel. Mary Hastings was not in the habit of obeying her uncle's commands in matters affecting her own comfort or safety.

"And leave Sir Lionel to go alone into the Gobi?"

The Desert

"Yes. He's bound to take the risk. You are not. I'm afraid your uncle is too wrapped up in his researches to pay much heed to possible danger. I don't think a white woman should take the risk."

Mary Hastings smiled slowly. She had a way of looking directly at a man—unlike most women—that disturbed Gray. He felt that he was blundering.

"Sir Lionel," she replied, "has set his heart on being the first white man in Sungan. He has staked his reputation as a scientist on this expedition. You do not know how much it means to him. If he finds the Sungan ruins and the descendants of the Wusun, he will have vindicated his judgment. If he fails it will be his last expedition. It is hard for a man of his age to fail. He has many rivals, at home and—in America."

"But you——"

"Sir Lionel needs me. I attend to the management of the caravan. And he can not spare Ram Singh."

She tossed her small head.

"Don't you think, Captain Gray, you've tried enough to spoil our chances of success? Isn't it rather mean of you to try to frighten me into leaving *Sher Singh?*" Mary Hastings was suddenly growing angry. Gray was committing the unpardonable sin of endeavoring—so she assured herself —to separate uncle and niece.

Marching Sands

She wanted to be angrier than she was. But the wall perch was a bad strategic position for a display of temper, which she considered he had earned.

"You know that it would weaken our chances of success to divide our caravan!" she accused, feeling for foothold on the stones beneath.

Gray was unable to account for the swift change in mood. What had he said to offend her? He had meant it only for her good.

"No, Miss Hastings," he flushed. "I simply wanted to warn you of real danger."

The girl slid down the rocks to the earth. She stamped a neatly shod foot disdainfully. Gray was oblivious of the fact that the maneuver had been planned for this purpose. She was plainly very angry. He wondered why, miserably.

"I thought you were a sportsman, Captain Gray —even if you were not a big game hunter as you pretended. I find I am mistaken. Good afternoon."

"Good Lord!" Gray watched her slight figure return to the tent and set his teeth. "Good Lord!" He smiled ruefully. "Horse thief—schemer—I wonder if there's anything else that she thinks I am. Guess there's nothing else bad enough."

He climbed down from his rocks and left the encampment, avoiding Ram Singh who was ushering in a line of coolies as he did so. The Sikh strode by with a scowl.

The Desert

So easily are quarrels made. And a woman, so fate has ordained, has the first voice in their making. But it is doubtful if Mary Hastings herself could have explained why she treated Gray as she did. Divinely is it decreed that a woman may not be asked to explain to a man.

Gray hesitated, half minded to seek out Sir Lionel and ask that the girl be kept in Ansichow. Realizing that this would be useless, he returned to his tent on the further side of the town. Mirai Khan was not there.

It was a good three hours before the Kirghiz appeared. Three hours in which Gray smoked moodily. Mirai Khan had news.

"Come, Excellency," he observed importantly. "Yonder is a sight you should see. Verily, it is a fine sight."

Gray took his hat and followed his companion to a knoll, where the Kirghiz pointed out to the plain.

Half a mile away a caravan of a dozen camels in single file was making its way into the sand dunes, leaving a dense haze of dust in its wake. He could see through his glasses Sir Lionel and Ram Singh on the leading beasts.

Near the end of the caravan he saw Mary Hastings. He thought that she turned and looked back at him. He could not be sure. He watched the slight figure with its veil about the sun helmet pass from view in the dust.

Then he walked back silently to the tent, beckoning Mirai Khan to follow.

"Have you the camels?" he asked when they were seated on the tattered rug that formed the tent floor.

"No, Excellency. The camels may not be hired."

"Then buy them."

Mirai Khan yawned and regarded his master with the benevolent scrutiny of the fatalist.

"It may not be. There were but eight two-hump camels in Ansichow, and these the Englishman bartered when he first came, in exchange for his tired beasts. He paid well."

"Well, buy the camels he left."

"That would be folly. A week must pass before these eight can bear burdens. They are nearly dead with hard use. The Englishman did not spare them."

Gray frowned meditatively. He must have beasts of burden, to carry at least ten days' stock of water, with necessary food. The Gobi was a barren land.

"Do you think a trader's caravan may visit Ansichow, Mirai Khan?"

"Perhaps. In another moon, or possibly three or four. Why should they come to this dung-heap in the sand?"

"Coolies might carry our supplies—if we paid them enough." Gray knew that this would be risky; but he was not in a position to choose. Time was

154

pressing. Mirai Khan smiled, showing yellow, serried teeth.

"No, Excellency. An ounce of gold apiece will not bribe these Chinese to come into the Gobi."

"The Kirghiz?"

Mirai Khan squinted thoughtfully at the glare of sunlight without the tent. "Is the Excellency determined to go into the Gobi?"

"Yes."

"What God wills, will come to pass. I, Mirai Khan, have helped you to safety. For the space of ten days I have eaten the food you have killed. Because of this, I shall go a part of the way into the Gobi. Also, a tribe of Kirghiz should be here within four days, from the northern steppe. It may so happen that some of these will come with us. I know not."

"Four days!" Gray groaned.

"Likewise, the men of this tribe will not be carriers of burdens. It is not their custom."

"Mirai Khan: why is it that you fear the city of Sungan? I thought you were a brave man."

Gray's purposeful taunt failed of its effect. Mirai Khan stared at him and spat out into the sand.

"The region of Sungan is unclean. It is the law of the Prophet that no one shall touch what is unclean."

"But you do not know that," cried the exasperated white man. "You are running from a shadow."

"A shadow may betoken evil. My father said it, and it is so."

Gray sighed. "Then buy a half dozen mules. They can carry our stores. Watch for the coming of the tribe you spoke of. When they are here let me know. Meanwhile, purchase water jars, flour, rice and tea sufficient for six men for three weeks."

The Kirghiz blinked understandingly.

"It is written that a white man shall go into the desert from here," he assented. "What is written will come to pass. It is also said by our priests that a white man's grave is waiting in the Gobi. If this thing also comes to pass, I and my comrades will bury you, so the kites will not make a meal of your eyes—for once you saved my life."

Whereupon the hunter turned over on his side and went to sleep, leaving Gray to his own thoughts. They were not cheerful.

The Hastings had left for Sungan. They had camels and would make good time. With luck, if they escaped the black sand-storms, they should be at their destination in seven or eight days. No wonder, he thought, Sir Lionel had spoken frankly to him about the inscription, when he had all the camels bought.

Camels could move faster than mules, over the bad footing. Gray would make his start four days —three if the Kirghiz arrived promptly—later than Sir Lionel. And he would fall behind steadily.

The Desert

If it had been possible, he would have gone alone. But he could not carry the necessary food and water for ten days. For a moment he pondered the advisability of pushing on alone as soon as the mules could be bought.

This plan he dismissed as useless. Mirai Khan had assured him that it would take at least two days to get the animals and the needed supplies. Also, he would be without a guide—for Mirai Khan would not start until the tribesmen arrived.

It would be tempting providence for one man to venture with a string of mules into the Gobi. Even so, Gray might have attempted it if he had a guide.

There was nothing for it but to wait. And Gray passed the time as best he could, overhauling his rifle and small stock of ammunition, and packing with the help of Mirai Khan the food the latter bought for him.

Fate moves in strange ways. If Gray had started before the four days were up, the events that took place in the Gobi would have shaped themselves differently. For one thing, he would not have seen the tracks of the wild camel in the sand.

Nor would he have heard the story of the pale sickness.

As Mirai Khan had assured him, the Kirghiz tribe appeared at Ansichow the evening of the third day. The hunter took Gray to their *aul* near where Sir Lionel's encampment had been.

157

Marching Sands

Acting as interpreter, he harangued the newcomers. Moreover, as he informed the American later, he did not translate what Gray said literally. If he had done so, he asserted, they would not have gone into the Gobi.

The reason that Mirai Khan set forth seemed sufficient, for after long debate, the elder of the tribe and two evil looking hunters consented to accompany Gray. They agreed to go on foot. Somewhat to the American's surprise nothing was said about turning back.

He broke camp at dawn, and the cavalcade of mules passed out of Ansichow with Mirai Khan leading. By the time the sun had broken through the mist they were well into the sand dunes.

There had been no wind-storm since the Hastings passed that way and Mirai Khan was content to follow the camel tracks.

CHAPTER XIV

TRACES IN THE SAND

It was monotonous work climbing the dunes that rose to meet them out of the ocean of sand. Added to this was the feeling of isolation, which is never so great as in the wastes of Central Asia. There were no birds or game to be met with. Only once did they hit on water. This was at their third camp, and the camel tracks showed that the Hastings had visited the oasis.

Owing to the high altitude, the exertion affected Gray; but he made the best of this necessary evil and pressed ahead. On the fourth day they lost the trail of the other caravan and Gray shaped his course by compass. He knew that Sir Lionel had planned to strike due west.

It was that night they discovered the tracks of the wild camel.

Gray had turned out from his blankets at sun-up and was warming his stiff limbs over the fire the others had kindled—for the autumn chill was making itself felt in the nights. He found Mirai Khan and the Kirghiz excited.

They had seen tracks about the encampment.

Marching Sands

The hunters showed them to Gray, who thought at first the imprints were left by the Hastings' caravan. Mirai Khan, however, assured him that the tracks had not been there the evening before. Also, the hoof marks were smaller than those of tne domestic camel, and not quite as deep in the sand.

Mirai Khan showed him where the tracks appeared, and passed around the camp twice, then led away over the dunes.

"It is the mark of a wild camel, Excellency," he said. "Of one that has come to look at us."

"And why should this not happen?"

Mirai Khan scratched his thin beard, plainly uneasy.

"It is a good omen," continued Gray, perceiving this. "For by this wild camel we may have meat."

He had heard that these animals, although rare, were sometimes seen in the southern Gobi. Beyond wishing that this particular camel had waited until the light was good enough for a shot, Gray thought little of the matter. Not so the Kirghiz. The hunters conferred earnestly with Mirai Khan and appeared reluctant to go on.

"If you see the beast," he added, impatient at the delay, "we shall try a stalk. We need meat."

Mirai Khan grunted and spat stolidly.

"Never have I shot a wild camel, Excellency. My father has said that when we sighted the tracks of one, it is well to return quickly."

Traces in the Sand

Inwardly, Gray consigned the spirit of Mirai Khan's ancestor to another region. Approaching the tether of the leading mule, he motioned to the Kirghiz to set out   They obeyed reluctantly.

"Are you men or children?" he asked. "You will have no pay until we sight the ruins of Sungan."

He wondered, as he trudged forward, whether this speech had been a mistake. The Kirghiz were clearly sulky. Mirai Khan was more silent than usual. Gray noticed that whenever they topped a rise he scanned the plain intently. The behavior of his guides at this point mystified him. The Kirghiz were naturally far from being cowards. Certainly they had neither fear nor respect for the Chinese of Ansichow. Being Mohammedans they were indifferent to the Buddhist priests.

Yet the glimpse of wild camel tracks had set these men—hunters by birth—into a half panic.

Gray gave it up. He was walking moodily by the leading mule, pondering his failure—for he could no longer conceal from himself the fact that he must reach Sungan a good week after the Hastings—when he saw Mirai Khan pause on the top of a dune. The hunter's figure stiffened alertly, like a trained dog at gaze.

Gray scrambled up the slope to the man's side. At first he saw only the brown waste of the dunes. Then he located what Mirai Khan had seen. He raised and focussed his glasses.

161

Marching Sands

Some distance ahead a man was moving toward them. It was a white man, on foot and walking very slowly. Gray recognized Sir Lionel Hastings.

Followed by the Kirghiz, he approached the Englishman. Sir Lionel did not look up until they were a few paces away. Then he halted, swaying from the weariness of one who has been walking for a long time.

He was without coat, rifle, or sun helmet. His lean face was lined with fatigue. The hand that fumbled for his eyeglasses trembled. His boots and puttees were dust stained.

"Is that you, Captain Gray?" he asked uncertainly.

"Yes, Sir Lionel. What's up? Where's the caravan?" Gray had been about to ask for Mary, but checked himself. "You'll want a drink. Here——"

The Englishman shook his head. Gray observed that his bald forehead was reddened with the sun; that his usually well-kept yellow hair was turned a drab with the dust.

"I had water, thanks. Back there, by the tamarisk tree. The caravan camped there for the night, two—or three days ago. I don't remember which." He wheeled slowly in his tracks. "Come."

A moment's walk took them to the few bushes and the tamarisk. There a well had been dug. Sir Lionel refused to mount one of the mules, although he was plainly far gone with exhaustion. At the

Traces in the Sand

time Gray was too preoccupied to notice it, but the Kirghiz—as he recalled later—were talking together earnestly, looking frequently in their direction.

The Englishman moved, as he spoke, automatically. He walked by dint of will power. When Gray, knowing the strength of the sun, placed his own hat on the man's head Sir Lionel thanked him mechanically.

It was this quiet of the man that disturbed Gray profoundly. There was something aimless and despairing in his dull movements. Gray, seeing how ill he was, refrained from asking further questions until they were seated in the small patch of shadow. The Kirghiz retired to a neighboring knoll with their rifles.

"It was near here we discovered camel tracks— wild camel tracks."

The words startled Gray, coming on top of the dispute with Mirai Khan that morning.

"Did you lose the caravan?" he exclaimed. "Good Lord, man! Where is Mary?"

"I've lost the caravan," said Sir Lionel. "And Mary as well."

Sudden dread tugged at Gray's heart.

"Where?"

"At Sungan."

Sir Lionel looked up at the American, and Gray saw the pain mirrored in his inflamed eyes.

"Was she with Ram Singh?"

163

Marching Sands

"Ram Singh is dead."

"The others?"

"Killed. I do not think that Mary was killed."

Gray drew a deep breath and was silent. From the knoll the hunters watched intently.

"I will tell you what happened." Sir Lionel drew his hand across his eyes. "The sun—I'm rather badly done up. No food for two days. No——" as Gray started to rise. "I'm not hungry."

He lay back on the sand with closed eyes. His face was strained with the effort he made to speak. Yet what he said was uttered clearly, with military brevity.

"The night after we sighted the camel tracks we were attacked in force. I think that was four nights ago. There was a crescent moon. Of course I had stationed sentries. They gave the alarm. There was a brisk action."

"Who attacked you?"

"Ram Singh said they might have been a party of wandering Kirghiz. We did not see them clearly in the bad light. Peculiar thing. They seemed to be afoot. When they beat a retreat, after exchanging shots, we looked over the ground. No footprints. Only camel tracks. And they carried off their wounded."

Gray wondered briefly if Sir Lionel's mind had been affected by the sun. But the Englishman spoke rationally. Moreover, Mirai Khan had been

164

alarmed when they first sighted the imprints in the earth.

"Our guides—Dungans, you know—said attackers were guards of Sungan. We did not see them again. Late the next afternoon a *kara buran* passed our way. We pitched tents when the wind became bad, inside the circle of our beasts. When the storm cleared off, I made out through my glasses the towers of Sungan."

Sir Lionel looked up with a faint flash of triumph.

"I was right. Sungan is a ruined city, buried in the sand. Only the towers are visible from a distance. We were about a half mile from the nearest ruins."

He sighed, knitting his brows. He spoke calmly. Gray was familiar with the state of exhaustion which breeds lassitude, when long exposure to danger, or the rush of sudden events, dulls the nerves.

"It was twilight when Mary and I started to walk to the towers, with two servants. I was eager to set foot in the ruins. And I did actually reach the first piles of débris. You won't forget that, will you, old man? I was the first white man in Sungan."

Gray nodded. He felt again the zeal that had drawn Sir Lionel blindly to the heart of the Gobi. And had perhaps sacrificed Mary to the pride of the scientist. But he could not accuse the wearied man before him of a past mistake.

"Go on," he said grimly.

"It was late twilight. I forgot to add that our Dungans deserted after the first skirmish. Frightened, I expect. Well, Mary and I almost ran to the ruins. She was as happy as I at our success— what we thought was our success. So far, we had seen no human beings in the ruins. There were any number of tracks, however, and vegetation that pointed to the presence of wells."

"Then Mary and I discovered the Wusun." Sir Lionel laughed suddenly, harshly. He gained control of himself at once. "They came—these inhabitants of Sungan—from behind the stone heaps and out of what seemed to be holes in the ground. As I said, it was late evening, and I could not see their faces well. Still, I saw——"

He checked himself, and fell silent, as if pondering. Gray guessed that he thought better of what he was going to say.

"They were unarmed, Captain Gray, but in considerable force. They ran forward with a lumbering gait, like animals. They were dressed in filthy strips of sheepskin, which gave out a foul smell. I had my revolver. Still, I hesitated to shoot down these unarmed beggars. They did not answer my hail which was given in Persian, then in Turki.

"Seeing that they were plainly hostile, I began

166

to shoot. They came on doggedly, apparently without fear of hurt. And my two men ran. One was a brave boy, Captain Gray—a *syce* who had been with me for several years. Yet he threw away his rifle and ran. I saw two of the men of Sungan pull him down."

Gray shivered involuntarily, thinking of the girl that Sir Lionel had brought to this place.

"I do not understand why it happened," the Englishman observed plaintively. "We had given these men no cause to attack us. I believe they were not the same fellows who rushed us the night before. For one thing, these had no arms. There were women among them. They gave me the impression of dogs, hunting in a pack. They must have been waiting for us in cover."

"What happened to the caravan?"

"Rushed. The Sungan people got to it before Mary and I could gain the camp. Our boys were surprised. Only a few shots were fired. The camels took fright and ran through the tents. I saw Ram Singh and another try to get out to me with spare rifles. The Sikh, who had the rank of Rifleman, shot very accurately. But the Sunganis came between us, and I saw him go down fighting under a pack of men. Mary and I turned aside and tried to escape into the sand dunes."

Sir Lionel raised himself unsteadily on an elbow.

"Do not think, Captain Gray, that I abandoned

167

Mary of my own will. It was dark by then. We could hear the men hunting us through the dunes. A party of them descended on me from a slope. My revolver was emptied by then. I knocked one or two of them down and called out for Mary. She did not answer. They had taken her away. If they had killed her, I would have come on her body. But she was gone."

"Did you hear her call to you?" Gray asked from between set lips.

"No. She is a plucky girl. In my search for her, I passed out of sight of the men who were tracking me. I could not remain there, for they were tracing out my footprints. They have an uncanny knack at that. Captain Gray. As I said, they reminded me of dogs."

He looked at his companion, despair mirrored in his tired eyes.

"I had two alternatives after that—to stay near Sungan, unarmed, or to return, in the hope of meeting you. I knew you would be likely to follow our tracks as far as you could. Possibly you would sight this brush. I made my way back here. A little while ago I sighted the dust of your caravan."

Gray was silent, breaking little twigs from the bush under which they sat and throwing them from him as he thought. Sir Lionel's story was worse than he had expected. Mary Hastings was in the Sungan ruins. She might even now be dead. He put the thought from him by an effort of will.

The full force of his feeling for the girl flooded in on him. From the night when her servants had seized him in the *aul* she had been in his thoughts. It was this feeling—the binding love that sometimes falls to the lot of a man of solitary habits, whose character does not permit him to show it—that had led him to warn her against going into the Gobi. And it was this that had urged him after her with all possible haste.

Now the Hastings' caravan had been wiped out and Mary was in the hands of the men of Sungan.

"We'll start at once," he said quietly. "That is, if you feel up to it."

The Englishman roused with an effort and tried to smile.

"I'm pretty well done up, I'm afraid, Captain Gray. But put me on a mule, you know. I'll manage well enough." Gray knew that he was lying, and warmed to the pluck of the man. "I must not delay you."

"We should be at the ruins in thirty-six hours."

"Right! Where's the mule——" he broke off as Mirai Khan appeared beside them.

"Excellency!" The Kirghiz's eyes were wide with excitement. "I have seen men with rifles approaching on two sides."

"Bring your mules into the brush, Captain Gray," said Sir Lionel quickly. "And place your men be-

169

hind the boxes of stores. You will pardon my giving orders? These are undoubtedly the same fellows who exchanged shots with us a little further on. If you can spare a rifle——"

The American handed him the piece slung to his shoulder, with the bandolier of cartridges. The Kirghiz hunters were already leading the mules to the brush.

CHAPTER XV

GRAY had no means of knowing who the new-comers were, but experience had taught him the value of an armed front when dealing with an unknown element. And Sir Lionel's story had excited his gravest fears.

Under the American's brisk directions the Mohammedans unloaded the animals and tied them near the well. The stores they carried to the outer bushes. Mirai Khan primed his breechloader resignedly.

"Said I not the wild camel tracks were a warning?" he muttered in his beard. "Likewise it is written that the grave of a white man shall be dug here in the Gobi. What is written, you may not escape. You could have turned back, but you would not."

"Take one man," ordered Gray sharply, "and watch the eastern side of the brush."

"A good idea," approved the Englishman, who had persuaded one of the hunters to place the roll of the tent in front of him. He laid the rifle across

171

the bundle of canvas coolly. "We must beat off these chaps before we can go ahead." He nodded at Gray, calmly.

Gray left one of the hunters with Sir Lionel, well knowing the value of the presence of a white man among the Kirghiz. He himself took the further side of the triangle to the north. The knoll was on a ridge that ran roughly due east and west. The nearest sand ridges were some two hundred yards away. Behind them he could see an occasional rifle barrel or sheepskin cap.

By this arrangement, at least three rifles could be brought to bear in any quarter where a rush might be started; likewise, they could watch all menaced points. But their adversaries seemed little inclined to try tactics of that sort. They remained concealed behind the dunes, keeping up a scattering fire badly aimed into the knot of men in the brush.

This did small damage. The Kirghiz, once the matter was put to an issue, proved excellent marksmen, and gave back as good as they received. Gray, watching from his post under a bush, fancied that two or three of Mirai Khan's shots took effect. He himself did not shoot. An automatic is designed for rapid fire at close range, not for delicate sniping.

But Sir Lionel was at home with a rifle. Glancing back under the tamarisk Gray saw him adjust his eyeglass calmly, lay his sights on a target, and press the trigger, then peer over his shelter to see if his effort had been successful. The Englishman evidently had seen action before—many times, Gray guessed, judging the man.

"A reconnoissance in force, I should call it, old man," the Englishman called back at him. "I think we are safe here. But the delay is dangerous."

He paused to try a snap shot at the dune opposite. Gray scanned the ground in front of him, frowning. He knew that Sir Lionel was as impatient as he to start for Sungan. There was no help for it, unless the attacking party could be driven off.

Gray had been pondering the matter. Their adversaries appeared to be a small party, and they had suffered at least three or four casualties in the first hour. Gray's force was still intact.

As nearly as he could make out the men behind the dunes were Chinese—border Chinese, and ill armed. Why they attacked him, he did not know. Mirai Khan had taken it for granted.

"Any one who enters this part of the Gobi seems to be marked for execution," he thought grimly. "If that's the case, two can play at it. And we've got to start before nightfall."

Cautiously he wormed his way back into the bushes to the side held by Mirai Khan. To this individual he confided what was in his mind. The Kirghiz objected flatly at first. But when Gray assured him that unless they did as he planned, night would catch them on the knoll, and they would be unable to fight off a rush, he yielded.

"If God wills," he muttered, "we may do it. And I do not think I shall die here."

Blessing the fatalism of his guide for once, Gray summoned one of the hunters. He removed a spare clip of cartridges from his belt and took it in his left hand. This done, he nodded to the two Kirghiz, straightened and ran out along the ridge, on the side away from Sir Lionel.

The maneuver took their enemies by surprise. One or two shots were fired at the three as they raced along the dune and gained the summit behind which the Chinese had taken shelter. Gray saw four or five men rise hastily and start to flee.

He worked the trigger of his automatic four times, keeping count carefully. Accurate shooting is more a matter of coolness than of skill. Two of the Chinese fell to earth; another staggered and ran, limping. The survivors picked up the two wounded and disappeared among the dunes.

"*Hai!*" grunted Mirai Khan in delight, "there speaks the little gun of many tongues. Truly, never have I seen——"

"Follow these men," commanded Gray sternly. "See that they continue to flee." Motioning to the other Kirghiz, he trotted back across the ridge to the further side. Here he was met with a scatter-

174

ing fire which kicked up some dust, but caused no damage.

The Chinese on this side of the white men's stronghold had learned the fate of their fellows and did not await the coming of the "gun of many tongues."

Gray saw a half dozen figures melting into the dunes, and emptied the automatic at them, firing at a venture. He thought at least one of his shots had taken effect. Pressing forward, he and the Kirghiz —who had gained enormous confidence from the display of the automatic—drove their assailants for some distance. When the Chinese had passed out of sight, Gray hurried back to the knoll.

There he found Sir Lionel seated with his back against the roll of canvas with the excited Kirghiz.

"The coast seems to be clear," observed Gray. "We can set out——"

The Englishman coughed, and tried to smile. "I stay here, I'm afraid," he objected. "It's my rotten luck, Captain Gray. One of the beggars potted me in that last volley. A chance shot."

He motioned to his chest, where he had opened the shirt. The cloth was torn by the bullet. "Touched the lung, you know"—again he coughed, and spat blood—"badly."

Gray made a hasty examination of the wound. It was bleeding little outwardly; but internal bleeding had set in.

"We'll have to get you back to Ansichow," he said with forced cheerfulness. "A mule litter and one of the Kirghiz will do the trick."

"No, it won't, old man." Sir Lionel shook his head. "I'd never get there. One day's travel would do me up. I'll stick—here."

Mirai Khan, who had rejoined the party, drew his companions aside and talked with them earnestly. Gray did what he could to make the Englishman comfortable. Assisted by the hunters, who worked reluctantly, he had the tent pitched, and laid the wounded man on a blanket, where he was protected by the canvas from the sun.

This done, he filled and lighted his pipe and sat beside his friend, smoking moodily.

"You'll find a cigarette in my shirt pocket," said Sir Lionel quietly. "Will you light it for me? I've enough lung—to smoke, and——" he cleared his throat with difficulty. "Thanks a lot. I've something to say to you. Won't take—a minute. Fever's set in. Must talk. Last message, you know."

He smiled with strained lips.

"Strange," he added. "Thought it only happened—in books."

Gray watched the shadows crawling across the knoll, and frowned. Sir Lionel, he knew, could not survive another day. With the death of his friend, he would be alone. And he must find Mary

A Last Camp

Hastings. He wondered what the Englishman wished to tell him.

"You know," began the other, seizing a moment when his throat was clear, "I said I'd seen the faces of the men of Sungan. They had their hands on me, and I saw them close. I did not tell you at first what I deduced from that."

Gray nodded, thinking how the explorer had broken off in the middle of a sentence in his story of two hours ago.

"Don't forget, Captain Gray——" a flash of eagerness passed over the tanned face—"I was the first in Sungan. I want the men who sent me to know that. Well, the faces I saw were white—in spots."

Gray whistled softly, recalling the words of Brent. The missionary had said that the man he saw in the Gobi was partially white. Also, Mirai Khan had said the same.

"Those men, Captain Gray, were not white men. They were afflicted with a disease. I've seen it too often—to be mistaken. It is leprosy."

Mechanically, Gray fingered his pipe. Leprosy! This sickness, he knew, caused the flesh of the face to decay and turn white in the process. And leprosy was common in China.

"I've been thinking," continued the Englishman, "while I was waiting to sight your caravan. There are lepers in the ruins of Sungan. That may be why the spot is isolated. The Chinese have leper colonies."

"Yes," assented Gray. Neither man voiced the thought that was uppermost in his mind, that Mary had been seized by these men. "Mirai Khan told me that Sungan was an unclean place. The Kirghiz —who are fairly free from the disease—avoid Sungan. Delabar, my companion, feared it, I think."

"This explains the myth of the white race in the Gobi—perhaps. And the guards."

"Mirai Khan said that men were brought from China, from the coast, to the sands of Sungan," added Gray grimly. "God—why didn't they warn us?"

"You were warned, Captain Gray. Our caravan traveled as secretly as possible. I—I paid no attention to what the Chinese said. They have their secrets. I should have been more cautious. I made the mistake of my race. Overconfidence in dealing with natives. I wanted to be the first white man in Sungan."

He paused, reaching for a cup of water that Gray had filled for him. The American watched him blankly. So the talk of the pale sickness had proved to be more than legend. And he had discovered the root of Delabar's dread of the Gobi. Why had not the scientist said in so many words that Sungan was a leper colony? Doubtless Delabar had known that Gray would not turn back until

178

A Last Camp

he had seen the truth of the matter for himself.

Had Wu Fang Chien reasoned along similar lines? It was natural that the Chinese authorities had not wanted the American to visit one of the isolated leper colonies. Wu Fang Chien had discovered Gray's mission. And the mandarin had been willing to kill Gray in order to keep him from Sungan. The Asiatic had tried to keep the white man from probing into one of the hidden, infected spots of Mongolia. Was this the truth? Gray, heart-sick from what Hastings had told him, believed so. Later, he came to understand more fully the motives that had actuated Wu Fang Chien.

"Remember," continued Sir Lionel wearily, "we learned that the Wusun were captives. The stone itself—the boundary stone we found at Ansichow—said as much."

"But the stone referred to the Wusun as conquerors."

"Some legend of a former century. Another of the riddles—of Asia. I'm afraid, Captain Gray, we've failed in our mission. And it has cost—much." He coughed, and raised his eyes to Gray. "We have found the lepers of Sungan. And we have let them take Mary. I'm out of the game, rather. And I'd prefer to die here than in a mule litter. You've done all for me you can."

Gray made a gesture of denial. The pluck of the Englishman, facing inevitable death, stirred his admiration. Lack of vitality, more than the wound, made it impossible to get Hastings out of the Gobi alive. Knowing this, Sir Lionel treated his own situation as indifferently as he might have disposed of a routine question of drill.

"I didn't tell you about the lepers at first," he continued, "because I was afraid you might lack the nerve to go on. I wouldn't blame you. But I've seen you under fire—and I know better."

"I'm going after Mary," said Gray grimly.

Sir Lionel nodded.

"Of course. Not much of a chance; but—I'm glad." He coughed and wiped his lips. "You were right, Captain Gray. She—she told me what you said at Ansichow. I regret that she—offended you. I have spoiled her, you know. A dear girl——" His cough silenced him.

Gray sought for words, and was silent. Neither man liked to reveal his feelings.

"My heedlessness brought Mary to Sungan, Captain Gray. Now I'm asking you to make good my mistake, if possible——"

"Excellency!" The shaggy head of Mirai Khan appeared between the tent flaps. "I must speak with you."

Gray went outside, to find the Kirghiz scowling and ill at ease. In their faces the sun was vanishing over the plain of the Gobi, dyeing the bare, yellow hillocks with deep crimson. A brown lizard trailed its body away from the two men, leaving the mark of its passage in the sand.

"Excellency, the hour of our parting is at hand. I go no further. The debt I owed you for saving my life I still owe, but—you will not turn back from Sungan. Hearken, hunter of the mighty little gun. I and my comrades followed the tracks of our enemies. They were camel tracks."

"Nonsense," growled Gray. "Those were men with guns. You saw them."

"And I saw the prints in the sands. They were not the tracks of men, but of camels. It is an evil thing when men are like to animals. My comrades were filled with a great fear. They have departed back to Sungan, taking the mules, for their pay——"

Gray glanced quickly about the encampment. It was empty, except for the tent.

"What is written may not be changed," uttered the Kirghiz sententiously. "The others are gone, and I will follow. God has forbidden that we remain in this evil spot. Because of my love for you, I have left you the rifle, standing against the wall of the cloth house, with its strap. If it is your will, you may shoot me with the little gun of many tongues, because I am leaving you. But I think you will not. I could have gone without your knowing."

Marching Sands

Gray surveyed the hunter moodily. Mirai Khan smiled affectionately.

"Even if you had threatened to shoot us, Excellency, we would not have taken another pace nearer Sungan. The spot is unclean. And why should you shoot us—for saving our lives? My comrades said that soon you will be dead, and would not need the mules, so they took the animals. I do not know if you will die, or not. You have the quick wits of a mountain sheep, and the courage of a tiger. But I fear greatly for you. He who is inside——"

Mirai Khan pointed to the tent.

"He who is inside will die here. Did I not foretell a white man would die? But you will go on, for the men of Sungan have taken the white woman who warmed your heart. I have eyes, and I have seen your love for the woman."

Gray walked to the rifle and inspected it. The chamber was empty, and the cartridges had gone from the bandolier. Sir Lionel had used up the small supply in the belt. Gray had no reserve ammunition. Wu Fang Chien had taken that. He handed the weapon to Mirai Khan.

"I have no more bullets for it," he said briefly. "Take it. Also, send word to the nearest white missionary behind Ansichow. Tell him what has passed here, and that I set out to-night for Sungan. Ask him to send the message back to my country, to this man."

182

A Last Camp

On a sheet of paper torn from a corner of the maps he still carried, Gray wrote down Van Schaick's name and address.

"It shall be done as you say," acknowledged the hunter, placing the paper in his belt. "The gun is a fine gun. But the little one of many tongues is better. Remember, we could have fallen upon you in the house of cloth and taken all you had. My comrades wished to do it, but I would not, for we have eaten salt together."

Mirai Khan lifted his hand in farewell, caught up the precious rifle, and hurried away, calling over his shoulder, "I must come up with the hunters before dark, or they will take the mule that is mine and leave me. As you have said, your message shall be sent."

He vanished in the dunes to the east, his cloth-wrapped feet moving soundlessly over the sand. Gray watched him go. He could not force the Kirghiz to continue on to Sungan. Even if he tried to do so, he had seen enough to know that from this point on Mirai Khan would be useless to him.

Before returning to Sir Lionel he made a circuit of the ridge and inspected the footprints where their enemies of the afternoon had passed. He saw a network of curious prints, marks of broad, splay hoofs. Occasionally, there was a blood stain.

He had been too far from the attacking party to notice their feet—and too busy to think about any such matter. But, undeniably, as Mirai Khan had said, here were camel tracks and nothing else.

"The devil!" he swore. "I certainly saw those Chinese—and they were men. Probably a trick—it certainly worked well enough to scare my guides."

He dismissed the matter with a shrug and made his way back to the tent.

"Anything gone wrong?" asked the Englishman.

"Nothing new," Gray evaded, unwilling to distress Sir Lionel with the truth.

"Then you'll be setting out, I fancy." He spoke with an effort. "I'll do nicely here—if you'll fill my water jar, and light the candle I see beside it. Don't leave me food—can't eat, you know. Deuced hemorrhage——"

Gray left him coughing, and filled the jar at the well. Also his own canteen which was slung at his belt. He lit the candle and placed it in the sand by the Englishman. Sir Lionel counted the cigarettes that lay beside the candle.

"They'll last—long enough," he whispered. "Close the tent, please, when you go out."

As if a giant hand had blotted out the light, the tent became darker. Sir Lionel looked up. "Sunset," he muttered, "no parade. I'll keep to my barracks."

Gray turned away. He could see that the man was nerving himself to be alone, and mustering his

184

A Last Camp

strength for the coming ordeal. The Englishman was utterly brave.

The American adjusted the blankets, and placed the remaining food—some flour cakes—in his shirt. Sir Lionel forced a smile.

"Right!" he whispered. "Strike due west— moonlight will show you compass bearings. Watch out for the ruins. Know you'll get Mary out, if it can be done. Good-by and good luck!"

"You're game!" exclaimed Gray involuntarily. "Good-by."

The Englishman adjusted his eyeglass as they shook hands. "Remember—due west."

Gray glanced back as he closed the curtains of the tent and tied the flap cords. Sir Lionel was lighting himself a cigarette at the candle.

That was the last he saw of Major Hastings. Sir Lionel died without complaint, a brave man doing his duty as best he could.

CHAPTER XVI

As his friend had predicted, Gray was able to watch his compass by moonlight, within an hour. It was a clear night. The stars were out in force with a trace of the white wisp clouds that hang above a dry, elevated plateau.

Sir Lionel was out of the game, and with him the Kirghiz hunters. Gray was alone for the first time since his visit to Van Schaick the evening that he had contracted to find the Wusun. He smiled grimly as he thought how matters had changed.

Here he was at the gate of the Wusun, the captive race. But Sir Lionel had found them hardly what Gray expected. A leper's colony is not a pleasant thing to visit. And this one was unusually well guarded. Behind these guards, in the ruins of Sungan, was Mary Hastings.

This thought had gnawed at the American's heart for the past twelve hours. The girl he loved—he could no more conceal that fact from himself than he could lose sight of the Gobi—was among the lepers. Was she alive? He did not know. The

186

guards of Sungan did not seem overmerciful. **But** why should they kill her?

No, he reasoned, she was alive. She *must* **be** alive. And she was waiting for help to come. She might have discovered that her uncle had escaped in the fight before the ruins. And she knew that Gray was coming to Sungan in their tracks.

What Gray was going to do after he found the girl, he did not know. He had long ago discovered that a multitude of difficulties confuse and baffle a man. He had trained himself to tackle only one thing at a time; not only that, but to think of only one thing. If he found Mary, there would be time to consider what would come next.

The thought of the girl urged him on, so that it was hard to keep an even pace. But he was aware of the uselessness of blind haste. He struck a steady gait which he could keep up for hours, a swift walk that left the dunes behind rapidly.

These dunes, he noticed, were not as high as at first. The desert was becoming more level, the soil harder. At some points the clay surface appeared between the sand ridges.

Gray did not try to eat. Nor did he drink, knowing the folly of that at the beginning of a march. In time he would do both, not now.

The man's powerful frame enabled him to keep up the pace he had set without fatigue or loss of breath. This was the secret of Gray's success as

187

an explorer—his careful husbanding of his great vitality, and his refusal to worry over problems that lay in the future.

When the vision of Mary flashed on him as he watched the summits of the dunes, silvered by the cold moonlight, he put it aside resolutely. The last sight of the girl—the slender figure perched jauntily on the camel as she rode away after their quarrel—tormented him from time to time. In spite of himself an elfin chord of memory visioned the friendly gray eyes, and the delicate face of Mary Hastings.

Gray set himself to considering his situation, realizing that he had desperate need of all his wits if he was to face Sungan and its people.

First there was the puzzle of the camel tracks that had frightened Mirai Khan. These tracks had been left by the party that had attacked Sir Lionel and himself. They had been sighted the day before.

It was possible that the first prints they had seen were those of one of their enemies, and that this man had carried the news of their coming to his companions. It would have been easy for the men of the camel feet—as Gray thought of them—to trail his party without being seen among the dunes. Or else, they might have been following Sir Lionel.

Gray decided that this was what had happened. The men of the camel feet had been tracking the Englishman.

Gray Carries On

This deduction led to another. The Hastings party had been attacked. Failing to turn them back, their assailants might have sent word of their approach to Sungan.

"Let's see what I know," mused Gray methodically. "Camel feet armed with guns beaten off by Hastings' caravan—send news to Sungan. Ambuscade prepared at Sungan ruins for Sir Lionel. He walks into it. After attack by lepers, camel feet take up pursuit of him, tracking him back to well, where they engage us."

Then the camel feet constituted a kind of outer guard of Sungan. They were poor fighters and seemed to have no heart for their work. The men who had wiped out the caravan were another kind. Sir Lionel had distinctly said they were not armed. They were lepers.

There was then an outer and an inner guard of Sungan. The outer—composed of an indifferent soldiery—had been seen by the missionary Brent. The captive these guards had been pursuing had undoubtedly been a leper, escaped from the colony.

Had Brent been done to death by the Chinese who knew what he had seen? If so, then Mary——

Gray groaned at the thought and the muscles of his jaw tightened.

"I'm through the outer guards," he forced himself to reason. "But there's one thing that calls for an answer. Why do the Chinese force the lepers to

189

drive off intruders? The poor devils are not good fighters. No better than the driven dogs Sir Lionel pictured them. They must have a hard master."

It was possible, of course, that the Chinese priests who were masters of Sungan had forced the lepers to attack the caravan as a last resource, after Sir Lionel's men had driven off the outer guards. In China human life has a low value, and that of a leper is a small matter. Such a proceeding would be in keeping with the cruelty of the priests—who saw their own power and the prestige of ancient Buddha waning with the inroads of civilization.

He was growing physically tired by now, to some extent. This growing weariness took toll of his thoughts, and brought the image of Mary before his memory.

He pictured her as he had first seen her—a slender figure in the bright tent, mistress of well-trained servants. Gray had loved her from the first. It seemed to him it had been a long time. As nearly as he had ever worshiped anything, he worshiped the girl.

There had been no other women in his life. He smiled ruefully, reflecting upon his blundering effort to help the girl. And she was now far removed from his help. It appalled him—how little he might be able to aid her.

With another man, this fear might have turned into reckless haste, or blind cursing against the

Gray Carries On

fate that had befallen Mary Hastings. Gray pressed on silently, unhurried, the flame of his love burning fiercely.

In this manner he would go on until he had found her, or those who had taken her. There was no alternative. Mirai Khan would have said that Gray was a fatalist, but Mirai Khan did not know the soul of a white man.

"If only I am not too late," he thought. "I must not be too late. That could not happen."

Gray had no words to frame a prayer. But, lacking words, he nevertheless prayed silently as he walked.

The stars faded. The moon had disappeared over the plain in front of the American. The dunes turned from black to gray and to brown, as the sunrise climbed behind him.

Gray sat down on a hillock, and drew out his flour cakes. These—some of them—he chewed, washing them down with water from his canteen.

Had Sir Lionel lived to see that day? Gray thought not. Mirai Khan's prophecy had born fruit.

A few feet away an animal's skull—a gazelle, by the horns—peered from the sand. Gray watched it quietly until the sun gleamed on the whitened bone. Then he rose, stretching his tired limbs, and pressed on.

Marching Sands

Late that afternoon he sighted the **towers of Sun**-gan slightly to the north of his course.

Working his way forward, Gray scanned the place through his glasses. He was on the summit of a ridge about a half mile from the nearest towers. The ruins lay in the center of a wide plain which seemed to be clay rather than sand.

At intervals over the plain sand drifts had formed. Gray wondered if it was from behind these that the lepers had advanced on the Hastings' caravan. In the center of the plain trees and stunted tamarisks grew, indicating the presence of water.

Throughout this scattered vegetation the ruins pushed through the sand. Sir Lionel had been correct in his guess that the desert sand had overwhelmed the city. Gray could see that only the tops of the tumble-down walls were visible—those and the towers which presumably had been part of the palaces and temples of ancient Sungan. Even the towers were in a ruined state.

They seemed to be formed of a dark red sandstone, which Gray knew was found in the foothills of the Thian Shan country, to the north. He judged that the structures were at least five or six centuries old. He saw some portions of walls which were surmounted by battlements. And the

towers—through the glasses—showed narrow embrasures instead of modern windows.

The sight stirred his pulse. Before him was the
ancient city of the Gobi that had been the abode
of a powerful race before it was invaded by the
advancing sands. Past these walls the caravan of
Marco Polo had journeyed. The great Venetian
had spoken of a city here, where no modern explorers had found one. He had called it Pe-im.

And in the ruins Mary Hastings might be still
living, in desperate need of him.

What interested Gray chiefly were the people of
the place. He was too far to make them out clearly,
and only a few were visible. This puzzled him,
for Sir Lionel had mentioned a "pack of lepers."

He was able to see that the people were of two
kinds. One was robed in a light yellow or brown
garment. Several of these men were standing or
sitting on ridges outside the ruins. Gray guessed
that they were sentinels.

Furthermore, he believed them to be priests. The
other kind wore darker dress and appeared from
time to time among the ruins. They were—or
seemed to be, at that distance—both men and
women.

The thought of the girl urged Gray to action. It
would be the part of wisdom to wait until nightfall before entering the city. But he could not
bring himself to delay.

He was reasonably sure, from the conduct of the men acting as sentinels, that he had not been seen as yet. He had planned no course of action. What he wanted to do, now that he had an idea of the lay of the land, was to get hold of one of the men of Sungan, leper or priest, and question him about the white woman who had been taken prisoner.

Mary had been in Sungan at least three days and nights. Surely the people of the place must know of her. Once Gray had an idea where she was kept, he would be able to proceed.

The venture appeared almost hopeless. How could he enter the ruins, find the girl, and bring her out safely? What would they do then? How was he to deal with the lepers, whose touch meant possible contagion?

But he was hungry for sight of Mary—to know if she was still alive. He could not wait until night to learn this. He marked the position of the nearest men in his mind, returned the glasses to their case, loosened his automatic in its sheath, and slipped down from his lookout behind the ridge.

"I've cut out sentries," he mused grimly, "but not this kind. They don't seem to be armed."

In fact, the men of Sungan were not armed—with modern weapons. But they had a deadly means of defense in the disease which bore a miserable death in its touch.

Gray, for once, blessed the continuous dunes of

194

the Gobi. He went forward cautiously, keeping
behind the ridges and edging his way from gully
to gully, crawling at times and not daring to lift his
head for another look at the sentinels he had located.

His sense of direction was good. He had crawled
for the last half hour and the sun was well past
mid-day when he heard voices a short distance
ahead.

Removing his hat, Gray peered over the sand
vigilantly. He found that he had come almost in
the line he had planned. A hundred yards away
two figures were seated on a rise. They wore the
yellow robes he had first noticed.

As he watched, one rose and walked away leisurely toward the ruins. The other remained seated,
head bent on his clasped arms which rested on his
knees. There was something resigned, almost hopeless, in the man's attitude.

Gray waited until the first priest had had time
to walk some distance. Then he wriggled forward
alertly.

He had no means of knowing that others were not
on the further side of the ridge where the sentry
sat. But he heard no further voices, and he had
ascertained carefully before he set out that these
two were isolated.

Reasonably certain of his prey, Gray pulled himself from stone to stone, from depression to de-

pression. Once the man looked up,—perhaps at a slight sound. Then his head fell on his arms again. Gray rose to his feet and leaped toward the ridge silently.

Eyes bent on the still figure of the priest, he gained the foot of the dune. The man stiffened and raised his ˉhead, as if he had sensed danger. Gray was beneath him by now, and stretched out a powerful arm.

His hand closed on a sandaled foot and he pulled the priest down from his perch. Gray's other hand clamped on the man's mouth, preventing outcry. They were sheltered from view from Sungan by the ridge, and the American believed no one would notice the disappearance of the priest.

"If you cry out, you will die," he said in Chinese, kneeling over the other. Cautiously he removed his hand from the priest's mouth.

"Tell me—" he began. Then—"It's a white man!"

He peered at the dark, sunburned face, and the newly shaven skull.

"Delabar," he said slowly. "Professor Arminius Delabar, minus a beard. No mistaking your eyes, Professor. Now what, by all that's unholy, are you doing here in this monkey rig?"

CHAPTER XVII

THE YELLOW ROBE

THE man on the sand was silent, staring up at Gray in blank amazement. It was Delabar, thinner and more careworn than before. Shaven, all the lines of his face stood out, giving him the appearance of a skull over which yellow skin was stretched taut—a skull set with two smoldering, haggard eyes.

"Speak up, man," growled Gray. "And remember what I said about giving the alarm. I don't know if this costume is a masquerade or not, but —I can't afford to take chances this time."

Delabar did not meet his gaze. He lay back on the sand, fingers plucking at his thin lips.

"I can't speak," he responded hoarsely.

"You can. And you will. You'll tell me what I want to know—this time. You lied to me before. Now you'll deal a straight hand. This is not an idle threat. I must have information."

Delabar glanced at him fleetingly. Then looked around. No one was in sight, as they lay in a pocket in the sand.

"What do you want to know?"

"A whole lot. First—how did you get here? I thought all white men were barred."

"Wu Fang Chien," said Delabar moodily. "He caught me the day after I left you. He shot the coolie and had me brought here."

"What's the meaning of that?" Gray nodded contemptuously at the yellow robe.

"Wu Fang Chien punished me. He forced me to join the Buddhist priests who act as guards of Sungan. He did not want me to escape from China. Here, I was safe under his men."

"Hm. He trusts you enough to post you as one of the sentries."

"With another man. The other left to attend a council of the priests. My watch is over at sunset. In two hours."

Gray scanned his erstwhile companion from narrowed eyes. He decided the man was telling the truth, so far.

"Will these Buddhist dogs come to relieve you at sunset, Delabar?"

"No. The priests do not watch after nightfall. Some of the lepers we—Wu Fang Chien can trust make the rounds."

"Is Wu Fang Chien in control here—governor of Sungan?"

Delabar licked his lips nervously. Perspiration showed on his bare forehead. "Yes. That is, the mandarin is responsible to the Chinese authorities. He has orders to keep all intruders from Sungan—on account of the lepers."

Gray smiled without merriment.

"You say the priests stand guard. Are they armed?"

"No. Not with guns. Any one who tries to escape from here is followed and brought back by the outer guards—if he doesn't die in the desert."

"I see." Gray gripped the shoulder of the man on the sand. "Did you hear me say I wanted the truth, not lies? Well, you may have been telling me the letter of the truth. But not the whole. Once you said 'we' instead of Wu Fang Chien. Likewise, I know enough of Chinese methods to be sure Wu wouldn't punish a white man by elevating him to the caste of priest. You're holding something back, Delabar. What is your real relation to Wu?"

Delabar was silent for a long time. Staring overhead, his eyes marked and followed the movements of a wheeling vulture. His thin fingers plucked ceaselessly at the yellow robe.

"Wu Fang Chien," he said at length, "is my master. He is the emissary of the Buddhists in China. He has the power of life and death over those who break the laws of Buddha. I am one of his servants."

Delabar raised himself on one elbow.

"A decade ago, in India, I became a Buddhist,

199

Captain Gray. Remember, I am a Syrian born. I
spent most of my youth in Bokhara, and in Kashgar,
where I came under the influence of the philoso-
phers of the yellow robe. I acknowledged the tenets
of the Buddha; I bowed before the teachings of the
ancient Kashiapmadunga and the wisdom that is
like a lamp in the night—that burned before your
Christ. And I gave up my life to 'the world of
golden effulgence.'"

A note of tensity crept into his eager words. The
dark eyes reflected a deeper fire.

"Earthly lusts I forswore, for the celestial life
that is born by ceaseless meditation, and contempla-
tion of the *Maha-yana*. I was ordained in the first
orders of the priesthood. That was the time when
foreign missionaries began to enter China in force,
in spite of the Boxer uprising and the revolt of
the Tai-pings. The heads of the priesthood wanted
information about this foreign faith, and the peoples
of Europe. They wanted to know why the white
men sought to disturb the ancient soul of China."

Gray whistled softly, as Delabar's character became clear.

"I was sent to Europe. At first I kept in touch
with the priesthood through Wu Fang Chien. Then
came the overthrow of the Manchus, and the republic in China. But you can not cast down the
religion of eight hundred million souls by a *coup
d'état*. The priesthood still holds its power. And

200

The Yellow Robe

it is still inviolate from the touch of the foreigner."

Gray knew that this was true. The scattered foreigners who had entered the coast cities of China, and the missionaries who claimed a few converts in the middle kingdom were only a handful in the great mass of the Mongolians. In the interior, and throughout Central Asia and India, as in Japan, the shrines of Buddha, of Vishnu, and the temple of the Dalai Lama were undisturbed. And here, not on the coast, was the heart of Mongolia. Delabar continued, almost triumphantly.

"Word was sent to me from Wu Fang Chien—who had heard the news from a Chinese servant of the American Museum of Natural History—that an expedition was being fitted out to explore Central Mongolia. I was ordered to volunteer to accompany it."

"And you did your best to wreck the expedition," assented Gray.

"I liked you, Captain Gray. I tried to persuade you to turn back. At Liangchowfu it was too late. When you escaped from Wu Fang Chien there, he held me responsible for the failure. The priesthood never trusted me fully."

"In my religion," said Gray grimly, "there is a saying that a man can not serve two masters and save his own soul."

Delabar shivered.

"The priesthood," he muttered, "will not forgive

201

failure. Wu Fang Chien is watching me. You can do nothing here. Go back, before we are seen together. Sungan is nothing but a leper colony. You were a fool to think otherwise."

"And the Wusun?"

"Lepers! They are the only ones here except the priests."

Gray's eyes hardened.

"A lie, Delabar. Why should Wu Fang Chien kill a dozen men to keep the English caravan and myself from Sungan?" He caught and held Delabar's startled gaze. "Where is Mary Hastings?"

"I—who is she?"

"You know, Delabar. The girl who came with the caravan. She was taken prisoner. Where is she?"

"I don't know."

Gray touched his automatic significantly.

"I want to know," he said quietly. "And you can tell me. It is more important than my life or your miserable existence. *Where is Mary Hastings?*"

Delabar cowered before the deadly purpose in the white man's eyes.

"I don't know, Captain Gray. Wu Fang Chien ordered that when the caravan was attacked, she should be brought to him. Not killed, but taken to him. Some of the priests seized her and took her to one of the inner courts of the city. At the time,

The Yellow Robe

Wu Fang Chien was directing the attack on the caravan. I have not seen her since."

"Where is this inner court?"

"You are a fool. You could not possibly get into the ruins without being seen. Wu Fang Chien would be glad to see you. I heard him say if the girl was spared, you would come here after her. He knew all that happened at Ansichow——"

"Then she is alive!" Gray's pulses leaped. "So my friend Wu is keeping the girl as bait for my coming. A clever man, Wu Fang Chien. But how did he know Sir Lionel had told me what happened at Sungan?"

"The Englishman was followed, back to where he met you. If he had been killed in the fighting here, I think Wu Fang Chien planned to send me to bring you here——"

"Yes, he is clever." Gray studied the matter with knitted brows. "So Wu wants to kill me off, now that I have come this far—as he did the men of the caravan? Look here! Does he know I'm near Sungan? Were you put here as—bait?"

"No," Delabar shook his head. "The men who were sent to attack you—the Chinese soldiers hired by Wu Fang Chien—lost track of you. Wu Fang Chien does not know where you are—yet. If he should find you here talking to me, it would be my death. I—I have learned too much of the fate of the Hastings. Oh, they were fools. Why should your people want to pry into what is hidden from them? Go back! You can do nothing for the girl."

Gray stared at the Buddhist curiously.

"You haven't learned much decency from your religion, Delabar. So the outer guards failed to make good, eh? By the way, how is it that they leave camel tracks in the sand?"

"They wear camels' hoofs instead of shoes. Hoofs cut from dead wild camels that the Chinese hunters kill for our food—for the lepers. It helps them to walk on the sand, and mystifies the wandering Kirghiz. Why do you want to throw your life away——?"

"I don't." Gray sat down and produced some of his flour cakes. "I want to get out of Sungan with a whole skin, and with Mary Hastings." He munched the cakes calmly, washing down the mouthfuls with water from his canteen. "And I'm going to get into the inner courts of Sungan. You're going to guide me. If we're discovered, remember you'll be the first man to die. Now, Delabar, I want a good description of Sungan, its general plan, and the habits of your Buddhist friends."

CHAPTER XVIII

NIGHTFALL comes quickly after sunset on the Gobi plain. Waiting until the shadows concealed their movements, Gray and Delabar started toward the city of Sungan.

The moon was not yet up. By keeping within the bushes that grew thickly hereabouts, Delabar was able to escape observation from a chance passerby. The man was plainly frightened; but Gray allowed him no opportunity to bolt.

"You'll stay with me until I see Mary Hastings," he whispered warningly.

A plan was forming in the American's mind—a plan based on what Delabar had told him of the arrangement of the buildings of Sungan. The lepers, he knew, lived in the outer ruins, where he had seen them that afternoon. In the center of the Sungan plain, Delabar said, was a depression of considerable extent. Here were the temples and palaces, the towers of which he had seen.

This, the old city, was surrounded by a wall. Delabar said it was occupied by the priests. And

205

in this place Mary Hastings might be found. It was a guess; but a guess was better than nothing.

When they came to the first stone heaps, Gray halted his guide.

"You told me once," he whispered, "that Sungan had a series of underground passages. Take me down into these."

"Through the lepers' dwellings?"

Gray nodded silently. Delabar was shivering— an old trick of his, when nervous.

"It is madness, Captain Gray!" he chattered. "You do not know——"

"I know what you told me. Likewise that you don't want me to get into these temples. Step out!"

Delabar glanced around in despair and led the way through the bushes. Once the American caught the gleam of a fire and saw a group of lepers squatting about a blaze in which they were toasting meat. At the edge of the firelight starved dogs crouched.

They came to an excavation in the ground, lined with stone. Delabar pointed to steps leading downward into darkness.

"An old well," he whispered. "It is dry, now. A passage runs from it to the inner buildings."

He seemed familiar with the way, and Gray followed closely. The steps wound down for some distance, the air becoming cooler. They halted on what seemed to be a stone platform.

"Here is the entrance to the passage," Delabar muttered. "It was used to carry water to the temple."

Gray put his hand on the man's shoulder and urged him forward, making sure at the same time that the other did not seize the opportunity to make his escape. He did not trust Delabar. He was convinced that the Buddhist had not made a clean breast of matters. For one thing, he was curious as to why the priests should take such elaborate precautions to guard the lepers. Elsewhere in China there were no such colonies as Sungan.

Why were armed guards stationed around Sungan? Why were the lepers barred from the inner walled city? Where was Wu Fang Chien?

The answer to these questions lay in the temple toward which they were headed.

They went forward slowly. Complete silence reigned in the passage. Occasionally Gray stumbled over a loose stone. Then he heard for the first time the chant.

It came from a great distance. It was echoed by the stone corridor, swelling and dying as the gust of air quickened or failed. A deep-throated chant that seemed to have the cadence of a hymn.

"What is that?" he whispered.

"The sunset hymn," Delabar informed him.

Gray, who had forgotten the council of the priests
—which must be nearby—wondered why the man
shivered.

"Does this passage lead direct to the council?" he
demanded.

Delabar hesitated.

"It leads to a cellar where two other corridors
join it," he muttered. "The chant is carried by the
echoes—the council is still far off." He moved
forward. "Come."

This time he advanced quickly. The song diminished to a low murmur, confused by distance.
Gray reflected that there must be many singers. If
all the priests were at the council, the corridors
might be clear. Wu Fang Chien would be with the
Buddhists.

A glimmer of light showed ahead. It strength-
ened as they drew nearer. Delabar broke into a half
trot, peering ahead. By the glow, Gray saw that
the passage they were in was a vaulted corridor of
sandstone carved in places with inscriptions which
seemed to be very old.

The chant swelled louder as they reached the end
of the passage. Before them was a square chamber
resembling a vault. Two large candles stood in
front of another exit. Gray thought he noticed a
movement in the shadows behind the candles. His
first glance showed him that the only other opening was a flight of stone steps, across from them.

Bassalor Danek

He reached out to check Delabar. But the man slipped from his grasp and ran forward into the room. Gray swore under his breath and leaped after him.

"Aid!" screamed Delabar. "Aid, for a follower of Buddha! A white man has come into the passages——"

He flung himself on his knees before the candles, knocking his shaven head against the floor. Gray halted in his tracks, peering into the shadows behind the candles.

"Help me to seize the white man!" chattered the traitor. "I am a faithful servant of Buddha. I have come to give warning. The white man forced me to lead him."

One after another three Buddhist priests slipped from the shadows and stared at Delabar and Gray. The former was in a paroxysm of fear, his knees shaking, his hands plucking at his face. Gray, silently cursing the trick the other had played, watched the three priests. They had drawn long knives from their robes and paused by Delabar, as if waiting for orders.

The alarm had been given. Footsteps could be heard coming along the hall behind the candles. Gray was caught. In the brief silence he heard the deep-throated chant, echoing from a quarter he could not place.

Still the priests waited, the candlelight gleaming

from their white eyeballs. Gray cast a calculating glance about the chamber. Two exits were available. The stairs, and the passage down which he had come. Which to take, he did not know. But he was not minded to be run down at the well in the dark.

A broad, bland face looked out from the corridor by the candles. He saw the silk robe and luminous, slant eyes of Wu Fang Chien.

"So Captain Gray has come to Sungan," the mandarin said calmly, in English. "I have been expecting him——"

"I did not bring him," chattered Delabar. "I gave the alarm——"

Terror was in his broken words. Wu Fang Chien scrutinized the kneeling figure and his eyes hardened.

"Who can trust the word of a mongrel?" he smiled, speaking in Chinese. "Slay the dog!"

Delabar screamed, and tried to struggle to his feet. Two of the Buddhists stepped to his side and buried their weapons in his body. The scream ended in a choking gasp. Again the priests struck him with reddened knives.

He sank to the floor, his arms moving weakly in a widening pool of his own blood. Wu Fang Chien had not ceased to smile.

Gray jerked out his automatic. He fired at the priests, the reports echoing thunderously in the confined space. Two of the Buddhists sank down upon the body of Delabar; the third wheeled wildly, coughing as he did so.

Gray laid the sights of his automatic coolly on Wu Fang Chien. The mandarin reached out swiftly. His wide sleeves swept against the candles, extinguishing them. Gray pressed the trigger and caught a glimpse of his foe's triumphant face by the flash that followed. Again he pulled the trigger.

A *click* was the only answer. The chamber of the weapon had been emptied. And Gray had no more cartridges. He threw the useless automatic at the spot where Wu Fang Chien had been and heard it strike against the stone.

He had no means of knowing if he had hit the mandarin with his last shot. He suspected that the trick of Wu Fang Chien had saved the latter's life. For a moment silence held the vault, a silence broken by the groans of the injured priests. The distant chant had ceased.

Gray turned and sought the stairs behind him. He had made up his mind to go forward, not back. He would not try to leave Sungan without Mary Hastings.

He had marked the position of the steps, and stumbled full upon them in the dark. Up the stairs he scrambled, feeling his way. What lay before him he did not know.

Marching Sands

A light appeared behind him. He heard footsteps echo in the vault. The glow showed him that he was at the top of the stairs. Into a passage he ran. It resembled the one that led from the well.

By the sounds behind him he guessed that the priests were following him. Either Wu Fang Chien had decided that Gray had taken to the stairs, or the mandarin was sending parties down both exits.

The feel of the air as well as the continued coolness told Gray that he was still underground. He ran forward at a venture. The passage gave into another vaulted room in which a fire gleamed in a brazier. The place was empty, but skins scattered around the brazier showed that it had been occupied not long since.

Gray took the first opening that offered and ran on. Glancing over his shoulder, he saw the Buddhists emerge into the room. He quickened his pace.

His pursuers had gained on him. Gray was picking his way blindly through the labyrinth of passages. He blundered into a wall heavily, felt his way around a corner and was blinded by a sudden glare of lights.

Gray found himself standing in a lofty hall in which a multitude of men were seated.

His first impression was that he had come into the council of the Buddhist priests. His second was one of sheer surprise.

Bassalor Danek

The hall had evidently been a temple at one time. A stone gallery ran around it, supported by heavy pillars. The embrasures that had once served as windows were blocked with timbers, through which sand had sifted in and lay in heaps on the floor.

The temple was underground. Openings in the vaults of the ceiling let in a current of air which caused the candles around the walls to flicker. Directly in front of Gray was a daïs. Around this, on ebony benches, an array of men were seated.

The floor between him and the daïs was covered with seated forms. All were looking at him. On the platform was, not the figure of a god, but a massive chair of carved sandalwood. In this chair was seated an old man. A majestic form, clothed in a robe of lamb's wool which vied in whiteness with the beard that descended to the man's waist. Each sleeve of the robe was bound above the elbow by a broad circlet of gold. A chain of the same metal was about the man's throat.

What struck Gray was the splendid physique of the elder in the chair. A fine head topped broad shoulders. A pair of dark eyes peered at him under tufted brows. High cheek bones stood out prominently in the pale skin. The figure and face were suggestive of power; yet the fire in the eyes bespoke unrest, even melancholy. The man addressed Gray at once, in a full voice that echoed through the hall.

"Who comes," the voice said in broken Chinese, "to the assembly of the Wusun?"

Gray started. He glanced from the figure in the chair to the others. There were several hundred men in the room. All were dressed in sheepskin, and nankeen, with boots of horsehide or red morocco. The majority were bearded, but all showed the same light skin and well-shaped heads. They appeared spellbound at his coming.

Footsteps behind him told him that his pursuers were nearing the hall. Gray advanced through the seated throng to the foot of the daïs. They made way for him readily.

Mechanically Gray raised his hand in greeting to the man on the throne.

"A white man," he answered.

At that moment several of the Buddhist priests entered the hall. He saw Wu Fang Chien appear. At the sight there was a murmur from the throng.

Gray was still breathing heavily from his run. He stared at the majestic form on the daïs. The Wusun! That was the word the other had used. The word that Van Schaick had said came from the captive race itself.

He glanced at Wu Fang Chien. The Chinaman was different from these men—broader of face, with slant eyes and black hair. The eyes of the man in the chair were level, and his mustache and beard were full, even curling. He resembled the type

Bassalor Danek

of Mirai Khan, the Kirghiz, more than Wu Fang Chien.

So this was the secret of Sungan. Gray smiled grimly, thinking of how Delabar had tried to conceal the truth from him—how the Buddhist had chosen to betray him rather than run the risk of his seeing the Wusun. And this explained the guards. The Wusun were, actually, a captive race.

Gray was quick of wit, and this passed through his mind instantly. He noticed another thing. Wu Fang Chien had left the other priests at the entrance and was coming forward alone. The mandarin folded his arms in his sleeves and bowed gravely. For the first time he spoke the dialect of the West.

"Greetings, Bassalor Danek, Gur-Khan of the Wusun," he said gravely. "It was not my wish to disturb the assembly of the Wusun during the hour of the sunset prayer, in the festival of the new moon. I came in pursuit of an enemy—of one who has slain within the walls of Sungan. You know, O Gur-Khan, that it is forbidden to slay here. When I have taken this man, I will leave in peace."

Bassalor Danek stroked the arms of the chair gently and considered the mandarin.

"Within the space of twelve moons, O Wu Fang Chien, the foot of a Buddhist priest has not been set within the boundary of my people. Here, I am master, not you. That was agreed in the covenant of my fathers and their fathers before them. You have not forgotten the covenant?"

"I have not forgotten," returned the mandarin calmly. "It is to ask for the person of this murderer that I come now. When I have him, I will go."

"Whom has he slain?"

"Two of my men who watched at one of the passages."

"Have the Wusun asked that guards be placed in the passages?"

Wu Fang Chien scowled, then smiled blandly.

"We were waiting to seize this man—a foreign devil. An enemy of your people as well as mine."

Gray watched the two keenly. He had observed that many of the Wusun near Bassalor Danek were armed, after a fashion. They carried bows, and others had swords at their hips. The followers of Wu Fang Chien seemed ill at ease. Moreover, their presence in the hall appeared to anger the Wusun.

Thrust suddenly into a totally strange environment, Gray had only his wits to rely upon. He was unaware of the true situation of the Wusun, as of their character. But certain things were clear.

They were not overfond of Wu Fang Chien. And they were bolder in bearing than the Chinese. Bassalor Danek, who had the title of Gur-Khan, had spoken of a covenant which seemed to be more

216

of a treaty between enemies than an agreement among friends.

On the other hand, Wu Fang Chien spoke with an assurance which suggested a knowledge of his own power, and a certainty that he held the upper hand of the situation.

The Wusun had risen to their feet and were pressing closer. They waited for their leader to speak. The Gur-Khan hesitated as if weighing the situation.

"This man," Wu Fang Chien pointed to Gray, "has come to Sungan with lies in his mouth. He has pulled a veil over his true purpose. And he is an enemy of Mongolia. You will do well to give him up."

Bassalor Danek turned his thoughtful gaze on Gray.

"You have heard what Wu Fang Chien has said," he observed. "You speak his tongue. Tell me why you have come through the walls of Sungan. In the lifetime of ten men no stranger has come to Sungan before this."

Gray's head lifted decisively.

"Wu Fang Chien," he responded slowly, "has said that I killed his men. Is this a crime in one man, when it is not such in another? Just a little while ago the soldiers of the Chinese surprised and destroyed a caravan of my people without warning and without cause."

"They had no right to come where they did," asserted the mandarin blandly.

"They were coming to Sungan."

Wu Fang Chien smiled and waved his brown hand, as if brushing aside the protest of a child.

"Foreign devils without a god. You were warned to keep away."

The white man's eyes narrowed dangerously.

"I came to find a woman of my people that you seized. She is here in Sungan."

Bassalor Danek looked up quickly. "When did she come to Sungan?"

"Several days ago. And Wu Fang Chien kept her. He planned to bring me here, in order to kill me." Gray met the gaze of the old man squarely. "This woman and I, Bassalor Khan, are descended from the same fathers as your race. We were coming to Sungan to seek you. And this man has tried to prevent that. A score of men have lost their lives because of it."

The mandarin would have spoken, but the Gur-Khan raised his hand.

"This is a matter, Wu Fang Chien," he said with dignity, "that cannot be decided in a wind's breath. I will keep this stranger. I will hear his story. At this time to-morrow, after sunset, come alone to the hall and I will announce my decision. Until then I will think."

Wu Fang Chien frowned, but accepted the verdict with the calmness that was the mark of his character.

"Remember, Bassalor Danek," he warned, "that these people are devils from the outer world. And remember the covenant which spares your people their lives. Sungan is in the hollow of the hand of Buddha. And Buddha is lord of Mongolia."

The Gur-Khan seemed not to hear him.

"Truly it is strange," he mused. "Twice in one moon strangers have come before me, with the same tale on their lips. This man, and the woman that my young men took from your priests because she had the face and form of one of our race. She, also, is in my dwelling."

CHAPTER XIX

CONCERNING A CITY

CONTRARY to general belief, a man does not sleep heavily after two days and nights of wakefulness. Gray had been without sleep for that time, but he was alert, although very tired. Continuous activity of the nervous system is not stilled at once.

As soon as Wu Fang Chien left the hall of the Wusun, the American had asked to be permitted to see Mary Hastings.

His request was refused by Bassalor Danek. The woman, said the Gur-Khan, was under his protection and could not be seen until daylight. Gray was forced to acquiesce in this. He felt that Mary would be safe in the hands of the elder, who seemed to enjoy complete authority in the gathering. This belief proved to be correct.

The knowledge that the girl was near him and reasonably protected from harm brought a flood of relief, and eased the tension which had gripped him for the past forty hours. He was exhilarated by the first good news in many hours.

Concerning a City

As a consequence, he now became acutely hungry. Bassalor Danek directed that he be taken from the hall and fed. Two of the younger men with the bows conducted him through a new series of corridors, up several flights of winding steps and into a small, stone compartment which, judging by the fresh air that came through the embrasures, was above the level of the sand.

Here they supplied him with goat's milk, a kind of cheese made from curdled mare's milk and some dried meat which was palatable. Gray fell asleep quickly on a pile of camel skins, while the men— Bassalor Danek had referred to them as *tumani*[1]— watched curiously.

Gray awakened with the first light that came into the embrasures. He found that he was very stiff, and somewhat chilled. At his first movement the *tumani* were up. One of them, a broad-shouldered youth who said his name was Garluk, spoke broken Chinese, of a dialect almost unknown to Gray.

He explained that they were in one of the towers of the temple which projected well above the sand. Gray, for the first time, had a fair view of Sungan from the embrasures.

It was a clear day. The sky to the east was crimson over the brown plain of the Gobi. The sun shot level shafts of light against the ruins.

[1] Possibly derived from the Tatar word *tuman,* a squadron of warriors, hunters.

Marching Sands

Gray saw the wall of the old city—the abode of the Wusun. Later in the day he wrote down some notes of what he observed on the reverse side of the maps he carried. They were roughly as follows:

The old city had been built in an oasis, apparently four or five centuries ago. Willows, poplars and tamarisks lined narrow canals which had been constructed through the ruins from the wells. By walling these canals with stone, the Wusun had kept them intact from the encroaching sand. There was even grass near the canals, and several flocks of sheep. The trees afforded shade—although the sun is never unendurable in the Gobi, owing to the altitude.

The buildings of the city had been more than half enveloped by the moving sand which was swept into the walled area—so Garluk said—with each *kara buran*. Owing perhaps to the protection of the wall, the sand ridges around the inner city were higher than the ground within. So it was difficult to obtain a good view of the city from the surrounding country.

Gray reflected that this must be why the Kirghiz had reported seeing only the summits of some towers; also, why he himself had taken the foliage that he made out through his glasses for bushes.

The buildings of Sungan were ancient, and fashioned of solid sandstone so that although partially covered with sand, their interiors—after

222

the embrasures had been sealed—were reasonably comfortable and warm dwellings. Delabar had been correct in quoting the legend that there were extensive vaults and cellars in Sungan. The underground passages communicated from vault to vault —a system that was most useful in this region where the black sand-storms occur every day in the spring, early summer and throughout the winter.

"Mighty good dugouts, these," thought Gray. "The Wusun have certainly dug themselves in on their ancestral hearths. Wonder how they manage for food?"

He asked Garluk this question. The Wusun responded that he and certain of his companions— the *tumani*—were allowed to go out on the plain through the lines of lepers and hunt the wild camels and gazelles of the plain. Also, the Buddhists maintained several shepherd settlements near the River Tarim, a journey of three or four days to the west.

Some citrons, melons and date trees grew by the canals of Sungan. At times a caravan would come to Sungan from China bringing other food.

Through his glasses Gray made out the figures of lepers outside the wall. Garluk explained that these were "the evil fate of the Wusun." They were put there to keep the Wusun within the wall. For centuries he and his people had been pent up. They were diminishing in numbers, due to the captivity.

Marching Sands

Occasionally some adventurous man would escape through the lepers and the Chinese soldiers, cross the desert to Khotan or Kashgar. These never returned. Death was the penalty for trying to escape.

Gray scanned the ruins through his glasses. Women were cooking and washing near the canals. Men appeared from the underground chambers and went patiently about the business of the day. They seemed an orderly throng, and Gray guessed that Bassalor Danek ruled his captive people firmly. Which was well.

He noticed pigeons in the trees. It was not an ugly scene. But on every side stretched the barren Gobi, encroaching on and enveloping the stronghold of the Wusun, the "Tall Men." The same resignation and patience that he had noted in the eyes of Bassalor Danek were stamped in the faces of Garluk and his companions. They were olive faces, stolid and expressionless. Gray had seen the same traits in some Southern Siberian tribes, isolated from their fellows, and in the Eskimos.

Among the notes, he afterwards jotted down some references for Van Schaick—on the chance that he would be able to get the data into the hands of his employers. Gray had a rigid sense of duty. His observations were fragmentary, for he lacked the extended knowledge of racial history and characteristics that Delabar was to have supplied.

In spite of their confined life, the "Tall Ones"

were above the stature of the average Mongol. Their foreheads did not slope back from the eyes as much as in the Tartar of the steppe, and the eyes themselves were larger, especially among the young women, who were often attractive in face.

Language: the Wusun had all the hard gutturals, and the forcible "t" and "k" of the Mongol tongue; but their words were syllabic—even poetically expressive. Many myths appeared in their songs— references to Genghis Khan, as the "Mighty Man-slayer" and to Prester John, by his native name— Awang Khan of the Keraits.

Intelligence: on a par with that of the middle-class Chinese, superior to that of the Kirghiz and Dungans of the steppe. Their characteristics were kindly and hospitable; their ideas simple, owing to the narrow range of objects within their vision. Of history and the progress of the world, they were totally ignorant, being kept so in accordance with the favorite practice of the Buddhists.

Arms and implements: limited to the bow, and the iron sword with tempered point. They had seen firearms in the possession of the Chinese guards, but were not allowed to own them. For cultivation, they dragged a rude, wooden harrow by hand, and used a sharply pointed hoe of iron. utensils, such as copper pots purchased from the As to cooking—this was done with rudimentary

Marching Sands

Chinese, makeshift ovens in the sand, and spits over an open fire.

As to religion, Gray was destined to make a curious discovery, as surprising as it was unexpected, but one which was beyond his limited knowledge to explain.

Such were the Wusun, as Gray saw them.

Garluk broke in on his thoughts with a guttural exclamation.

"How can you see so far," he demanded, "when we can not see?"

Gray smiled and was about to hand the Wusun his glasses when he checked himself. The binoculars might prove useful later, he thought. As it happened, they did.

Meanwhile, Gray's mind had reverted to the thought that was last with him when he had gone to sleep the night before and was first to come to him with awakening. He had neither washed nor eaten, but he would not delay.

"Take me to the white woman," he ordered.

Still staring at him in bewilderment, the two hunters led him down the stairs, through a postern door, and out on the sand. After a brief word with some older Wusun who were squatted by the tower, Garluk struck off through the ruins, waving back the throngs that came to gaze at Gray.

The American noticed that there were few children. Some of the women carried water jars.

226

Concerning a City

They were not veiled. They wore a loose robe of clean cotton—he learned that they worked their own looms, of ancient pattern—bound by a silk girdle, and covered by a flowing *khalat*. All were barefoot.

Gray was conducted to a doorway outside which a *tumani* stood, sword in hand. After a brief conference with his guides, the guard permitted them to enter. Throughout his stay in Sungan, Gray was watched, quietly, but effectively.

His heart was beating fiercely by now, and he wanted to cry out the name of the girl. He walked down into semi-darkness. A smell of musk and dried rose leaves pervaded the place. A woman rose from the floor and disappeared into the shadows. Presently Garluk drew aside a curtain. Gray entered what seemed to be a sleeping chamber and found Mary Hastings standing before him.

"Captain Gray!" she cried softly, reaching out both hands. "Last night they told me you were here. Oh, I'm so glad!"

He gripped the slim hands tightly, afraid to say what came into his mind at sight of the girl. She was thinner and there were circles under the fine eyes that fastened on him eagerly.

He could see her clearly by the glow from a crimson lamp that hung overhead. The room was comfortably fitted with rugs and cushions. A jar of water and some dates stood near them.

"How did you get here?" she echoed. "Where is

Sir Lionel?" A shadow passed over her expressive face. "I saw the attack on the caravan. Did he——"

"Sir Lionel made his way back to me," said Gray, his voice gruff and tense. "He was the only survivor of the caravan."

"Then he is dead," she responded slowly. "Or he would have come with you." She bit her lip, bending her head, so that Gray should not see the tears in her eyes. "Oh, I have feared it. The Buddhist priests said that their guards would find and kill him. An old man of the Wusun who speaks Turki repeated it to me."

Gray was glad that Mary was prepared, in a measure, for the death of her uncle. He had found the sight of her distress hard to bear. He turned away.

"Yes. Sir Lionel died—bravely."

She released his hands, and fumbled with a torn, little square of linen that had once been a handkerchief.

"Oh!"

Fearing that she would break down and weep, Gray would have left the room, but she checked him with a gesture. She looked up quietly, although the tears were still glistening on her eyelids.

"Please, Captain Gray! I've been so—lonely. You won't go away, just for a while?"

For a while? He would have remained at her

side until dragged away, if she wished it so. He saw that she had changed. Some of the life and vivacity had been driven from her delicate face, leaving a wistful tenderness.

He himself showed little sign of the hardships of the last two days, except a firmer set to the wide mouth, and deeper lines about the eyes. He was unshaven, as he had been for some time, and the clothing on his rugged figure was rather more than usually the worse for wear.

The girl noticed a new light in his eyes—somber, even dogged. There was something savage in the determination of the hard face, born—although she did not know it—of his knowledge that the life and safety of Mary Hastings was now his undivided responsibility.

CHAPTER XX

"Poor Uncle Lionel," she said sadly, "he never knew that—the Wusun were here, as he had thought they would be."

"He will have full credit for his achievement when you and I get back home, out of Sungan, Miss Hastings."

She looked at him, dumbly grateful. Gone was all the petulance, the spirit of mockery now. But her native heritage of resolution had not forsaken her.

"Thank you for that, Captain Gray. I—I was foolish in disregarding your warning. I was unjust —because I wanted Uncle Singh to be first in Sungan." She sighed, then tried to smile. "Will you sit down? On a cushion. Perhaps you haven't breakfasted yet. I have only light refreshments to offer——"

A fresh miracle was taking place before Gray's eyes. He did not know the courage of the English girls whose men protectors live always in the unsettled places that are the outskirts of civilization.

The Talisman

His nearness to the girl stirred him. Her pluck acted as a spur to his own spirits. In spite of himself, his gaze wandered hungrily to the straying, bronze hair, and the fresh, troubled face.

Unconsciously, she reached up and deftly adjusted a vagrant bit of hair. He wanted to pat her on the back and tell her she was splendid. But he feared his own awkwardness. Mary Hastings seemed to him to be a fragile, precious charge that had come into his life.

He drew a quick breath. "I *am* hungry," he lied.

She busied herself at once, setting out dates and some cakes. While he ate, she barely nibbled at the food.

"Now," he began cheerfully, having planned what he was to say, "I'm indebted to you for breakfast. And I'm going to question you."

He realized that he must take her mind from the death of her uncle.

"How have our new allies, the Wusun, been treating you, Miss Hastings?"

"Very nicely, really. But not the priests. They took all my belongings except a little gold cross under my jacket. You see, the priests came with the—the lepers who attacked us."

Gray nodded.

"And the Buddhists seized me, not the poor, sick men. They carried me off after gagging me so I couldn't call out."

"Wu Fang's orders."

"They took me down into some kind of a tunnel and kept me there until the shooting had ceased. They were escorting me along the passages when we met a party of Wusun, armed with bows. They talked to the priests, then they seemed to become angry, and the Buddhists gave me up. I don't know why the Wusun wanted me."

Glancing at the beautiful girl, Gray thought that the reason was not hard to guess. He did not then understand, however, the full significance that the woman held for the Wusun.

"Perhaps they recognized you as a white woman —one of their own kind," he hazarded.

She shook her head dubiously.

"I thought the Wusun did not know any other white people existed, Captain Gray. One of them— I heard them call him Gela, the Kha Khan—was a young man, as big as you, and not bad looking. He was angriest of all—with the priests, that is, not with me."

Gray frowned.

"Gela led me to the council hall of the 'Tall Ones,'" she continued, looking at him in some surprise, for the frown had not escaped her. "There I found old Bassalor Danek. I could not speak their language, but Uncle Singh taught me quite a bit of the northern Turki. Bassalor Danek was really a fine old chap, but I like Timur better."

"Timur?" he asked. "One of the *tumani?*"

"I don't see why you don't like them. They helped me. No, Timur seems to be a kind of councilor. He's white haired, and limps. But he speaks broken Turki, which I understand. So—I have been well treated, except that they will not let me out of this building, which belongs to Bassalor Danek."

"What did the Turki-speaking fellow have to say for himself?"

"He asked my name. Of course he could not pronounce it, so he christened me something that sounds like Kha Rakcha. I think Kha—it's a Kirghiz word, too—means 'white' in their tongue."

"Rakcha is western Chinese for some kind of spirit," assented Gray, interested. "So they've named you the White Spirit—or, in another sense, the White Woman-Queen. Your coming seems to have been an event in the affairs of the Wusun——"

"That is what Timur said." She nodded brightly. "He is one of the elders of the *kurultai*—council. I hope I made a good impression on him. He seemed to be friendly."

"I think," pondered Gray seriously, "that you have made a better impression than you think. That helps a lot, because——" he was about to say that his own standing with the Wusun was none too good, thanks to Wu Fang Chien's enmity, but broke off. He did not want to alarm her. "Because

233

they've let me come to see you," he amended awkwardly.

The girl's vigilant wits were not to be hoodwinked.

"That's not what you meant to say, Captain
Gray," she reproached him.

"It's true—" he was more successful this time—
"that your coming probably earned me a respite."

"A respite?"

When is a woman deceived by a man's clumsy
assurance? Or when does she fail to understand
when something is kept back?

"Captain Gray, you know something you won't
tell me! Did the Wusun threaten you?"

"No. They shielded me——"

"Then you were in danger. I thought so. Now
what did you mean by—respite?"

Instead, Gray told her how he had found his way
into Sungan, omitting the details of the fighting, or
his own achievement. Mary considered him
gravely, chin on hand.

"I prayed that you would follow our caravan,"
she said. "I wished for you when every one was
fighting so. Somehow, I was sure that you would
reach Sungan. You see, you made me feel you
were the kind of man who went where he wanted
to go."

Gray looked up, and she shook her head reproachfully.

"You're just like Uncle Singh. You won't tell

234

if there's any danger. Will not the Wusun protect us from the priests?" She stretched out a slim hand appealingly. "There's just the two of us left. Shouldn't you be quite frank with me? Now tell me what you meant by 'respite'!"

He cordially regretted his unfortunate choice of the word. Perforce, he told her of Wu Fang Chien, and the dispute in the council.

"So you see our case comes up for trial to-night," he concluded. "It's a question of the Gur-Khan's authority against the power of Wu Fang Chien. I'm rooting for old Bassalor Danek. I think he'll treat us well. For one thing, because he's curious about us. In a way, we're his guests. I hope he checkmates Wu, because—to be frank—we're better off in Sungan than with the Buddhists."

This time she was satisfied.

"Of course," she nodded. "Wu Fang Chien would not let us go free easily. He would have to answer, then, for the attack on the caravan. To answer to the British embassy."

Gray reflected that they were the only survivors of the fight and that the Chinese could not afford to permit them to escape.

"I'll appear to argue for immunity—our immunity—to-night," he smiled.

"Are you a lawyer, Captain Gray?" The girl tried to enter into the spirit of his remark. "Have we a good case?"

"Chiefly our wits," he admitted. "And perhaps the tie the Wusun may feel for us as a kindred race."

"Splendid!" She clapped her hands. "I think you're a first-rate attorney."

Gray recalled the majestic face of Bassalor Danek, and the anger of the Wusun at the entrance of Wu Fang Chien.

"They made some kind of a covenant, didn't they, with the Chinese Emperor?"

"Timur said it was an agreement by which the Wusun were to keep their city inviolate, and not to leave its boundaries. Even the invading sands have not dislodged them. Timur described them as numerous as the trees of the Thian Shan, the Celestial Mountains, at first. Now only a few survive. The Chinese have posted lepers around them."

Gray nodded. Slowly the history of the Wusun was piecing itself out. A race descended from invaders from Europe before the dawn of history, they had allied themselves with the might of Genghis Khan and earned the enmity of the Chinese. Since then, with the slow persistence of the Chinese, they had been confined and diminished in number.

"You remember the legend of Prester John—in the middle ages," continued the girl eagerly. "Marco Polo tells about a powerful prince in mid-Asia who was a Christian. I have been thinking about it. Isn't the word Kerait the Mongol for

236

Christian? Do you suppose the first Wusun were
Christians?"

"They don't seem to have any especial religion,
Miss Hastings—except a kind of morning and evening prayer."

"I've heard them chant the hymn. Timur says it
was their ancestors'." The girl sighed. "To think
that we should have found the Wusun, after all. If
only my uncle——" She broke off sadly.

A step sounded outside the room and Garluk
thrust his shaggy head through the curtain.

"I come from the Gur-Khan," he announced.
"The Man-Who-Kills-Swiftly must come before
Bassalor Khan."

"They are paging me," said Gray lightly, in answer to her questioning look. "I've got to play
lawyer. But I have an experiment to try. Don't
worry."

He rose, and she looked up at him pleadingly.

"Come back, as soon as you can," she whispered.
"I—it's so lonely here. I was miserable until Timur
told me they had heard shooting during yesterday's
sunset chant. I guessed it was you——"

"My automatic," explained Gray with a grin. "I
missed Wu Fang Chien, which is too bad." He was
talking cheerily, at random, anxious to hearten the
girl. She winced at mention of the fighting.

"I'll be back to report what is going on."

"If anything should happen to you——"

"I seem to be accident-proof, so far." He smiled lightly, masking his real feelings. "And there's a plan——"

"Come," said Garluk. "Bassalor Khan waits at his shrine."

"I'll have a better dinner to offer you," Mary smiled back. "Don't forget!"

"I'll make a note of it—Mary."

Gray stepped outside the curtain. In spite of his promise, he could not return to the girl's room.

He found Bassalor Danek waiting in a chamber under the temple, to which he was conducted by the impatient Garluk. The Gur-Khan was seated on a silk carpet beside an old man with a face like a satyr, whom Gray guessed to be Timur. They looked up silently at his approach. The *tumani* withdrew.

At a sign from Bassalor Danek, Gray seated himself before the two. They regarded him gravely. He waited for them to speak.

"Wu Fang Chien," began the Gur-Khan at length, "will come to the hall to hear my word at sunset. His ill-will might bring the dark cloud of trouble upon my people. If I give you up, he will thank me and bring us good grain and tea from China in the next caravan."

He paused as if for an answer. But Gray was silent, wishing to hear what more the two had to say.

The Talisman

"Yet, O One-Who-Kills-Swiftly," put in Timur mildly, "you are of the race of the Kha Rakcha and she has found favor in our hearts. You say you came here to seek her. That is well. But we must not bring trouble upon our people. They have little food. There is none to place before the shrine of our race."

He glanced over his shoulder at a closed curtain. Here one of the Wusun stood guard. Gray guessed that this was their shrine. He was curious for a glimpse of it.

"What is the will of the Gur-Khan?" he asked quietly.

Bassalor Danek glanced at him keenly.

"I have not made ready my answer, O Man-from-the-Outside. Wu Fang Chien cried that you had come unbidden to meddle with what does not concern you. The Kha Rakcha is very beautiful, and the light from her face will be an ornament to our shrine. You have said that you came to seek us. But that cannot be. For no word of us has passed the outer guards. Even the wandering Kirghiz that we see at a distance do not know us."

Gray had been waiting for a lead to follow. Now he saw his chance and summoned his small stock of poetical Chinese to match the oratory of Bassalor Danek.

"Hearken, O Gur-Khan," he said, and paused, knowing the value of meditation when dealing with

239

an oriental. Inwardly, he prayed for success in his venture, knowing that the fate of the girl depended greatly on what he said.

"It is true," he resumed, "that I was sent to seek the Wusun. Beyond the desert and beyond the border of Mongolia live a people whose fathers a very long time ago were the same as your fathers. They have means of seeing across great distances. They have the Eyes-of-Long-Sight. With these eyes they saw the Wusun in captivity, and they sent me with a message. This message I shall deliver when it is time."

Timur shook his gray head shrewdly.

"Can a fish see what is on the land? A gazelle has keen eyes; but a gazelle cannot see across the desert, much less can a man. What you have said is not true."

"It is true. Not only can my people see beyond any distance, but they can hear. Behold, here is proof."

While the two watched curiously, Gray pulled his maps from his shirt and spread them on the floor before him. Bassalor Danek glanced from the paper to him expectantly.

"Here is what we saw, with our Eyes-of-Long-Sight. See, here is the last village of China, Ansichow, and the desert. Here, by this mark, is where we knew Sungan to be. And beyond it is the River

The Talisman

Tarim, as you know, and the Celestial Mountains. By this paper I found my way here."

Bassalor Danek fingered the map curiously. Then he shook his head.

"This is a paper, like to those of the priests of Buddha. It is a kind of magic. With magic, much is possible. But these are signs upon paper. They are not mountains and rivers."

Gray sighed, confronted with the native incredulity of a map. The Wusun, despite their natural intelligence, were bound by the stultifying influence of generations of isolation. In fact, their state of civilization was that of the dark ages. It was as if Gray and Mary Hastings had wandered into a stronghold of the Goths.

Still, he felt he had made a slight impression. He drew the field glasses from their case.

"I have been given a token," he explained slowly, making sure that the two understood his broken Chinese. "It is a small talisman of the Eyes-of-Long-Sight. With it, you can see what is far, as clearly as if it lay in your hand."

Timur stroked his beard and smiled.

"It may not be. Even with magic, it may not be."

"Look then." Gray lifted the glasses and focussed them on the guard who stood by the shrine curtain. "With this you can bring the man's face as near as mine."

241

He handed the glasses to Bassalor Danek who turned them over curiously in his hand. Obeying Gray's direction, he leveled them on the guard. The man stirred uneasily, evidently believing that some kind of magic was being practiced upon him. Bassalor Danek gave a loud exclamation and the glasses fell to his knees. He peered from them to the man at the curtain and muttered in his beard.

"I saw the face within arm's reach of my own," he cried. "Truly, it is as this man has promised!"

"Nay," Timur objected. "The one by the shrine did not move, for I watched. It may not be."

Nevertheless, his hand trembled as he lifted the glasses to his feeble eyes. Gray helped him to focus them. He, also, gave an exclamation.

For a while the two Wusun experimented with the binoculars, scrutinizing the walls, the floor and the rugs with increasing amazement. Gray kept a straight face. The glasses were powerful, with excellent lenses. The Wusun had never seen or heard of anything of the kind.

"This is but a token," he reminded them gravely, "of the Eyes-of-Long-Sight that my people have. If this talisman can bring near to you what is afar, do you doubt that we could know what is beyond the desert? Is not the coming of the White Spirit proof that we knew?"

This was a weighty matter and Bassalor Danek

and Timur conferred upon it, putting down the glasses reluctantly.

"I know not," hazarded Timur. Gray saw that his double question had confused them. To remedy his error he turned to Bassalor Danek.

"Keep these small Eyes-of-Long-Sight," he said. "I give them to you."

Despite his accustomed calm, the chieftain of the Wusun gave an involuntary exclamation of pleasure. Gray pressed his advantage.

"Further proof I will give, O Bassalor Danek. Draw the curtains of the shrine that I may see the god of the Wusun. Then I will show you that my people beyond the desert knew of the god."

He reasoned swiftly that the Wusun, if Timur's account of their history had been correct, must have in their shrine some emblem of the Tatar deity—the god Natagai which Mirai Khan had described to him—or possibly some Mohammedan symbol. He rather guessed the former, since the Wusun had been isolated before the Moslem wave swept over Central Asia.

"It is not a god, O Man-from-the-Outside," demurred Timur. "It is a talisman of our fathers. Once, the Wusun had priests. In the time of Kubla Khan. Now, all that we remember is the hymn at sunset and sunrise. Almost we have forgotten the words. We have kept the talisman because once our priests, who were also warriors, cherished it."

Gray nodded, believing now that it was an image of Natagai, the Tatar war deity.

"It is said," continued Timur meditatively, "that the talisman was fashioned by a chieftain of our people. I have heard a tale from the elders that this khan lived when the Wusun were in another land, before they crossed the mountains on the roof of the world. Draw the curtain!"

At the command the guard drew back the heavy folds of brocade. Gray saw a stone altar, covered with a clean cloth of white silk. On the cloth stood a cross.

CHAPTER XXI

MARY MAKES A REQUEST

The cross was jade, in the shape of the medieval emblem—the Greek cross. Before it burned a candle. Gray stared at it silently while Timur limped forward and trimmed the wick of the candle.

"We do not remember the faith of our fathers," the old Wusun said sadly. "But we have kept the talisman. It is not as strong as the bronze Buddha of Wu Fang Chien. We will not give it up, although he has asked to buy it. Truly, no man should part with what was precious in the sight of his fathers."

Thoughts crowded in upon Gray. Was this the cross left by a wandering missionary—one of those who followed the footsteps of Marco Polo? Were the ancient Wusun the Christians mentioned in medieval legends as the kingdom of Prester John, sometimes called *Presbyter* John? The Wusun had been warriors. Was the symbol of the cross adapted from the hilt of a sword? Was it one of the vagaries of fate that had brought the cross into the hands of the Wusun, who were descendants of the Christians of Europe? Or had they of their own accord become worshipers of the cross? What did it mean to them?

He recalled the sunset hymn. Was this their version of the vespers of a forgotten priest? He did not know. The problem of the cross existing among the remnants of the Wusun remains to be solved by more learned minds than his. It was clear, however, that beyond the cross, they retained no vestige of their former religion.

Abruptly his head snapped up.

"I promised you, Bassalor Danek," he cried, "that this would be a symbol. As I have promised, you will find it. We—who are of the same fathers—have also this talisman of our God."

The Wusun stared at him. There was a ring of conviction in Gray's words. He recalled Delabar's words that the talisman of the Wusun had earned the captive race the hatred of the Buddhists. He saw now how this was. Fate—or what the soldier esteemed luck—had put an instrument into his hand. For the defense of the girl. He must make full use of it.

He pointed to the jade cross.

"The Kha Rakcha and I are of the same blood as the Wusun. We came in peace to seek you. The Kha Rakcha claims your protection. Will you not grant it? Thus, I have spoken."

Mary Makes a Request

Bassalor Danek folded his lean arms, tiny wrinkles puckering about his aged eyes.

"I hear," he said. "The tale of the Eyes-of-Long-Sight is a true tale. But this thing is another tale. Have you a token to show, so that we may know that it, also, is true?"

In the back of Gray's mind was memory of a token. Something that Mary had mentioned. In his anxiety, he could not recall it.

Thus did Gray miss a golden opportunity. If he had been alone, his natural quickness of thought would have found an answer to the Gur-Khan's question. With the life of the girl he loved at stake, he hesitated.

It was vitally important that Bassalor Danek should believe what Gray had said about the cross. Believing, he would aid them, for he reverenced the cross. Doubting, they would be exposed to the wiles of Wu Fang Chien.

"If I spoke the truth in one thing, O Gur-Khan," he parried, "would I speak lies concerning another?"

"The two things are not the same," put in Timur, logically. "The talisman is precious—like to the gold in the sword-hilt of Gela. Yet what is it to you?"

"It is the sign of our faith. It is the talisman of Christianity."

"I know not the word."

Marching Sands

"You know the name of the ancient khan of the Wusun—Awang Khan?"

Gray hazarded a bold stroke, on his knowledge of the legend of Prester John of Asia. Timur considered.

"The name is not in our speech," he announced.

Bassalor Danek looked up sagely.

"You speak of faith, O One-Who-Kills-Swiftly. Is that a word of a priesthood?"

"Yes."

"Then," said Bassalor Danek gravely, "it is clear that your talisman is not like to this. Nay, for the only priesthood is that of the false Buddhists."

"Our faith is different from theirs—even as a grain of sand is different from a drop of clear water."

The Gur-Khan's hand swept in a wide circle.

"Nay. What can we see from Sungan save the grains of sand? Everywhere, beyond, is the Buddhist priesthood. We have seen this thing. It is true." He lifted his head proudly. "Behold, youth, here is the talisman of a warrior. From chieftain to chieftain, it has been handed down. It is the token of a chieftain. Of one who safeguards his people. None can wear it but myself, or another of royal blood who has fought for his people."

For the first time he showed Gray a smaller cross, fashioned from gold which hung from a chain of the same metal across his chest under the cloak.

Mary Makes a Request

"Because I am khan of the Wusun, this thing is mine," he added. "If my father and his before him had not been strong warriors, the Wusun would have passed from the world as a candle is blown out in a strong wind."

"Aye," amended Timur. "It is a sign of the rank of the Gur-Khan. Has it not always been thus?"

Both men nodded their heads, as at an unalterable truth. Age and isolation had made their conceptions rigid. The safety of the Wusun was their sole care.

"Your sign is not like to ours," said they. "Is the moon kindred to the sun because both live in the sky?"

"There is but one Cross," cried Gray.

They shook their heads. How were they to alter the small store of belief that had been their meager heritage of wisdom?

"You are not kin to us, but the Kha Rakcha is a woman, and so may become kin to the Wusun," announced Bassalor Danek. "Go now, for we must weigh well our answer to Wu Fang Chien."

Gray rose, his lips hard.

"Be it so," he said slowly. "If it is in your mind that you must yield to Wu Fang Chien, give me up into his hands. I will take a sword and go to seek him. Keep the Kha Rakcha safe within Sungan. She is, as you have seen, the White Spirit.

Her beauty is not less than the light of the sun. Guard her well."

Gray had spoken bitterly, feeling that he had failed in his plea. He had not sensed the full meaning of the other's words. He knew that his own death would be the most serious loss to the girl. Without him she was defenseless.

He did not want to leave her. She had been so childlike in her reliance upon his protection. And he was so helpless to aid her.

But Gray had weighed the odds with the cold precision that never left him. There was a slight chance that he might be able to kill Wu Fang Chien, and if so, Mary might be safeguarded.

He walked away from the shrine, and, unconsciously, bent his steps toward the house of Bassalor Danek where the girl was. Then he turned back, resolutely. He could not see Mary now. She would guess instantly—so quick was the woman's instinct—that something was wrong.

Gray retraced his steps to the tower and to his own chamber where he would await the decision of the Gur-Khan.

For the space of several hours the two Wusun debated together. They glanced from time to time at a water clock which creaked dismally in the corner furthest from the shrine. Their brows were furrowed by anxiety as they talked.

Outside the sun was already past its highest point,

and the sands burned with reflected heat. The people of Sungan had taken shelter under the canal trees and in the underground buildings. Even the dogs and the lepers were no longer to be seen. Quiet prevailed in Sungan, and in the armed camps of the guards without the wall.

No glimmer of sunlight penetrated into the shrine of Bassalor Danek. The attendant lighted fresh candles and stood motionless. Then he stirred and advanced to the doorway. He uttered a gruff exclamation.

Mary Hastings pushed past him and stood gazing at the two Wusun.

"Timur!" she cried. "Where is the One-Who-Kills-Swiftly?"

The councilor of Sungan glanced at her wonderingly. She was flushed, and breathing quickly. Her bronze hair had fallen to her slim shoulders. Tall and proud and imperious, she faced him—a lovely picture in the dim chamber.

"He said that he would return to me," she repeated. "And he has not come. Well do I know that this could only be because of something evil that has happened. Where is he?"

The two were stoically silent. She approached them fearlessly. To the guard's amazement, she stamped an angry foot, her eyes wide with anxiety.

This, to the guard, was something that should not be permitted in the high presence of the Gur-

Khan. He laid a warning hand on her shoulder. Startled, the girl drew back and struck down his arm. Abashed by her flaming displeasure, the warrior glanced at Bassalor Danek.

The Gur-Khan frowned.

"Touch not the Kha Rakcha, dog!" he growled. "Soon the woman is to be allied to me by blood." Then to Mary: "It is not fitting, maiden, that even one such as you should come to this place in anger. Cover then the flame of spirit with the ashes of respect."

Timur interpreted his stately speech. But the girl was wrought up by fear for Gray. Not until he had failed to rejoin her did she realize how much his coming had meant.

It was not loneliness alone. She yearned to hear the soldier's quiet voice, to feel the reassurance of his eyes upon her. Womanlike, her anxiety had grown. Perhaps—so close had the two become in thought after their meeting of the morning—her intuition had whispered that Gray was in trouble.

So she was not minded to respect the dignity of the two aged men. Mary Hastings had been mistress of native servants. She knew how to exact obedience.

"Tell the chieftain," she cried, "to answer when I speak. Am I one to hide the fire of spirit under the cloak of humiliation? Speak! What has become of the white man?"

Mary Makes a Request

Timur rendered the Gur-Khan's reply in Turki.

"The tall warrior has offered his body to cool the anger of Wu Fang Chien, who demands him."

The girl paled.

"How? When?"

"He will take a sword that we will give him this night and go to seek the ruler of the Buddhists. Even so shall it be. We have decided, in council. In this way Wu Fang Chien will be appeased, and the Wusun will drink of the solace of peace in their trouble. Furthermore——"

"Stay!" The girl drew a quick breath. She guessed why Gray had not come to her. The knowledge of his danger steadied her tumultuous thoughts. The danger was worse than she feared. But—such was the woman's strength of soul when the man she loved was menaced—she became strangely calm.

She had not admitted to herself until now that she loved the American. With the understanding of the fresh sacrifice he was prepared to make for her, she could no more deny the truth of her love than she could question the fact of her own life.

"Will you give me up as well?" she asked scornfully.

"Nay. You will have a place by the side of the Gur-Khan, because of your beauty which—so said the One-Who-Kills-Swiftly—is like to the sun.

The Wusun will safeguard the Kha Rakcha, even as *he* demanded."

Mary Hastings sighed softly. Then lifted her head stubbornly. She flushed rosily.

"The white man is precious in my sight," she said clearly. "His life is like to the warmth of the sun, and if he dies, my life would pass, even as water vanishes when it is poured upon the sands."

"Verily," pondered Timur, stroking his beard, "is he a brave man. But how then may Wu Fang Chien be appeased?"

Anger flashed into the girl's expressive face.

"So the Wusun are weak of soul," she accused. "Their heart is like the soul of a gully jackal. They would give up the warrior who came to be their friend, to buy their own comfort! *Aie!* Are you such men?"

Timur stared, confronted for perhaps the first time in his life with the scorn of a woman who thought as a man.

"Think you I will buy my comfort, upon such terms?" she continued mercilessly. "Or remain in the shadow of those who are not men but jackals?"

Timur raised his hand. The decision of the leaders of the Wusun had been actuated by their jealous care of their people, not by selfish motives. But the girl's swift words had sadly confused him.

"If you yield him up," said Mary Hastings, "I also will go. I will not part from him."

Mary Makes a Request

And she would not. If Gray was to face the Chinese, she would be at his side. How often do men judge correctly the true strength of a woman's devotion?

"We have planned otherwise," pointed out Timur. "For you——"

"I have spoken, you have heard."

Bassalor Danek questioned the councilor as to what had been said. Then the chieftain rose.

"Say to the woman," he announced, "that I, the leader of the Wusun, have decided. What my wisdom decides, she cannot alter by hot words. Who is she, but a fair woman? I am master of the talisman of the Wusun."

He pointed to the altar. Mary, intent upon his face, followed his gesture swiftly. She gave a little cry at seeing for the first time the cross. She caught Timur's arm.

"What is that?" she begged. "What—does it mean?"

Timur explained the symbol.

"It is the sign of the Gur-Khan alone," he concluded. "None but those of a chieftain's rank bear it." He touched the smaller cross lying upon the broad shoulders of Bassalor Khan.

Radiantly the girl's face brightened. She smiled, drawing nearer to the two old men. No need for a woman's wit to reason logically!

She drew back the throat of her jacket, revealing

the tiny gold cross which had been her sole belong-
ing left by the avaricious Buddhists. If Wu Fang
Chien had known of the token, he would have torn
it from her.

"See," she said softly. "I also am a bearer of
the cross."

The Wusun stared from her excited face to the
glittering symbol on her breast.

To their limited intelligence two things were plain.
The girl's talisman had not been in Sungan before
she came. So it was clearly hers. Also, she wore
it as by right.

They recalled her pride, and her angry words.
Verily, she wore the sign of rank by right. Timur
stepped back and bent his head.

"O, Queen," he said, "I was blind. Will you
pardon the dog who was blind?"

Bassalor Danek had been frowning, somewhat
jealously. But as he stared into the woman's open
face, his brow cleared.

"It is well, Kha Rakcha," he observed slowly.
"This is truly the token that witnesses the truth of
your coming. None but a woman royal-born can
wear such a talisman as this. It is well."

He touched the cross curiously, comparing it with
his own. Timur bent over his hand, watching.
The girl was silent, holding her breath in suspense.

The minds of the Wusun were wise in their way,
but their wisdom was that of simplicity.

Mary Makes a Request

"None but a queen may carry this on her breast," they assured each other. "So in very truth this *is* a woman royal-born."

She seized swiftly upon her advantage.

"Then you know that I am one who commands."

"Aye," they said, each in his tongue, "we were as blind dogs before."

"Guard then," she said, her lips trembling, for she felt the strain, "the life of the One-Who-Kills-Swiftly. For he is of my blood."

Bassalor Danek pondered, and spoke with grave decision.

"We will safeguard him within Sungan. Wu Fang Chien will ask in vain."

CHAPTER XXII

M ARY laughed a little unsteadily. Surely it was
a strange miracle that her gold cross had worked.
She did not think it luck. In her woman soul there
was no thought of fate. God's care had shielded
the life of the man she loved.

Timur was speaking.

"Bassalor Danek is well content," she heard.
"Beforetimes, he was warmed by the sight of your
fairness. But now it is verily a thing assured.
Gela, the Kha-Khan, son of my son, commander of
the *tumani,* has conceived love for you. Bassalor
Danek has granted his wish that you may become
the wife of his abode and hearth."

Hearing, she did not yet understand.

"Gela?"

"He who took you from the evil priests. Because
of the talisman you wear it is fitting that you should
be his bride."

She looked from one to the other, in sudden discomfort.

The Answer

"Thus will you truly become kin to the Wusun," nodded Timur.

"I?"

"Bassalor Danek, in his wisdom, has decided."

The joy of her brief victory faded swiftly. The reaction weakened her, made this new obstacle disheartening. But she drew strength from a fresh thought.

"Take me to the white man!"

"Nay—it is not fitting. The bond of Gela's love is upon you."

To their bewilderment, the girl laughed. For a brief moment hysteria had claimed her, wearied by the hardships she had undergone. In her sudden stress she clung to the thought that had brought her consolation.

She was a woman unnerved. In reality, she was instinctively calling upon the aid of Gray's strength.

"Are you still blind?" she begged unevenly, the tears not far from her eyes. "Have you not seen the love of the white man for me? How can Gela take me from him, when I am already bound to him?"

Gray had said nothing to her of his love. But she had read in his face what he had not spoken.

"Fools!" she stamped angrily. "You cannot take me from the arms of the One-Who-Kills-Swiftly. He will hear of this." She was speaking somewhat wildly now, feeling all her strength ebb from her.

"He will claim me. He will keep me—— Oh, truly, you are blind."

To the Wusun her sudden emotion was a display of the temper that undoubtedly was the heritage of her royal blood.

Mary was, however, on the verge of a breakdown, and sought the shelter of her own room, since she could not see Gray. She hurried hither, with the woman who had waited without the shrine, at her heels. To tell the truth, she fled.

In her chamber she flung herself down on the cushions and gave herself up to a most unqueenly fit of weeping. The woman waited stoically.

When Mary sat up and dried her tears, the woman smiled. Mary's face was wan, and her hair disheveled. Glancing into a bronze mirror that the woman brought her, she was almost glad that Gray could not see her now. Whereupon she fell into reflection, and presently sent the handwoman for brush and black ink-like paint which is the writing fluid of the Wusun.

Then she diligently sought for any scraps of white stuff that might serve as paper. She selected her handkerchief, but was forced to place it in a window to wait until it dried.

She watched it in the process, a very sad looking woman, her hands clasped about her knees and her head resting sidewise on her hands.

Meanwhile, the post-meridian shadows were

The Answer

lengthening across the enclosure of Sungan. Shepherds were driving their few flocks from the outer strips of grass; children who had bathed in the canals were playing in the last of the sunlight. Groups of warriors emerged from the ruins and walked slowly toward the fires where the evening meal was preparing. Elders sought the council hall.

There was even greater bustle without the wall, where the Chinese were gathering.

It was now the time of the sunset hymn. Gray, pacing the stone floor of his tower room, heard the chant of many voices. It came from the temple below, and the voices were repeating words the meaning of which the owners no longer knew. Gray glanced impatiently from his window, wondering why he had not heard from Bassalor Danek.

It might have been an hour after sunset that steps sounded outside the door of the chamber. Garluk opened the door and stepped back with a gesture of respect.

Gray looked up eagerly, thinking that Bassalor Danek or the lame Timur had come. Instead a tall figure strode into the room.

It was a young man of powerful bearing. He carried his shapely, olive head proudly. His dress was the white lambskin of the Gur-Khan, but without the gold ornaments. A broad, leather belt girdled his waist, and from this a straight sword hung in a bronze scabbard.

Marching Sands

The newcomer lifted his hand in greeting—a gesture that Gray returned. He squatted down on the carpets silently, beckoning to Garluk. Gray eyed him appraisingly, thinking that he had seldom seen a man of such fine physique. The stranger's shoulders were shapely, his arms heavily thewed, his waist slender. He moved with the ease of a man poised on trained muscles.

The three sat in silence until Garluk bethought him to speak.

"This is the Kha Khan, O Man-from-the-Outside," the *tumani* observed. "Gela, the leader of the *tumani*, and grandson of Bassalor Danek."

"I give him greeting," returned the white man, wondering what his visitor had to say.

Presently Gela turned his dark head to Garluk and spoke in a low tone that carried resonantly, from a deep chest. Evidently he did not know the dialect that Gray spoke. The majority of the Wusun were ignorant of Chinese.

"Bassalor Danek," interpreted Garluk, "has seen the talisman on the breast of the Kha Rakcha. He has pondered, in his wisdom, the words you spoke. And he has made answer to Wu Fang Chien."

Once more Gela spoke, while Gray waited impatiently.

"Bassalor Danek, who is lord of the Wusun, listened to the complaint of Wu Fang Chien, governor of Sungan. And his decision was as follows: Undoubtedly both you and the white woman came to seek the Wusun. While you have slain many of the men of the Buddhists, they also have killed the men of the caravan. So, there is no debt to be avenged."

Gray smiled at this simple, but logical way of looking at the situation.

"Furthermore," interpreted Garluk, at Gela's prompting, "since you have sought the Wusun, you may stay here. In the covenant it was agreed that the penalty of attempting to escape is death; still, there is no punishment for entering Sungan. You and the Kha Rakcha will stay in Sungan."

This was good news. Gray was surprised, but he did not permit this to appear in his face.

"What said Wu Fang Chien?" he asked.

"He will try to seize you and the woman. He will call in the soldiers with guns from the desert."

"Will Bassalor Danek protect us?"

"He has given his word. Moreover, he is bound to guard the woman."

Gray did not at first heed this last remark. He was wondering just how far the Chinese would go in their attempt to gain possession of himself and the girl. Probably, he decided, Wu Fang Chien was not over-desirous of forcing an entrance into Sungan. But the mandarin would lose no chance of capturing himself, or possibly of sniping him from the outer wall.

263

But for the present he reasoned that they were safe. Then Garluk's reference to Mary returned to his mind. He recalled that Timur had mentioned that Mary must remain with the Wusun.

Gela had risen, his message delivered. Gray halted him with a gesture.

"Why is Bassalor Danek bound to keep the Kha Rakcha?" he asked, inspired by a new and potent uneasiness.

Gela himself answered this, and Garluk interpreted.

"Have you not heard?" he smiled. "Gela, the Kha Khan, desires the White Spirit for himself. To-morrow night he will marry her, according to the custom of the Wusun. Bassalor Danek has agreed."

Gray checked an exclamation with difficulty.

"That may not be," he said sternly. "The White Spirit is not one to marry among the Wusun."

Garluk laughed. "Did not Gela, the strongest of the Wusun, take her from the yellow priests? Does she not wear the talisman which is the same as that of our shrine? Gela as yet has no wife. Why should he not marry?"

While the two watched him, Gray considered the new turn affairs had taken. All his instincts prompted him to cry out that the thing was impossible. Mary must be protected. Yet he knew the futility of a protest.

The Answer

"Has the Kha Rakcha agreed to this?" he asked, playing for time.

"She does not know of it," asserted Garluk complacently. "Why should a maiden be told before she has the armlet"—he pointed at the bronze circlet about Gela's powerful arm—"of her lord bound about her throat?"

Gela interrupted brusquely.

"The Kha Khan asks," said Garluk, "if you are the husband of the Kha Rakcha?"

"Good Lord!" meditated the American. He thought of asserting that he was. Then reflected that Mary, who knew nothing of what was passing, would hardly bear out his story. But he could not let the opportunity go by without asserting some claim to the girl. "I was to marry her," he compromised, "when we returned from the desert."

Gela barked forth a curt word and strode from the door, after a keen glance at the American.

"The Kha Khan says that he will take her. Doubtless there are many women where you come from. He desires the Kha Rakcha, whose life he saved. Wu Fang Chien would have slain her. So said the yellow priests."

Gray glowered at Garluk, who smiled back.

"Gela has never seen such a woman as the Kha Rakcha. She is as beautiful as an aloe tree in bloom," chattered the *tumani*. "She will bear him strong children, and a son to wear his sword when he is old."

"If she does not agree—what then?"

"It will make no difference. Bassalor Danek has said that she will be a worthy wife to his grandson. Does she not wear the talisman at her throat? That is a good omen for the Wusun. Did she not come here to seek the Wusun? Moreover, if Gela marries her, then Wu Fang Chien cannot take her."

"What if I forbid?" asked Gray dryly.

"No one will heed you," explained Garluk frankly.

Gray considered the matter, frowning.

"Take me to the Kha Rakcha," he ordered.

Garluk made a gesture of denial.

"It is forbidden. To-morrow night the maiden is to be married. There will be a feast, and a great chant. We will drink wine of mare's milk."

"Then send Timur to me."

"It is night, and he is lame. After sunrise, perhaps he will come."

With that Garluk slipped from the door. Gray heard the sound of a bar falling into place. He was shut in for the night.

CHAPTER XXIII

He slept little. The fate destined for Mary had come as a complete surprise. It was not strange, he reflected, that Gela should want her for a wife. Nor that Bassalor Danek should approve the marriage. He might have foreseen something of the kind.

No wonder the Gur-Khan had taken excellent care of the girl, when she was marked for the bride of his grandson. Gray swore fluently, and vainly. The calmness with which the Wusun had put him aside was irksome. He wished that he had claimed to be the husband of Mary. It was too late now.

Nor did he hope that the girl's objection, once she heard of the proposed match, would carry weight. Evidently marriage among the Wusun was arranged by the parents of the parties concerned, as in China. Bassalor Danek's word was law. And the old chieftain fully appreciated the beauty of the girl.

Gray groaned, reflecting that the coincidence of the cross that the girl wore had rendered her doubly desirable in the eyes of the Wusun. He wondered how they had seen the cross. Was the marriage to be the price of his safety? He groaned at the thought.

Flight, even if he could reach the girl, from Sungan, was not to be thought of for the present. Wu Fang Chien would be alert for just such an attempt. And Gray did not see how he could hope to win through the lepers.

"They say blood calls to blood," he muttered. Then he scowled savagely. "Confound Gela!"

He was hungry for sight of the girl. She must be worried about him, as he had not been able to visit her yesterday as he had promised. His involuntary protest had excited the suspicions of Garluk. He would find it difficult now to escape from the surveillance of the *tumani*, if he should make the attempt.

And beyond the Wusun was Wu Fang Chien, watching keenly for any effort on the part of Gray or Mary to leave Sungan.

It was clear to Gray that the mandarin could not permit them to leave the place alive. For one thing, they would carry the news of the massacre of the caravan. And the tidings of the existence of the Wusun.

It would be fatal to the plans of Wu Fang Chien and the Buddhists if the Wusun should be discovered. The knowledge of a race of ancient Asia that worshipped the cross would be a severe blow

The Challenge

to the Mongolians. The Wusun were dying out. Soon they would be extinct, and the danger over. Until then Wu Fang Chien must guard his prisoners.

The situation afforded little comfort to Gray. At daybreak he pounded on his door. In time Garluk came with food. Timur, he said, would visit Gray presently, in the morning. No, the Man-from-the-Outside could not leave the tower. Bassalor Danek had issued orders. He was concerned for the safety of his guests as the soldiers of the Chinese had been seen assembling outside the wall.

The Wusun, said Garluk, had mustered their fighting men at the wall and in the passages, under Gela. After the wedding the Chinese could not interfere with the Kha Rakcha, for she would be the wife of the Kha Khan.

Gray dismissed Garluk, to hasten the approach of Timur, and watched moodily from the embrasure. He knew that he was little better than a prisoner. Hours passed while the sun climbed higher. He noticed an unusual activity in Sungan, and saw bodies of armed men pass from point to point.

The discipline of the place was strict. Probably, he reflected, a heritage from the military ancestors of the Wusun. It was noon when Timur entered the chamber and seated himself calmly on the rugs.

Gray curbed his anxiety, and greeted the lame councilor quietly. He had a desperate game to play with nothing to rely upon but his own wits.

269

Marching Sands

"Garluk said that you had need of me," observed Timur, scanning him keenly.

"I have a word to say to you," corrected Gray quietly.

"It is said," he added as the old man was silent, "that the Kha Rakcha is to be asked in marriage by Gela, the Kha Khan. Is this so?"

"They said the truth. The wedding will be to-night, after sunset."

Gray's heart sank at this. He had hoped, illogically, that Garluk had exaggerated the state of affairs. Timur stretched out a lean hand. In it was a small square of linen, Mary's handkerchief.

The American took it eagerly. It was a message from Mary, written in the Chinese ink, and it ran as follows:

> Bassalor Danek has ordered me to marry Gela. I have said no, a hundred times, but they will not listen. It will be to-night. They will not let me see you. I don't know what to do, Captain Gray. Please, please think of something—to delay it. I did not dream they wanted to do anything like that. I would rather face Wu Fang Chien. Why could not you come to me? Please, help me. Timur has agreed to carry this.

It was signed with Mary's name. The girlish appeal stirred Gray strangely. She had sent to him for aid. Yet there was little he could do. He followed the note mechanically and faced Timur, thinking quickly.

"In her own country," he said slowly, "the Kha

The Challenge

Rakcha has high rank. Because of this it is not fitting that she should marry among the Wusun. She does not want to stay in Sungan. It will kill her. This is the truth."

"I have seen that you speak the truth," assented the chieftain. "And my heart is warm for love of the woman who talked with me. Yet Gela has rank among us."

"But she does not wish the marriage."

"It is the word of Bassalor Danek."

"You know that I speak what is so. The woman will die, if not by her own hand, from unhappiness."

Timur looked sadly from the embrasure.

"It may be. But death is slow in coming to the young, O Man-from-the-Outside. Before she dies the Kha Rakcha will bear Gela a son. That is the wish of Bassalor Danek."

Gray's lips tightened grimly.

"Is that a just reward for coming over the desert to find the Wusun and lighten their captivity?"

"It is fate."

"If it comes to pass the White Spirit will never leave Sungan, but will die here. Will you lay that black fate upon her?"

"Will she not be kept here, if she does not marry Gela?"

Gray looked up hotly. "The Kha Rakcha is not a subject of Bassalor Danek. She is a servant of a mightier king——"

Timur raised his hand.

"Harken, youth," he said gravely. "I have seen your love for the Kha Rakcha, and I know that she has love for you in her heart——" Gray's pulses quickened at this—"but the will of Bassalor Danek must be obeyed. I know not if it is fitting that she marry among the Wusun. But the Gur-Khan has said that by the marriage, aid may be obtained from her people for the Wusun. Blood ties are strong. And the Wusun are fast dying out. If the marriage takes place, the Kha Rakcha will remain in Sungan. That is the word of the Gur-Khan. It may not be altered."

Silently, Gray studied the pattern of the carpet at his feet. His firm mouth was set in hard lines. Argument was gaining him nothing. And he must make his effort to save the girl now or never.

"I claim the White Spirit as my bride," he said. "By right of love. She is mine."

Timur combed his white beard thoughtfully.

"How can it be?"

"In this way. Bassalor Danek has given to Gela what is mine. Since the time of Kaidu and Genghis Khan it has been the law of Mongolia that a maiden should not be taken from the man to whom she is betrothed."

"Bassalor Danek has decided. It is for the good of his people."

The Challenge

"I, who have come across the desert to the Wu-sun, know that it is not so. I call upon the Wusun to abide by the law of Mongolia."

"The marriage feast is being prepared. The White Spirit will be clothed in the robe of blessed felicity."

"Let it be so." Gray looked at the old man steadily. "Let there be a marriage this night, according to the custom of the Wusun. But I, as well as Gela, claim the girl. You know the law?"

"If two men say that a woman is theirs, they must decide the matter with weapons in their hands."

"That is the law, Timur. From across the desert I have known it. I will fight Gela. Thus it will be decided."

Timur glanced at him curiously.

"The Kha Khan is no light foe. He will fight with swords. He has learned the art of sword play from his fathers."

"Be it so." Gray rose. "Bear this message to the Kha Khan. Say that the White Spirit is mine."

The Wusun sighed.

"It is the way of the hot blood of youth. You are foolhardy. Why should friends fight when Wu Fang Chien is approaching our gates? Still, what fate has written will come to pass. I will tell Bassalor Danek your message."

Marching Sands

That night there was a stir in Sungan. Rumor of the coming event had spread through the ruins, and, with the exception of the guards that Gela stationed to prevent any attempt at entrance on the part of the Chinese, the whole of the Wusun men flocked into the council hall.

Gray, from his tower, watched the glow of the sunset and saw the shadows form about the gardens of Sungan. The evening chant floated up to him, mournful and melodious. Occasionally he saw a sentry pass along the outline of the wall.

He wondered grimly whether he would see the next sunrise. Timur had announced, by Garluk, that Gray's challenge to the chief of the *tumani* had been accepted.

Garluk was voluble with excitement. He made no secret of his belief that the American would die at the hand of Gela. It would be an excellent spectacle, he said. He asked if Gray intended to protect himself by magic during the combat.

Gray did not answer. He had had no experience in handling a sword; the primitive blades of the Wusun were clumsy weapons. Doubtless Gela was skilled in their use.

The situation afforded little ground for hope. Certainly Gray, who had had an opportunity to measure his adversary, was not overconfident. He was resolved to make the best of it. He was doing the only thing he could to aid the girl.

The Challenge

He was not sorry. Gray was the type that did
not shirk physical conflict. And his love for Mary
Hastings was without stint. He did not know how
much she cared for him. He was incredulous of
Timur's words—that she could love him.

At Garluk's summons, he followed the *tumani*
down the stairs. The corridors were thronged with
men who stared at him avidly. So great was the
crowd that Garluk could barely force his way into
the hall.

The place was brightly lighted with candles.
Overhead, the gallery was filled with the Wusun.
On the daïs Bassalor Danek was talking earnestly
with Timur and the other elders of the tribe.

A murmur went up at Gray's entrance and the
throng turned, as one man, to stare at him. He returned their scrutiny, from the doorway, hoping
that he might see the girl. Would she be brought
to the hall? He did not know. Timur limped
forward.

"The bronze bracelet," he ordered Garluk. The
tumani produced a metal armlet which he clamped
upon Gray's left forearm. It was an ancient ornament, engraved with lettering unfamiliar to the
American. He wondered idly what Van Schaick
would have thought of it.

"It shall be as you wish," said Timur gravely.
"Bassalor Danek is just. He has granted your

275

claim. If you are the victor, the White Spirit shall be yours."

"It is well," assented Gray.

He spoke mechanically, feeling the phenomena known to men who are about to go into bodily danger—the acute interest in all about him, merged into indifference.

"We have sent for the White Spirit," added Timur. "Gela will bring her."

A fresh murmur caused Gray to raise his eyes. He searched the throng greedily. At the door behind the daïs Mary Hastings had appeared. The murmur changed into a loud exclamation of astonishment.

The girl had been forced to discard her own clothing for a loose garment of white silk, fitted with a wide girdle of the same material and a veil that covered her face below the eyes. Her hair hung over her slender shoulders in bronze coils on which the candlelight played fitfully.

Her arms were bare. Thrust into the glare, she shrank back. Then she caught sight of Gray and would have started forward, but the women around prevented her. For a moment her eyes sought his pleadingly.

"The Kha Rakcha," murmured those near him. "*Aie*—she is fair."

Gray's heart leaped at the sight. Then Gela appeared at the girl's side, his tall bulk towering

The Challenge

above the women. He was armed with his sword and appeared well pleased with the situation.

"A fine stage setting," thought Gray whimsically. "Just like the plays at home. Only the savage in this case isn't ready to drop by the footlights when the time comes. And his sword isn't *papier maché*."

His mind ran on, illogically. But his gaze fastened hungrily on the girl. He admired the pluck which kept her erect and calm in the face of the multitude.

"A thoroughbred!" he muttered. He wanted to call to her, but the commotion would drown his voice. He did not look at her again. The appeal in the girl's mute eyes was too great.

With this came a quick revulsion of feeling. His stupor of indifference vanished at sight of the slight figure among the staring Wusun. A hot longing to fight for her swept over him—a desire to match his strength with her enemies, to win her for himself and keep her.

The thought sent the blood pulsing through him quickly. He smiled and waved at the girl, who responded bravely.

Gray moved toward her, followed by Timur. He wished to speak to her. And then came the incident which altered matters entirely and which set in motion the strange events of that night.

Gela had been talking with Bassalor Danek. In a burst of pride, the Kha Khan turned to the girl,

Marching Sands

caught her about the knees and lifted her easily for all to see. Surprise caused the girl to cry out.

"Gela!" Gray called angrily, "that was ill done. The Kha Rakcha is not for your hands to touch!"

The youth did not understand. Mastered by an impulse of passion, he laughed, pressing the white woman closer. An echoing cry came from the Wu-sun. Gela kissed the bare arm of the girl, running his free hand through her hair.

The sight was too much for Gray's prudence. Pushing Timur aside, he sprang forward. Several of the *tumani* stepped into his path. Gray struck at them viciously.

He was in the grip of a cold rage which renders a man doubly dangerous. His powerful body flung forward through the group of his enemies. Love for the girl blinded him to the consequences of his mistake.

An outcry arose. Gray paid no heed to it, his fists smashing into the faces of those who tried to hold him. He wrenched free from men who caught his legs.

"Peace!" cried the great voice of Bassalor Danek.

An injured Wusun, bleeding from the mouth, struck at Gray with his sword. The white man stepped under the blow and twisted the weapon away from its holder.

Aflame with the lust of conflict, he swung his blade against the others that flashed in his face.

278

The Challenge

The force of his trained muscles beat down their guard and cleared him a way to the foot of the daïs.

Then the Wusun gave back, at a sharp command. A space was cleared around him. He saw Gela standing alone before him, smiling, weapon in hand.

CHAPTER XXIV

A STAGE IS SET

"Ho!" cried the voice of Garluk. "It is come."
Others caught up the words. "It is come. Gela
is ready. One must die!"

"One must die," echoed Garluk, "or give way to
the other."

A quick glance upward showed Gray that Bassalor Danek was leaning forward in his chair. Mary
was watching tensely from the group of women.

Gray had little time to think. The man who now
confronted him was a more formidable adversary
than those he had knocked aside. Gela stood, poised
easily, his bare sword swinging in a knotted arm.

Gray smiled and moved forward, while the throng
of the Wusun watched greedily.

The thought of what he was to do had come to
him. And he acted on it instantly.

Swinging his weapon over his head he leaped at
Gela. The Kha Khan's sword went up to guard
the blow. As it did so, the white man dropped his
blade and caught the other's arm.

It had been done in the space of a second, coolly

A Stage is Set

and recklessly. Gray drew the arm of Gela over his own shoulder, turning as he did so. It was a wrestling trick and it brought the Wusun's weight full on the sword arm.

A wrench, a quick change of footing, and Gela's sword dropped to the floor. Both men were now unarmed.

Gray had taken the only course that would save his life. Unskilled in use of the sword, he had reduced the fight to even terms. But he felt at once the great strength of the Wusun.

Gela gripped him about the waist, crushing his arms to his side. Gray felt a sharp pain in his back, and stiffened against the hold. Slowly he forced his arms up until his fists were under the other's chin.

It was now a trial of sheer strength. Gela strained at his grip, locking his iron-like muscles in an effort to bend his foe back. Gray brought one knee up into the Wusun's stomach and pressed up with his fists.

For a long moment the two were locked motionless. Silence held the hall.

"Ho!" came the voice of Garluk, "we will see the man crushed. Gela will crush him as a bullock beats down a sheep."

They were panting now, and the perspiration streamed down into Gray's eyes. He had not guessed the Wusun was so strong. The scene and

281

the spectators faded from his sight, leaving the vision of Gela's set face staring into his own.

In weight and muscle the Wusun had the advantage of his adversary. But Gray was not putting forth his strength to the utmost, knowing that the hold must be changed when Gela tired.

Seeing that he could not snap Gray's spine by sheer weight, Gela shifted his grip swiftly, reaching for a lower hold.

Gray had been waiting for this. As the other released his pressure, he struck. It was a hurried blow, but it jerked back the Wusun's head and rocked him on his feet.

Instantly Gray struck with the other hand. This time his fist traveled farther and Gela fell to the floor.

He was up at once, growling angrily. As he rushed, Gray beat him off coolly—short, telling blows that kept him free from the other's grasp.

"Ho!" laughed Timur, "which is the bullock now? The man has sharp horns."

Gela hesitated, bleeding from nose and mouth. He had never been forced to face a man who was master of such blows. He swayed, gasping with his exertions, his brown head thrust forward from between his wide shoulders.

Gray waited, poised alertly, regaining his breath.

Then Gela lowered his head and sprang forward.

A Stage is Set

Gray caught him twice as he came—with each fist. But this time the man was not to be stopped.

Gray was caught about the shoulders, swung from his feet and dashed to the stone floor. He felt the other's knees drive into his body, and rolled to one side as Gela's hands fumbled for his throat. He knew it would mean death to be pinned to the floor by the Wusun.

Lights were dancing before his eyes. The hall had grown dark, for Gela's arm was over his eyes.

For a long space the two were locked almost motionless on the floor.

He heard Mary cry out. The sound was drowned in an exultant shout from the watchers. Gray was on his knees. He drew a long, painful breath. His lungs had been emptied by the fall to the hard floor.

Silently, he set his teeth and warded off the hands that sought his throat. With an effort he rose to his feet, throwing off the weight of his enemy. He staggered as he did so, and realized that he was on the point of utter exhaustion.

The shout grew in volume as Gela, still vigorous, advanced on Gray with outstretched arms. The white man stepped back. Again he avoided the clutch of the Wusun who was grinning in triumph. As he did so he summed his remaining strength with grim determination, watching Gela.

Again the Wusun advanced. This time Gray did not draw back. He launched forward bodily, eyes

283

fixed on his foe's face. His fist caught Gela full on
the cheek-bone, under the eye.

Watching, and fighting off the stupor of weakness, Gray saw Gela's head jerk back. The Wusun
slipped to the floor, and lay there.

It was all that Gray could do to keep his feet.
His head was on his chest, and his dull sight perceived that Gela was trying to crawl toward him.

The muscles of the Wusun moved feebly, pulling
his body over the floor. His splendid shoulders
heaved. The blow that he received would have
knocked out an ordinary man.

Gray, his shirt torn from his back, and blood
dripping from his mouth, watched. Gela edged
nearer. There was silence in the hall.

Then the Wusun's head dropped to the floor and
his shoulders fell limp. He ceased moving forward.
Gray's blow had ended the struggle. Both men
were exhausted; but the white man was able to keep
his feet.

As his sight cleared, he looked up at Mary. The
girl's gaze burned into his. Gray moved toward her,
fumbling at his left arm.

He mounted the steps of the daïs. He took the
bronze armlet weakly in his hand. Barely, he was
able to raise it and place it around the girl's throat.
She did not draw back.

Then he put his hand on her shoulder and turned
to face Bassalor Danek. As he did so, there was a

commotion in the crowd at the hall entrance. A Wusun stepped forward. He held a strung bow in one hand.

"I bring news, O Gur-Khan," the newcomer cried. "Wu Fang Chien is within the gate of Sungan."

At this, confusion arose among the Wusun. Women screamed and the *tumani* shouted angrily.

"The Chinese soldiers have driven back the sentries on the wall," repeated the messenger. "Wu Fang Chien sends word to you. He has come for the two white people. They must be given up to him. Or he will search the whole of Sungan."

The uproar died down at this. All eyes were turned to Bassalor Danek. The Gur-Khan sat quietly in his chair, but the hand that stroked his beard trembled.

"Will Wu Fang Chien break the covenant of our people?" he demanded sternly.

"Aye; he has mustered his soldiers with guns."

Gray felt the girl draw closer to him. She did not know what was going on, yet guessed at trouble in the air. He put his arm over her shoulders, thrilled that she did not protest.

Instead, her hand reached up and pressed his softly. Her hair touched his cheek. He had married Mary Hastings, by the law of the Wusun. It was not marriage as their customs ordained; but he felt the exultation that had come when he bound

the circlet of bronze about her slim throat. She
was his! He had won her from Gela. And—mi-
raculously—she was content to have his arm about
her. Of course he could not urge the claim of this
barbaric ritual on her—if they ever won free from
Sungan. For the moment, however, he joyed in
the thought that he had fought for and won the
woman he loved. The new menace, voiced by the
messenger, slipped from his mind. He saw only
the girl.

Then he realized that she was blushing hotly.

"Please," she whispered, "I—I must get my
clothes. This dress is not—I don't want to wear
it."

"It's mighty becoming," he said, laughingly.

He spoke haphazard, his triumph still strong upon
him.

"Oh!" She smiled back. "Now that you are my
—master, they'll let me change to my own things,
won't they? I'll run back to Bassalor Danek's
house."

He saw that she was disturbed by the multitude.
But the lines about his mouth hardened. His arm
tightened about her.

"You won't leave me—now," he whispered. Then
he saw sudden alarm in her eyes. "We're in trouble,
as usual. I'll send a woman for your clothes." He
spoke lightly, trying to reassure her. "Here's
Timur——"

A Stage is Set

At his request, the lame chieftain curtly dispatched an attendant for Mary's garments. Timur was watching Bassalor Danek. The Gur-Khan was staring blankly before him. He was called upon to make a decision which meant much to his people.

Gray also was watching the ruler of the Wusun, wondering whether the latter's pride would lead him to resist Wu Fang Chien.

Then a figure pushed through the *tumani* at the foot of the daïs. It was Gela, staggering with weariness, the blood still flowing from the cuts in his face. In spite of this he carried himself proudly, and there was a savage light in the eyes that peered at Bassalor Danek and the two white people.

He pointed at Gray and growled something that the American did not understand.

"He says," interpreted Timur, "that you are a brave man. That the word of Gela will not be broken. He will guard the Kha Rakcha from the Buddhists. And he will protect you who are the husband of the woman."

A murmur of approval came from the ranks of the *tumani* at the words of their leader. Bassalor Danek looked troubled.

"It is well said," cried Gray. He stepped forward, holding out his hand. Gela drew himself up defiantly. It may have been that he did not understand the gesture of the white man.

"Gela says," explained Timur, "that he will do this for the Kha Rakcha. Not for you."

But Gray had seen his chance, and turned to Bassalor Danek.

"Harken, Gur-Khan of the Wusun," he said clearly. "You must answer Wu Fang Chien. You have heard the word of Gela, who is a generous foe. Have you forgotten that your fathers and mine were once the same? Or the talisman in the shrine? By this thing, I ask a favor. It will be the last."

"Speak," responded the chieftain quietly. "I have not forgotten."

"The Kha Rakcha and I have come across the desert to Sungan to seek the Wusun, who are of our blood. Many died, that we should come here. And"—he recalled the words Mirai Khan had once used—"we have eaten your meat and bread. What we came for has been accomplished. Why should we stay here? Would it not be better to bring word of what we have seen to those of your blood who are across the desert?"

Bassalor Danek meditated, stroking his beard.

"Once I said to Wu Fang Chien and the priests, O Man-from-the-Outside, that you are my guest. So it shall be. I will not give you up."

"The time of the Kha Rakcha in Sungan is ended," returned Gray boldly. "Like the crescent moon she has come and will go. She must carry the word of the talisman in the shrine back with her. It was for this that the Kha Rakcha was sent. She will return to a king who is greater than the Manchu emperor once was."

The Gur-Khan shook his head shrewdly.

"What power is greater than the Dragon Empire? What other people are there than the Mongols, the Kirghiz and the Buddhists priests?"

"Beyond the desert is a sea, and beyond the sea are those whose blood was once yours. We will take our message to them and they will know of the Wusun."

Timur limped forward to the Gur-Khan's side.

"A thought has come to me, O Khan of the Wusun," he said slowly. "It is a high thought and an omen. It is that this man and woman will return whence they have come, with speech of what they saw in Sungan. It is written in the book of fate that this shall be. Why else did the white man overcome Gela?"

He turned to Gray, with a moody smile on his lined face.

"Your people, O Man-from-the-Outside, will not find the Wusun, if they send again. That is my thought. The sun passes from the heavens and it is night; the camel leaves his bones to dry in the sands. So will the Wusun pass from Mongolia. The priests of Buddha are powerful. Soon the sands will climb over the walls of Sungan."

A murmur from a hundred throats, a muttered lament, greeted this.

"We will deliver our message," said Gray.

Timur was silent, standing beside the troubled Gur-Khan. A quick emotion of friendship for these resigned captives of Sungan swept over Gray. He turned to Gela.

"Will you do this for the Kha Rakcha?" he asked. "Will you escort us through the ranks of the Buddhist priests and the soldiers? It will not be an easy task. There will be bloodshed. But it would save the life of the Kha Rakcha."

Timur interpreted his request. The Kha Khan lifted his head proudly. He spoke rapidly, harshly, pointing to the watching warriors.

"He will do what you say," assented Timur. "The *tumani* will take you through the guards of Sungan. It has not been done before——"

"Wu Fang Chien first broke the covenant," reminded the American.

"*Aie!* It will be a hard struggle. The soldiers have guns——"

Gela broke in sternly. Already the light of conflict showed in his keen eyes. He issued a series of guttural commands to the *tumani*. The women began to press from the hall, uttering wailing laments. The young men clustered around the Kha Khan.

A Stage is Set

"Wu Fang Chien will scourge us for this," muttered Timur.

"Wu Fang Chien," pointed out Gray grimly, "may not live to do it. Likewise, it is better, for the peace of the Wusun, that we should go from Sungan."

He thought, also, of Gela's savage love for the girl. For the moment the Wusun was their friend. But the future might alter that. He had seen his opportunity, and seized it. The *tumani* were drawing their weapons and chattering excitedly.

Gray had reasoned that now the Buddhists were assembled at the gates of Sungan. If he and the girl could penetrate their ranks, they might obtain a good start over the desert, which was now free of the outer guards.

"As you have said," announced Bassalor Danek, rising, "it shall be done."

"What is happening?" Mary asked anxiously. Sensing the importance of what was passing, she had not spoken before.

Gray laughed. He touched her shoulder shyly.

"Come to me, as soon as you are ready, Mary. Gela is a generous foe. He will guide us beyond the wall."

She looked at the young Kha Khan gratefully. Well she knew what the danger would be, although Gray had not mentioned it. On a quick impulse the girl stooped and picked up Gela's weapon from the floor. She placed it in the hand of the Wusun. The action caught the fancy of the *tumani*.

"The Kha Rakcha is one at heart with the Wusun!" they cried, looking eagerly at the beautiful woman.

"Aye, the Kha Rakcha!" shouted Gela, his moodiness vanished. "We will shed our blood for the white queen."

"Ho—the white queen!" echoed the *tumani*.

CHAPTER XXV

WHAT happened now came swiftly and with little warning. Bassalor Danek, once the die was cast, ceded his authority to Gela. The traditional leadership of the Wusun was the Kha Khan's in time of war. Now, for the first time in generations they were to resist the authority of their gaolers.

Gray remembers clearly that Bassalor Danek bade them a solemn farewell standing in his white robe at the foot of the daïs. Then the Gur-Khan, who was impressed with the importance of the occasion, raised his hand with dignity.

"By the talisman at your throat, O Kha Rakcha," he said, "do not forget the Wusun—if it is the decree of fate that you should pass from here in safety."

"She will not forget," promised Gray. He watched the aged figure depart for the tower where Bassalor Danek intended to watch what was to happen through the Eyes-of-Long-Sight.

Gela assumed command impetuously. Gray watched him muster the *tumani*. The young men

293

were afire with anticipation of a struggle. The long pent up enmity against their captors was about to be released. From the dwellings of Sungan came the lament of the women. It shrilled in the night air—the world-old plaint of women before battle.

Timur lingered with them. The three were surrounded by the hunters who had strung their bows and unsheathed their heavy swords.

There was only a half-light in the upper hall of the council-temple where they now stood. It reflected faintly upon the red sandstone of the walls, with the faded, painted figures of an older age looking down upon them.

Gutturally, the warriors spoke under their breath to each other, laughing much, although not loudly. Some, however, leaned upon their bows silently, their eyes blank. This note of tensity was familiar to the American. Gray had watched men go forward under fire with the same forced merriment, the same semi-stupor.

But the hunters were contented. Young men, for the most part, their lean faces hardened and lined by exposure to the sun, their bloodshot eyes narrow, their lips thin and cracked—they smiled more frequently than not. A savage pleasure lurked in their eyes. They were to lift their swords against the oppressors of the Wusun. Gray counted the swords. They were all too few.

Wearied of confinement, they were, for a brief

moment, to strike into the desert as free men. Perhaps. For they might never win beyond the wall.

They shuffled their yak-skin boots, breathing heavily. The air in the gallery became close and hot with scent of soiled leather. Mary stood close to Gray, her shoulder against his. She had changed to her torn dress and crumpled jacket. Her glance was on him.

"Robert!"

"Yes—Mary." He looked down, his face alight at hearing her speak his name.

"You were frowning. Will it be so very bad?" Her slender body pressed against his so that he could feel the pulse of her heart. "Then you mustn't leave me—this time."

"No."

He wanted to take her in his arms, to call her his wife. But he checked the swift impulse sternly. He had no right. How was he to know that she was yearning for just this comfort?

Gela waved his arm, and there was a shuffling of many feet, moving forward.

"Robert!"

Her eyes, shining with faith in him, drew nearer and held his own. His arm drew her closer to him, savagely. Perhaps he hurt her. But she did not protest.

Blindly, he pressed his mouth against the fragrance of her hair. Clumsily, with dry lips, he kissed her throat and cheek, marveling at the pulse that beat so strongly where he touched.

Two swift, slender arms closed around his neck. The girl sighed, quivering, uttering a soft, happy murmur. Gray, unbelieving, tried to look into her face, but tender, moist lips touched his in a quick caress. Her eyes were half closed, and she was strangely pale.

"Mary!" he whispered, and again: "Mary."

She was smiling now, the gray eyes glad.

Gela cast an appraising eye over the assemblage and gave a command. The *tumani* pressed forward to the stairs that led to the entrances above ground.

Gray felt Mary's hand seek his. A cool breath of air brushed their hot faces. He saw the glitter of torches, lighted by the *tumani*. Then they passed out into the night.

The sands of Sungan were vacant except for the group of warriors under Gela. A slight breeze stirred among the aloes and tamarisks, lifting tiny spirals of dust under their feet and causing the torches to flicker.

Then the torches were dashed into the sand, and the warrior groups became shadowy forms, moving against the deeper shadow of the towers.

Overhead the moon was cold and bright. Its radiance showed the dark figures of Chinese on the wall, and glittered on their guns. At the gate in

the wall in front of them was a group of priests.
Wu Fang Chien was not to be seen.

Between the *tumani* and the wall was a level
stretch of sand perhaps two hundred yards in length.

"See!" chattered the old Timur, "the message of
Bassalor Danek has been sent. They are waiting."

"It would not be well to rush the wall," cautioned Gray quickly, sizing up the situation. "They
have guns——"

"If I had a bow!" Timur's reluctance had vanished under the growing excitement. "Ho! The
hunters will hunt new prey."

One of the priests cried out something that Gray
did not understand. Gela answered defiantly, and
the *tumani* rushed forward, carrying Gray and
Mary with them.

A shot sounded from the wall, greeted by a defiant
shout from the Wusun. A scattering volley followed. The guards—Chinese irregulars, Dungans,
bandits, followers of the priests, what-not—were
poor marksmen. But the range was close. And the
Wusun, ignorant of tactics against gunfire, were
bunched close.

Gray saw several stumble and fall in the sand.
More shots. The torches wavered. Timur stooped
and picked up a bow and arrow from one of the
fallen.

The priests had vanished from the gate. This had
been closed. But not before Gray sighted groups

of the lepers running about in confusion. Some seemed to be armed.

The Wusun wavered under the fire, as undisciplined men are bound to do. Gray forced the girl to crouch in the sand with Timur while he ran forward to Gela. The Kha Khan was shouting angrily at his followers.

"The passages!" Gray seized Gela's arm. "Here, you will be killed. Go down to the passages."

Gela, the hot light of battle in his scarred face, stared at him unheedingly. But Timur, who was not to be left behind, limped forward and echoed Gray's words.

Comprehension dawned on the Kha Khan, and his eyes narrowed shrewdly. He shouted to his men. The *tumani* began to run back, leaving dark bodies prone in the sand.

Gray made his way to the temple with Mary. A shout of triumph sounded from the wall. The firing did not cease. The blood-lust had been aroused in the men on the wall, who had found the killing of the poorly armed Wusun an easy matter.

But Gray, seeing the set faces around him, realized that the *tumani* were not going to give up the struggle. It was an age-old feud—the struggle of the oppressed Central Asians against their Mongol captors.

He and the girl were swept along at Gela's side like leaves in a swift current. Down into the temple the Wusun pressed, silent this time. They streamed into the underground corridors, led by men with torches. The shouting over-ground grew fainter.

Once Gray stumbled over a body. It was a woman, bleeding from a death wound in the throat. The priests had been here, and warfare in the Gobi reckons not of sex.

The flutter of a yellow robe appeared in the corridor in front of them. A bow twanged, and Gray saw an arrow appear between the shoulders of the fleeing priest. A knife that the Buddhist held clattered to the floor.

The *tumani* shouted and pressed forward. They were under the wall now, and the passage began to rise. Gray saw that it was the same that led to the well.

A sharp command from Gela silenced the Wusun. They ran out into the well and up the steps, savagely intent on their purpose.

They emerged into confusion. Gray saw that other Wusun were running out from the adjoining passages, driving the priests before them. The Chinese on the wall had turned. Taken by surprise, they were firing hastily. Their foes were scattered now, and the fight became a hand-to-hand affair.

One by one the torches dropped to the sand. Swords flashed in the moonlight. Gray saw some of the men of the leper pack, led by priests. These were met with arrows of the *tumani* and driven back. They fled easily.

Forced to hand-grips, the Chinese at the wall wavered.

"*Aie!*" cried Timur. "The fight goes well. I am young again." He pointed exultantly at the leaping forms of the hunters.

The girl walked quietly at Gray's side. The American picked up an empty musket and went forward. It was a poor weapon, but it served. Gela was in advance of his followers, who had cleared the wall now and were pacing forward, seeking out the groups of Chinese.

By now the soldiers were running back through the outskirts of the city.

Gray could see the leper pack mingling with the shadows among the sand dunes. Occasionally, there was a shrill cry as the Wusun hunted out a yellow-robed Buddhist. The Chinese were fleeing in earnest. The only light now came from the moon. It was a battle of shadows, wherein dim forms leaped and struck with bared knives, peering at each other's face.

"*Aie!*" echoed the old chieftain, who was leaning on the shoulder of a *tumani*, "this is the way our fathers drove their foes before them. It is a goodly sight."

He hobbled on, refusing to be left behind. Gray drew a deep breath, surveying the scene with ex-

perienced eye. The smoldering anger of the
Wusun had cleared a temporary passage. "We are
outside the city, Mary," he said.

"It is not over yet," she responded quickly.
"See—there are lights ahead, to the right."

Gela had seen the same thing. He gathered together the hunters that remained about him and
advanced cautiously. Rounding some dunes, they
came full on the lights.

It was the camp of the Chinese guards. Camels
and horses were tethered among some make-shift
tents. Lanterns flickered as coolies sought to as-
semble the beasts.

A group of men were facing them standing uneasily in front of the tents. Gray saw the bulky
figure and mandarin hat of Wu Fang Chien. The
light from a lantern struck across his broad face,
savage now with baffled anger. He held a rifle.

CHAPTER XXVI

THE girl gave a quick cry. It was answered by
a shout from Gela.

One of the Chinese fired. The man who was supporting Timur dropped to the ground with a moan,
hands clasped to his stomach.

Both Gela and Gray sprang forward at the same
time. Wu Fang Chien caught sight of them and
lifted his rifle. His followers shot wildly, doing
no damage in the uncertain light.

The mandarin, Gray thought swiftly as he ran,
had rallied some of the fugitives at the camp.
Possibly he had guessed Gray's intention to leave
Sungan, and was determined to prevent it at all
costs.

Gray could see the man clearly as he peered at
him over the sights of the rifle. The weapon was
steady. Behind him, a warning shout echoed from
the Wusun. Gela, at his side, did not slacken his
pace.

Still Wu Fang Chien held his fire. Gray, watching intently, saw that the rifle the mandarin held

was one of his own—stolen from his luggage. The thought wrought on him with grim humor. It did not occur to him to turn back. He could not leave Gela to go forward alone. The Kha Khan was panting as he ran, wearied by his efforts, but grimly intent on Wu Fang Chien.

Behind Wu Fang Chien, he saw the horses struggling at their tethers. His senses were strangely sharpened by the tensity of the moment. He heard Gela pant, and even caught the distant lament of the women of the Wusun. The coughing of frightened camels came to him clearly.

The lantern glinted on the rifle barrel that was aimed full at him. He saw Wu Fang Chien's evil eyes narrow. Then they widened. The rifle barrel wavered. And dropped to the sand. Gela and the white man halted in their tracks.

From the throat of Wu Fang Chien projected an arrow shaft, the feathers sticking grotesquely under his chin.

Slowly the mandarin's knees gave way and he fell forward on the sand, both hands gripping the arrow that snapped the thread of his life.

"*Aie!*" the voice of Timur rang out. "I have taken a life. I have slain an enemy of my people!"

Gray turned and saw the old chieftain standing bow in hand beside Mary. His cry had barely ceased when a yellow-robed priest sprang at him from a tent.

Marching Sands

The Buddhist held a knife. His course took him directly toward Mary. The girl waited helplessly. Gela's warning cry rang out. Several of the Wusun were running toward her. But too far away to aid.

The priest was within a few paces of the girl, too near for Gela or Gray to interfere in time.

Then the figure of Timur limped forward. The old man struck at the priest feebly with his bow. And caught him by the shoulders.

The Buddhist stabbed the Wusun viciously, burying his knife in Timur's back. The old man uttered no sound, but kept his hold, snarling under the bite of the knife. Gray stepped to the side of Wu Fang Chien and caught up the mandarin's rifle.

It was his own piece and loaded. He laid the sights on the man in the yellow robe as the latter threw off the clinging form of Timur. The rifle cracked as the Buddhist stepped toward Mary.

The priest staggered to his knees. It had been a quick shot, and an excellent one, considering the light. Gela grunted approval.

Gray saw the girl go to the side of the stricken Timur. Then he looked about the camp. Wu Fang Chien was dead, and his remaining followers had run from the camp into the desert. Only Gela's band of the Wusun were visible, thinned in numbers, but triumphant. They thronged toward their leader, bearing useless rifles as spoil, tired, yet chuckling loudly.

The Bronze Circlet

The fight was over.

Gela motioned significantly to the moon which was high overhead. Time was passing, and the white man must be dispatched while the coast was free. He had not forgotten his promise in the council hall. The Kha Khan returned to Mary and led her away from the old chieftain.

Gray saw that the girl was crying. Not noisily, but quietly, trying to keep back the tears. The strain of the night was beginning to tell on her, and the death of Timur at her side had been a shock. She did not want to look back.

"I—I liked Timur," she said softly. "He was good to me."

"He was a good sort," assented Gray heartily.

For the girl's sake, he wished to leave the camp at once. Delay would mean peril. Gela seemed to have guessed his thought. The Kha Khan issued brisk orders to his followers. Then he threw his own warm, sheepskin *khalat* over the girl's shoulders.

Two camels, the pick of those in the encampment, were produced. These were fitted hastily with blankets. A third was loaded—protesting loudly after the fashion of the beasts—with foodstuffs and water, commandeered from the supplies of the Chinese. Gela examined the goat skin water bags attentively and nodded with satisfaction. They were all-important.

This done, he turned to Gray and pointed again to the moon Then he motioned out over the desert to the west to a gray expanse of shimmering earth, with scattering wisps of stunted bushes.

"He wants us to go in that direction," said the girl, "not back to China."

Gray had already reasoned out their best course. The direction of Gala agreed with his own conclusion. To the west four or five days' fast ride on camels was the river Tarim, with isolated settlements of shepherds. Here they would be across the boundary of Kashgaria and free from the authority of the Chinese Buddhists. And beyond the Tarim was Khotan—just north of the Karakorum Pass to India. He still had his maps and compass.

"From there," assented the girl, "we can reach Kashgar, where there will be merchants from Kashmir. My uncle has been at Khotan with me. It is not hard to travel to India from there."

Urged by Gela they mounted the kneeling camels. The Wusun clustered around. Out of the camp they led the white man and woman until the towers of Sungan were barely visible on the horizon.

Here they were beyond danger of meeting with Chinese fugitives. Gela halted and raised his hand in farewell. Gray and the girl did likewise.

"He has kept his word to us, and he is proud of it," whispered Mary, "and we can't thank him." For neither could speak Gela's tongue.

306

The Bronze Circlet

"Good-by, old man, and good luck," said Gray heartily, in English.

Turning back after an interval, he saw the Kha Khan and the Wusun watching them. They were seated in the sand, their faces bent toward the departing camels. Until the two were out of sight, Gela remained there.

The camels were fresh and moved swiftly. It was a clear night, with a touch of cold in the air, a forerunner of the winter that was settling down on Central Asia. The miles passed swiftly behind, as Gray, guided by his compass, kept on to the west.

They did not speak. Behind them the crimson of dawn flooded the sky. The moon paled, coldly. Early morning chill numbed the man and the girl. The long shadows of the camels appeared on the sand before them. Mists, wraith-like and grotesque, receded on the skyline. From black to gray, and then to brown the sand dunes turned. Waves of sand swept to the sky-line on either side.

They were alone in the infinity of Asia.

Gray wanted to speak, but a strong shyness gripped him. He urged his beast beside the girl's and took her hand. She did not withdraw it. This made him bold. Already the sun warmed their backs. The camels slowed to a steady trudge.

"Our honeymoon has begun," he said. His heart was beating in unruly fashion. "And in Kashgar, we can find a missionary, to—to make you really my wife—if you will."

She did not answer. Instead, she drew back the *khalat* that the Wusun had given her. Gray saw that the bronze circlet was still about her throat.

THE END